Truffles by the Sea

JULIE CAROBINI

BETHANY HOUSE
MINNEAPOLIS, MINNESOTA

Published by Bethany House Publishers
11400 Hampshire Avenue South
Bloomington, Minnesota 55438

Bethany House Publishers is a division of
Baker Publishing Group, Grand Rapids, Michigan.

Printed in the United States of America

Library of Congress Cataloging-in-Publication Data

Carobini, Julie.
    Truffles by the sea / Julie Carobini.
       p. cm.
    ISBN 978–0–7642–0427–2 (pbk.)
1. Florists—Fiction. 2. Beaches—Fiction. 3. Conduct of life—Fiction. I. Title.

    PS3603.A7657 T78   2008
    813'.6—dc22

                                    2007034451

For my mom, Elaine F. Navarro,
my hero

One

I, GABY FLORES, WILL BE gullible no more.

There. I said it. And I mean it this time, my friend. No more believing the unbelievable. No more living like a patsy. No more dating guys from the dark side. The time has come for me to shake those things, those issues, those people in my life that just don't make sense. *¿Comprende?*

Deep breath in. Start fresh.

So...here I sit in my newly rented loft on the third story of a fantastic house overlooking one of the prettiest neighborhoods you've ever seen. The house sits perched at the edge of a channel that's swollen with ocean water. From my vantage point, I can see the open arc of the harbor mouth, where the seawater flows in and out. I've got the outfit I'm wearing, the remnants of my recently ransacked floral shop, and a new (so what if it's a little rundown?) place to live—and all with a view of the sea.

What better place to start fresh?

My friend Bri huffs up the final step to the third floor. "Is that it?" she asks.

I drag my gaze from the window where I've been watching a kayaker pull her paddle against high tide and look across the nearly empty loft. "Unless you've knocked over a Nordy's lately."

Bri blows out a weary breath, drops the last box onto the hardwood floor, and slides it against the wall with one flip-flop-shod foot. Standing there with a garbage bag of hand-me-downs in one hand, she says, "Sorry, Gaby. I didn't mean . . . Anyway, you know my offer still stands. Let me buy you some new things—I really want to." When I don't answer right away, she scrunches up her brow. "Please just get over yourself, will ya? Take me up on it."

I manage a smile. A girl's—no, this girl's—got her pride. Without that, thanks to the fire that leveled my apartment building, I got nothin'. (Unless you count my Visa card, that is.) I sneak another peek through the silt-smudged window, toward the water below, and see that sunny-yellow kayak continuing to rock its way toward the harbor mouth. The sight cheers my wounded heart.

When I turn back, Bri's still pacing, her forehead scrunched, the bag now at her feet.

"Bri-Bri, stop fretting. That closet full of things I had left at the shop should be enough to help me get by. Plus all that stuff you collected for me. All I've really got to do now is hang them up in here and I'll have the neatest closet in town."

"And skimpiest."

I glance down at my roundish hips, dreaming of slimmer days. "Skimpy's good."

Bri rolls her eyes. "At least that criminal you had working for you wasn't into women's clothing."

I shrug. "Not that I knew of anyway."

Bri grunts and wags her head. "You amaze me. For someone who's been ripped off all the way around, you're far too chipper." She leans her head to one side and stares at me. "Gaby, you're usually so dramatic about everything. What's gotten into you anyway?"

"*Moi?* Dramatic?"

"Don't deny it, girlfriend. I've known you way too long."

I shake it off. "Well, I have had my moments, *chica*. You know it. It's just that the sickly smell of my burnt-out apartment made me realize how blessed I really am. Can you imagine?"

Bri's face softens, because, yes, she knows what I mean. Because my mind whirs like a fan on fast all day long, I tend to be a deep sleeper. By the time I turn out the light each evening, I get so lost in slumber that it would probably take one of California's super-sized earthquakes to shake me awake.

My point is this: Had I been home when the fire broke out and before all those hottie fire fighters showed up, my dead-to-the-world slumber habit may have kept me from noticing in time. Sure, a working fire alarm would have helped. By order of the fire department, our landlord had finally installed one in each apartment. For some reason, though, none of the tenants, yours truly included, actually verified that he'd also put batteries in them. They don't work without them, you know.

Bri glances around my new digs, her eyes settling on a flat brown-bag-wrapped package. She bends to pick it up. "Where would you like this?"

"Just stand it up against the kitchen cabinet."

Bri snickers.

"What?"

"I'm so sorry, Gaby. That just sounded kinda funny. Most people say kitchen cabinets. You know, with an *s* at the end."

I take the package from her arms and feign a scolding. "Just give me that, silly girl. If I had more than one, I would have said so." I lean the package against the solitary cabinet.

Bri sighs. "Okay, okay. I guess you are blessed, girlfriend. Although these walls have seen better days." She stares at what looks to be soot embedded into the plaster. "Wonder why Livi didn't grab it for herself?"

"I can't imagine. The rent's incredibly low for this area. I mean—come on—the beach is close enough to walk to, yet it's a community all its own. I've no idea why she passed this up." Livi's our mutual friend, even if she is a bit of a doormat. She heard about this loft coming up for rent and told me about it—even though she'd love to get away from her punk-loving roommate who swears over every little thing. "Anyway, God probably just whispered this find into her ear just for me. The timing was perfect, you know."

"I know." Bri paces. "Um, Gaby?"

"You don't have to worry, Bri-Bri."

She swallows a sigh.

"I can afford it. I have some savings, and my insurance will help me with what Sammy took from the shop." Sammy's the delivery guy who cleaned out my floral shop—literally—the day I was picking through the rubble of my apartment building, hoping to find at least one unscathed tube of Aloha Red lipstick.

"After your huge deductible."

I glance at my deceased grandmother's old peanut jar, the one filled with spare change, and bite back the sting of self-pity. "Stop. You've got to have faith, my friend."

"I do. You just bring out the mothering instinct in me."

"Quit worrying. I've got this fabulous roof over my head now. I'm just looking forward to a nice quiet life by those calm waters out there." I toss a wave toward the filthy window with a lone spot rubbed clean, trying not to gag. "Oh, to start fresh . . . . I want that. It'll be perfect. You'll see."

"Knock, knock!"

Bri spins around, and my eyes flicker toward the door. A lanky woman with blunt-cut brown hair peeks in.

"I hope you don't mind me barging in before you're all settled." She steps inside my loft. "Are you Gaby?"

My forehead arches toward the sky. "I'm her."

"Wonderful! I'm Iris Hornsby. We're neighbors. I live with my husband and daughter in the fourplex just across the street." She leans close and whispers, "We own it."

I nod.

My new neighbor wrinkles her nose and squeezes her shoulders together, her smile bright. "I figured you'd be busy, but I didn't want to wait to welcome you to our neighborhood." She thrusts a jar of hard candy into my hand. "These are for you and . . . ?" Her voice trails off as she glances over her shoulder at Bri.

Bri reaches out her hand. "I'm Gaby's friend, Bri Stone. Just helping her move in."

Iris grins cheerily. "Aw, you're a great friend, then. It's a good thing you're just a helper today. Loft occupancy is limited to one." She laughs a gravelly laugh and bows her head my way. "Wouldn't want to have to turn you in."

I remember the jar of candy in my hands and glance down. "Thanks for the gift, Iris. Very nice of you." I rub the price tag still stuck to the side of the jar with my thumb.

"You're very welcome! Just a little something to help you feel at home in our Harborwest family." Her face scrunches like a prune when she says *family*, and I dare not catch eyes with Bri.

We all stare at each other over an awkward silence. I wear a smile, willing Bri with my infamous eyebrow arch not to roll her eyes in front of company. If it had been offered, Bri could've received a Ph.D. in Sarcasm. I just know she's having issues with my new neighbor's enthusiasm, but what-ev! This knowing-your-neighbors thing is a brand-new concept for me.

Iris backs up. "Well, ladies, I'll let you two get back to all your—" she hesitates while taking another quick survey of my nearly empty loft—"unpacking."

"Thanks again, Iris, for stopping by."

On her way out, she halts near the stairway and does this strange sort of lunge backward, like she's been snagged at the collar with fishing line. She cocks her chin. "By the way, Gaby. How did you learn about this rental's availability?"

I hesitate. "A friend mentioned it. Why do you ask?"

She just smiles. "No reason, really. But may I ask how your friend learned of this rental?"

I freeze in place, my tongue tied. The past few weeks of turmoil rush to mind, and I'm feeling like naked prey in a sea of sharks. I brush off my reticence and snap out of my trance when Iris scrunches her shoulders together and shakes her head. "Never mind, never mind," she says. "I see you're busy. No matter. I'm sure we'll have plenty of chances to chat soon."

I'm embarrassed by my knee-jerk reaction to Iris's kindness.

She continues. "By the way, you'll want to watch out for some of the neighbors around here. That one across the street?" She points to a small shingled house with a couple of beach chairs set up on a square wooden deck. "Went a little loony after a bad incident. And your next-door neighbor Sarah . . . is more than a little crazy. She hardly talks and is up all night. Suspicious, you know? Well, bye now. I'm sure we'll be seeing each other around the 'hood."

Afterward Bri snorts. "What'd she say her name was? Iris Kravitz?"

I hold up a palm for the second time today. "Oh, Bri-Bri. She seemed nice. A little inquisitive, but . . ."

"Inquisitive? Right. I think she's nosey." Bri's staring at the loft's front door.

"So we'll probably never have tea?" I shrug. "So what?"

"Tea?!"

I plunk down the canister of hard candy onto the counter of my tiny new kitchen, which actually juts out into the living room. "Coffee, water, whatever," I say with resolve. "All I'm saying is that God gave me this great place to live." I say that meaning *location, location, location*. "And so what if Iris is a little interested in her new neighbor?"

"I thought you turned over a new leaf." Bri's accusing me now. "Whatever happened to 'meaning what you say and saying what you mean'?"

"Yes, well, I really meant it when I thanked her for the jawbreakers."

"Pffst!" Bri smirks. "She was fishing, Gaby. And I want to know why."

"That's so silly. She's probably just a talker, and as you well know, I could talk that woman under the table. But that's not going to happen."

"Oh, really. And why's that?"

"I'm through, Bri. This is my watershed moment—it really is. I'm staying out of the fray, chica, by reining in this mouth o' mine. No longer will this tongue be getting Gaby-girl into trouble. I just want to live my life, and do it well."

"Sounds like you're dodging. If you're not careful, you'll slip into those old passive-aggressive ways."

"I will not. I'm becoming wary, that's all. But I figure the best way to stay a step ahead of other people's strangeness is to keep my opinion to myself."

"You're so dramatic. You don't talk too much."

I swing her a doubtful look.

"Okay. So you're a bit, uh, chatty. In this case, that just might be a good thing. It would keep Iris on her toes."

"That remains to be seen." I wink at Bri. "Listen, I know you worry about me. Granted, I've given you lots of reasons to do just that, but

I'm really hoping to start fresh here. And that includes not allowing myself to get sucked into neighborhood drama, if there really is any. Besides, even if she is nosey—and I'm not saying she is—she's just one lady. How much trouble could she be?"

Bri folds her arms across her chest. She sneaks a peek out the window to the street below, where Iris is hosing down her lawn and staring up toward my loft. Water has pooled around the base of a queen palm and trails slowly down the sidewalk.

"Yeah," Bri says, casting a skeptical glance my way. "Good luck with that."

Two

MY LAST BOYFRIEND STOOD TALL with chiseled features and a mane of silken hair that would make Black Beauty sob with envy. He was also a liar, a scoundrel, and . . . did I mention a liar? It's a ridiculous story, really, but one that's helping me redefine my gullible ways. Ty—the ex-boyfriend—dated me to keep watch on the woman he really wanted, and that would be my best friend, Bri. Not that she noticed. Bri's a smart chick but dumb when it comes to men who openly ogle her. Ty also happened to be Bri's boss, and that girl was just too crazy-in-love with her husband, Doug, to see that all the private meetings Ty scheduled were more about his desire for her than, well, her business acumen.

I want a love like that. Can you imagine? To be so blind to the near-groping of strangers because you only have eyes for your husband?

"Yoo-hoo."

It's late, and I'm in front of the dilapidated mansion-of-sorts I now call home, chewing on thoughts while clipping back a bougainvillea gone wild. I swivel around to face Iris, her arms folded across the front of her polo shirt. Everything about her screams "matron of the neighborhood," except her face. Her skin's smooth, and I realize she's probably younger than she acts. Or maybe she's had an excessive amount of skin peels.

"Hello, Iris. How are you this evening?"

"Hello, Gaby."

A woman, sylphlike in tight leggings, jogs by. Iris leans toward me. "We call her Barbie Runnergirl."

Who's "we"?

Iris pauses. "Look at this," she says. "Jake's got you doing the gardening. Hope he doesn't recruit you to paint the whole place too. It certainly needs it."

Jake McGowan's the landlord I've yet to meet. When I called about the loft, I had to leave a voice mail, and he phoned me back all the way from Spain, where he was attending his fifth *corrida de toro*, or bullfight. *¡Ole!* Jake asked me a few questions and surprised me by telling me where I could send the check. He then directed me to a conch shell propped up against the side of the house, where I found two keys: one to the main house and the other to my loft.

I swipe at a strand of hair with the back of my gloved hand. I could use a bangs trim, but right now my paltry savings is set aside for rent and food. "I just thought I'd clip this vine back a little—you know, so that the flowers would have more breathing room." Like Mama would do.

"Hope Jake discounts you for that!" Iris smiles, but I'm not so sure what I see in those round eyes of hers. "He's an interesting man, your landlord. Wouldn't you agree?"

I keep clipping, glad that utilities are paid by the homeowner. Otherwise, I'd probably be taking my baths in the channel of ocean water flowing behind my house. "He's very nice, but we've never actually met."

"Really? He's a wicked world traveler. Absolutely wicked."

"Is that right?"

"Hardly shows up around here at all. But that's obvious, isn't it? Most of the homes around here are beauties by the water—even the tiny ones—but Jake has failed to keep his up to neighborhood standards. The only reason he's kept the house this long is because it's paid for. You know, his father owned this place before him."

"Hmm."

"His father bought this property more than thirty years ago. He was already a retired police officer at the time. The neighbors around here thought the man was positively ancient to be building a house here so late in life."

How Iris knows so much about things that happened most likely when she was still toddling around in Pampers and eating cereal off the floor, is a mystery to me.

She drones on. "The old man had little Jake with him at the time; it was just the two of them. When he died, Jake took the place over and lived here with his young daughter, even after his wife divorced him. It's no wonder she did! Jake's not the kind of man who can commit to just one woman. My friend Shonda and I have lost count of all the girls he's brought home—"

"Well," I cut in. "Jake's a nice man. Sounds like his life isn't perfect, but really, whose is?" I'm hoping she gets the hint that I've no desire to engage in speculation about someone I've never met—especially someone who's giving me a steal of a price on my loft. It's a risk I can't afford to take.

Instead, her eyes bug out, startling me by their wideness. "Well, well. Sounds like you two really hit it off."

Instant heat saturates my cheeks. Like I meant it that way. I hear my mama's voice in my head telling me to *escapa*—meaning escape! In my panic I don't notice my friend Livi drive up in her hybrid until she's parked in front of us, waving out the window.

I drop my pruning shears into the dry grass and nearly skip to the sidewalk. "Hey, friend!"

"Buona sera! Is this a bad time?" My Italian-wannabe friend carries a basket of goodies from Trader Joe's and the kindest smile this side of California. Is that chocolate poking through the plastic?

I hug her and sense Iris's stare boring into the back of my head. "Not at all!" I turn and discover my neighbor just as I had imagined. "Livi, this is my new neighbor, Iris."

"Hello," Livi says.

"A pleasure." Iris glances my way. "See you around the 'hood, Gaby."

I turn back to see Livi nodding at me, her smile confident.

"What?"

"I just came from the mechanic."

I scrutinize her trendy Prius. "What's wrong with it?"

"Nothing. Nothing. Just had the fluids changed. Max asked about you."

"Max. He's so good with cars, isn't he? And honest too. He works on my gently worn Volvo sometimes. Did he tell you?"

Livi digs a balled-up fist into her side, almost like she's angry, which she almost never is. "I said he asked about *you*, Gaby. Tsk, tsk. Didn't you hear that?"

My face feels warm again. "Okay, so . . . did you tell him about my sudden move?"

Livi's sigh sounds more like the ripple of a baby's voice at naptime. "I told him about the fire at your apartment building and he was shocked. He wanted to know if you were okay, and where you were now. He said to give you this." She hands me a business card. "Said you could bring your car in anytime, free of charge. I think he's got the hots for you, Gaby."

I nearly scream with laughter.

Most of the time, Livi's as gentle as a shore bird, unless she's selling something. Livi's a Realtor, and although she's yet to own a piece of property of her own, she's quickly learning that to sell it, boldness counts.

I flop an arm around her perfectly-sculpted shoulder, and we walk toward the entry. "Max is just enamored with my car. Nice of him to ask about my well-being, though. He's been friends with Bri and Doug for years, so we bump into each other bunches over there. There's never been any spark between us." I bite my lower lip. "Sorry to disappoint you."

Livi stops and roots her sinewy legs in place. "Is that a duck?" She points into the cloudless, yet darkening, sky. Sure enough, a mallard's honking and gliding over the rooftops toward the open channel.

I make a face. "Quack."

Her smile falters. "I'd forgotten that you'd have ducks living near you."

"It could've been you." I hate to admit the obvious because if Livi had decided to rent this place, where would I be? "I'm thrilled to be here but feeling guilty that you passed on it."

Livi brightens. "Don't! I was only kidding. I'm so glad you're here. Really." Livi's got a lovable disposition, if not a lot of guts (except when selling real estate, that is). She may not realize this yet, but Livi epitomizes the "do unto others" Scripture to heart, often at her own peril. Exhibit A for atrocious is her roommate, Jet. It's tough to understand why Livi continues to share an apartment with an aging punk-loving Goth. Still, her fortitude inspires me.

That and her fit little body. We step into the house and in the midst of the second flight of stairs up to my loft I realize I'm winded. She's not. Talk about unfair. Add *out of shape* to my list of misfortunes.

"Is this view not just absolutely beautiful, Gaby? Like the canals of Venice." Her voice sounds wistful.

"I know. Million-dollar view." On a dollar-a-day budget.

A sound like a lawn mower cranked up to full speed draws our attention. Livi thrusts her chin forward. "Who's that?"

A kid with oily beige hair zips around the corner, the bow of his inflatable dinghy rising up off the water. He steers an outboard from the back end of the boat to the home next to mine, drops something onto the dock, then starts up again. We watch as he drops a couple of sheets of paper onto my dock below.

I shake my head. "Can't say that I know."

"I'm all over it. You want me to go grab that, right?"

Climbing those stairs any more than is necessary doesn't thrill me. With legs like hers, Livi could probably take them two at a time and be back before the wind of her stride settles. That is just so wrong.

I shrug one shoulder. "If you really want to."

Livi hands me the basket of goodies I've been dying to wrest from her. "*Ciao*, baby." I watch her dart for the stairs, her ponytail bouncing behind her, and make a mental note to send that girl to Italy someday.

She's back in a snap, waving a flyer, and not a bead of sweat to be seen anywhere on her skin. "It's the *Reef Report*, one of the benefits of your new neighborhood, Gaby. You'll find it comes in so handy." Spoken like a true real-estate professional, although by the way she's peering over my shoulder, something tells me it's news to her.

I scan the page. *Rad Reminders:* details about trash pickup and street sweeping days; *Rare Ruminations:* notes from the association president; *RomanticRewards.blogtown.com:* tips for the lovelorn from Iris. And *Rumor Ruckus:* a welcome wagon of sorts, listing the neighborhood's newest residents.

Livi laughs and says, "You're listed in here!"

"Where?"

She points to my name, spelled incorrectly there in blazing hunter green. "See, it says, 'Welcome Gabby Flores.' They spelled it with two *b*'s. You just moved in this morning—talk about news traveling fast."

I huff and set the page aside to read later. "Forget this for now. Since you haven't seen this place lived in, let me show you around. There's the kitchen." I point to a microwave circa 1997 on top of a small counter, next to a wet bar. "And there's the living room." I point again, this time at Bri's old denim couch shoved up against one long wall. "And we also happen to be standing in my bedroom." Once again, I gesture to Bri's sofa, which unfolds into a bed. Thank goodness Bri never cleans out her garage.

Livi's shoulders slump. "And all I brought you was that silly basket. I'm so sorry about the fire and all, Gaby."

I force a smile. "It's all part of the Big Plan," I say, trying to assure both of us that God really is in all of this.

"What're you going to do about the shop?"

I meet her eyes with mine. "I'm going to open those doors tomorrow and hope that my puny inventory will bring in enough for me to buy more."

"Alone?"

"It'll be fine."

"No, it won't. I'm offering my services, free of charge."

"I can't pay you."

"Tsk, tsk. Didn't you hear me? Free of charge. That means no money is to change hands in this deal."

This is so like Livi. The giver who keeps on giving. I'm desperate for the help, but at what cost?

She breaks into my thoughts. "I'm not taking no for an answer. I still have to show properties when clients call, but you know, my degree's in accounting. I'll come in to help you every afternoon until business is back to its former glory."

Former glory. That's rich. All my business's former glory got me was a slumlord apartment manager and a juiceless fire alarm. I nearly gag on the pride that's wrapped around my neck, tightening its noose with every offer of help bestowed upon me. Who am I to turn down such care, though? Livi's perky, hopeful presence around the shop would be a great help.

I avoid answering her until later, when we're standing on the sidewalk in the twilight, talking about nothing much at all. "Livi, I'm determined to make Florally Yours work. I humbly accept your offer. I owe you, sweet girl, and I'll find some way to pay you back."

She wags her head with determination. "Not necessary."

I wave good-bye to my friend as she pulls away from the curb, hesitating only when I notice Iris, half-hidden by a concrete light pole, a taut leash jutting from one hand. Other than the quiet purr of Livi's car heading north on Harborwest Court, the only sound in the air is the whimper of Iris's floppy-haired mutt fighting the very real threat of strangulation.

Three

"I THINK YOU SHOULD START a blog, Gaby."

I shrug.

"A blog. You know what a blog is, right?"

I hold up my two-week-old French manicure, the one I've been preserving with clear gloss applied each night. "Do these fingers look like they spend much time pounding on a keyboard?" Sure, I know that blogging's still all the rage, but considering that my laptop went up in flames (and if I'd have left it in the shop, Sammy would be using it to IM his supplier about now), I doubt I'll be joining the masses on the Internet anytime soon. E-mail's still my main reason for using the computer at all.

Livi stares at my fingernails. "They're beautiful, Gaby. I envy how nice they are for someone who works with plants."

I grab the broom that's leaned up against my shop's counter. Florally Yours is a sliver of a place in downtown Ventura, but it's plenty for me to handle. Unfortunately, not only did Sammy steal my money, wire, moss, and raffia—he also tracked in a ton of dirt from the planter out front.

Livi continues, spreading out invoices on the counter like a hand of cards. "I don't want to push. It's just that as your new business advisor, I think that a blog would be such a nice way to advertise your talents."

"You do?"

"Gaby, you've noticed the big emporium that's just opened down the street, right?"

I sigh. *Don't remind me.* "Yes, I'm aware of it."

"So I was thinking. You could give advice on caring for flowers or how to create spectacular floral arrangements. When you give you always get something in return."

"Ooh, that sounds like a Bible verse."

"Well, I was thinking that I could get you started and then let you loose with the advice. Maybe you could divide your posts into five topics, one for each day of the week. For example, on Mondays you could talk about choosing the right flowers for every occasion, then on Tuesday, something else, and on and on."

I wrinkle my nose and inhale a puff of dusty air. "Sounds pretty regimented, sweet girl. Thank you, anyway."

"I like to think of it as just being very organized. You give people what they come to expect, and after a while they'll be calling you for orders. You could be sending orders clear across the country by next week!"

I'm sparked by a thought. "Didn't the neighborhood newsletter mention a blog? What was it . . ."

"RomanticRewards.blogtown.com."

I jerk upright. "That's it. Wonder what it's really about . . . maybe coupons for dates or something. Kind of a strange thing to find in a community newsletter, don't you think?"

"Actually, it's advice for keeping the home fires burning, if you know what I mean."

I glance at Livi.

She shrugs. "I checked it out last night."

"Oh."

"Seems like pretty good advice. Although I'm not interested in that kind of thing right now."

"About that . . ."

Livi forges ahead. "By the way, your landlord called when you were at the post office. He asked how you were doing."

"You're kidding. I don't even know who owns this building. I've just always paid my rent through an agency."

"I meant your loft landlord, Jake, called. We've never met in person, but I almost feel as if I know the man."

I stop sweeping.

Livi shrugs. "I've heard things."

"Like?"

"Oh, I don't know. Something about him being a chef who travels the world." She taps her keyboard. "Actually, I understand he's more of a consultant now."

"Consultant of what?"

"Chef things, I guess. He's also a pretty popular date, from what I hear."

You and me both, sister. I slide the dustpan under a pile of dirt. "Did he leave a message?"

"Yes. He said he wanted to make sure that the neighbors were being nice to you. Then he laughed so loud I had to hold the phone away from my ear. Anyhow, he said to tell you that he may be occupying the lower floors sooner than he had originally planned. He didn't give a date, but said if you had questions, you could drop him an e-mail." She holds up a three-by-five card. "I wrote down his addy here."

I glance at it, then start swishing the broom around again. He's moving back. An uncomfortable chill alights on my skin as I resist speculations about my elusive landlord. None of my business. I straighten and feel my back crack. "Getting back to my earlier question, Livi . . . why not?"

"Why not what?"

"We were talking about Iris's romance blog, and I was wondering why you never date anyone." Livi's divorce has always been a fragile subject, and I wonder if I've just gone too far.

Livi looks up.

"Too personal?"

She looks back down at the stack of my bills in front of her. "No, of course not. I fell in love once. Well, you know that. It didn't work out for me, but I'm not against love or anything. I'm just not particularly interested in going through that again."

I sigh. "Can't say that I blame you."

Livi laughs. "Right. You?"

"All right, I deserved that. I guess I have been man-crazy over the years. But I've changed. Yes, chica! I've changed. If it happens, fine, but I won't go searching for it. As Bri would say, 'I'm so done with that!' "

Livi smiles but squints like a skeptic. No matter. I'll prove to her—and the rest of my friends—that I've grown up. I've finally realized that life is not a Hollywood romance. Mr. Fabulous will not be waltzing through that door to save me from my current pickle, and I won't suddenly burst forth in song out of gratitude. In other words, unless Richard Gere swoops in here at the end of the day, I'm sunk.

Livi breaks through my reverie. "I've brought you my old laptop. You can have it. And I will set up that blog for you, Gaby, when you're ready."

I look up from sweeping to find Livi's earnest face staring back at me. That hopeful expression of hers is hard to turn down. What could it hurt? "Sure. You do that, and I'll try to come up with something spectacular to say."

"*Arrivederci!*"

That phrase about "best-laid plans" hurtles through my mind after I turn the key to rev up my worn-out Volvo at lunchtime and all I hear is the steady click of a dead starter. My eyes glare into the sky's clouds, the ones threatening to do more than block the sun. "God, I can't afford another thing!"

Determined, I turn the key again, and this time even the clicking slows. I wrench myself from the car, muttering that God must've misunderstood my prayer.

Livi looks up as I blast through the front door. "Back already?"

"My car's dead." I grab the counter and drop my head and pink clutch onto it.

Livi slides a key over to me. "Take mine."

I drag myself up. "No!" My eyes fixate on the antiqued-frame mirror that's listing to the right on the wall in front of me. Sammy must have bumped it when he was slithering through here in the dark. Why he took all my favorite artwork from the walls, yet left that, I'll never know. If not for the mirror and my wall-mounted stem cutter, the place would be as empty as Jesus' tomb. Tears threaten to come, but I force them back. Mama always frowned when I cried.

"You could always call Max," Livi says tentatively.

Max Rispoli. Dependable and gracious, my friendly neighborhood mechanic would know what to do. I wince, remembering Max's offer of help for such a time as this. I don't want to take advantage of his kindness, nor do I want him to think I'm some kind of leech, suctioning away every bit of generosity.

"He'll think I set you up to tell him my tale of woe," I whine. "How convenient is that? Just one day after he offers me free services, I'm taking him up on them." I grunt, trying to figure out a way to come up with enough cash to pay for what just may be a substantial repair bill.

"You're so dramatic, Gaby. He asked about you, remember? I just told him the truth. That's when he offered to help you out if you ever needed it. He sounded really sincere."

I grimace, my lips pressed together.

Livi holds up her hands. "You know me; I don't say anything." She leans over the counter and lowers her voice like we're being monitored. "But I've just reviewed your bills and I think you'd better take advantage of any freebie you can."

I pick up the phone.

"Can it be salvaged?"

Max grins at me, his eyes soft and wise, like he's lived far longer than his thirty-five years. "Don't worry about a thing, Gaby. Just needs a new starter . . . and maybe a few other things." My mouth pops open and I start rifling around in my bag for my Visa card.

Max laughs. "It's on me, Gaby."

I shake my head. "I don't know what to say. I'll pay you back someday; I really will."

He fishes a set of keys out of a greasy pocket. "Like I said, forget it. Now here, take these keys. I brought you a loaner."

I glance over at the sunset red Jeep Liberty parked behind my pale white Volvo. I thought maybe he'd borrowed a customer's car to drive over here, but now he's offering it to me? "I-I couldn't."

He hardly moves, but his eyes crinkle into a smile as he continues to hold out the keys. "Sure you can. Just take it, and I'll let you know when yours is fixed up. One thing I ask, though. . . ."

I gulp, feeling as dependent as a toddler. "Anything."

"I need a ride back to my shop to grab the tow."

We meander through Ventura streets until we reach Max's shop some three miles away, my cheeks blushed and warm the entire time. What is up with that? There's just something about a man in uniform, even a mechanic's shirt, that messes with a girl's mind. Again, I'm thinking of Richard Gere in *An Officer and a Gentleman*.

Anyway, we're in front of his shop, and let me just say, for a mechanic's garage, it's impressively pretty, with walls coated in crisp white paint and a shiny blue stripe stretching like a headband just below the roofline. The bays are another matter. Three are occupied with cars wearing more layers of grime than a coal miner after dark. If not for the exotic car the color of a yellow highlighter in bay number four, the garage's interior would be awash in muted grunge. Max hops out and stands in the street. He rests one hand on the doorframe of my stylish new ride and leans in from the passenger side. "You look right at home driving this thing."

Again with the warm cheeks.

"I'll be back to pick up your car within the hour. I should have it fixed up by tonight or tomorrow at the latest. Okay with you?"

"Max . . . I don't know what to say."

"You?"

"Funny. I'm trying to say thank you. This leaning on others thing is very humbling."

"You're welcome." Max continues to lean against the car but turns his gaze toward an indistinct spot in front of us. "I'm not trying to humble you, Gaby. I just want you to know that I'm here for you. If you ever need me." He swings his gaze back toward me until his eyes catch mine head on.

Bri's right. She always says that Max bears a striking resemblance to a young Clint Black, and—oh my—I can see that now. He implores me with those chocolaty brown eyes and lopsided smile, and I feel a major sugar rush coming on. At the moment, country crooner Clint has nothing on the inquisitive eyes staring back at me.

But this is Max we're talking about. We've been bumping into each other for ages at Bri's house, and there's never been anything but friendly hellos between us. I delve back into those eyes of his and get a revelation of sorts: Max, the man who lost his wife to cancer five years ago and who's raising his surf kid alone, feels sorry for me.

The realization catches my breath, and I sense the rosy glow of my cheeks draining away.

I compose myself. "I appreciate that, Max. You're the best mechanic around, you know."

He straightens abruptly and gives the hood of the car a slap. "I'll give you a call when she's ready."

He walks toward the small office at the front of his shop and steps inside with nary a glance in my direction. I put the Jeep back in gear and try to shake away the feeling that somehow my compliment was lacking.

Four

AMAZING WHAT A TANK FULL of gas in a new-ish car does for the psyche. I've been buzzing around Ventura like a woman who has it all together rather than one who's unraveling by the moment. More than once my eyes have picked up on a chip the size of a pinhead on the nail of my right index finger. I don't have money for luxuries, and for the time being, a manicure falls into that category. But the comfy seats I've sunk myself into have helped me manage not to internalize my dire situation. Not too much anyway.

My cell rings again, and I sigh, believing I'm about to hear Livi's apologetic voice on the other end. She's called twice already, asking for forgiveness both times for bothering me. Doesn't she get it? I'd be desperate without her. I lean the phone to my ear and all I hear is, "Have you eaten?"

It's Bri, and what comes to my mind is that it is truly ungodly to lie, but I clear my vocal cords anyway. "Of course I ate, Mother."

"Good. What?"

"What . . . what?"

"What did you eat?"

I gulp. Do I tell her about the half-empty jar of candy sitting on my kitchen counter? Do I mention that I'll be living off of Livi's gift from Trader Joe's for as long as I'm able? Because although Bri's known for mothering her friends, she's equally known for her lack of culinary skills. Not that I'd ever tell her that too harshly. She does, after all, make a mouth-watering chocolate chili. Oh, and her brownies are to die for. Truly. Just the thought makes my stomach grumble, but are my problems hers?

I pull over to the side of the road. "Oh, honey," I say, "stop worrying. Anyway, how's the tour-boat business?"

"Four dolphins at the harbor mouth. Need I say more?"

I giggle. Bri's a sucker for sea life, which is why her new gig as a harbor cruise guide fits her so well. I thought she'd die when she left Coastal Tours after her boss made overtures toward her that were, let's just say, extremely inappropriate. That and the fact that he was dating me at the time just about put poor Bri-Bri over the brink.

I'm taking my lessons from her, though. Because, wouldn't you know it? Bri picked herself up, invested in a gently used cabin cruiser, enlisted the services of her old bus driver, Ned—although I do question that choice—and can now be found giving sightseers the grand tour of our small harbor. I'm straining to face my trials *con buen gusto*—with good taste—like my friend, but a sheath of dark moodiness that raises up on a whim may be my undoing.

Bri's peppy voice breaks into my thoughts. "I've got to get back to the boat, girlfriend, but I wanted to invite you to dinner tonight. Can you make it? Doug's made chowder."

My stomach cries out, and I slap a hand over the mouthpiece of my phone. Not only will this keep Bri from hearing my loud tummy rumbling, but it also allows me, without my friend hearing, to whisper a thanks to God that Doug's doing the cooking. "I'll be there, girlfriend," I tell her.

"Beautimus! Come as you are!" With that she's off on her next adventure at sea, and I've pulled up in front of my shop with its sad little Closed sign dangling in the window. I flash on my mama, standing along the highway next to a dozen buckets of freshly picked and sorted flowers, her proud smile willing customers to stop for a bundle—whether they need them or not. *I'm trying, Mama . . . trying not to give up. You'll see.*

Inside, Livi's laptop buzzes, and she hardly notices that I've stepped inside. Her eyes follow the path of words flitting across her screen. I lean in next to her, but she pulls the screen shut. "Max called. Says your car'll be ready"—she glances at her watch—"in about an hour."

"Max," I sigh. "My hero."

"He sounded grumpy."

"Car's old. Probably a bigger job than he'd originally thought. I feel sorry for him."

Livi sighs that babyish sigh of hers.

I stop. "And that means?"

Livi's chin pulls her face downward. Only her eyes meet mine, briefly. She reminds me of the stereotypical timid librarian, a woman whose head is buzzing with a million thoughts yet is unwilling to let them spill out.

"You do think I'm taking advantage of Max. Don't you?"

She spits her sigh this time and adds a shrug. "That's *amore*, I guess. I'm just giving you the message, Gaby. I don't have an opinion."

Everybody has an opinion. I bite back the sting of sarcasm rising in my throat. I know my friends think I've butchered my life plan, the one to get married just once and forever, to have a quiver full of *bambinos* and to do it all while managing a successful small floral business. I can tell by the way Livi avoids my eyes that she thinks I should give up. Maybe get a job somewhere or move back home. I can think of a whole string of things to say to her, but I don't. Instead I do the breathing exercise I've read about, the kind that women in labor try when the pain attempts to control them and turn them into tortured animals instead of the glowing new mother they'd dreamed about.

I'm calm by the time Livi opens up her extra laptop, the one she insists that I borrow, and turns the screen toward me. "What do you think?" she asks.

Wow. A field of baby blue forget-me-nots splashes across the screen. Blue on green with touches of white to outline thousands of petals. Striking. Beautiful. Alive. Yet somehow disconcerting.

Livi cuts into my thoughts. "It looks familiar, doesn't it? I got the idea from your doodles on that legal pad over there." She points toward the phone.

I perk. That's why it looked familiar. "You captured that so well, Livi. You're a genius!"

I glance back at the screen, and my momentary elation pales again. In the right-hand corner, I read *Florally Yours, Gaby Flores, Owner.* I want to add *Always the Florist, Never the Bride,* but would that be tacky? I swallow my doubts and the taste of pride. I should be thrilled, but my pop's gone. Maybe Sammy stole my enthusiasm for running a business too.

I suck in a breath. "It's amazing, Livi. You have a gift," I tell her. "You truly do!"

"So you like it?"

"It's . . . wow. What can I say? How did you do this so fast?"

"I just found the template and then added your info. And see?" She points to the blank spot beneath the floral banner. "This is where I'll add your daily posts. Unless you'd like to do that yourself."

I hold up all ten of my long fingernails.

"Right. So I'll add them."

I reach out and hug Livi then. While I'm internalizing her judgment of me, she's building my blog. I'm an idiot.

"No big," she says and smiles shyly.

The bell on the front door rings and we both look up. Max sticks his head in, obviously trying not to track in any of the dirt encrusting his work boots. "Gaby, can I see you outside?"

I oblige and walk cautiously outside, aware that a cold sweat has begun its descent along my arms. One little suggestion from Livi, and I find that I'm reacting to Max like he's a blind date dropped from heaven itself—and did I mention he has hair the color of dark chocolate? Before he turns to talk with me, I resolve to treat him as I always have. This is *Max*, I tell myself, *a friend*. A sigh escapes me, but it sounds more like a sneeze.

"Gesundheit."

I blush. "Thanks." I avoid his eyes and glance absently at my car instead. "So, you got the work done on it already. You're fast."

He kicks a pebble to the curb. "Actually, Gaby. I'm going to need to keep it longer. I fixed the starter, but it gave me some trouble on the way over here. Was afraid of that." He leans his hip against my Volvo and crosses his arms. "I could've called, but I was almost here anyway, so I dropped by."

I groan. "So . . . . it's pretty bad?"

"Dunno. But I'd like to check it out before giving you back something that may not be safe to drive. When's the last time you had a tune-up?"

"No sé . . . I mean, I don't know. I can't remember."

He fights a grin.

"Is that really so bad?" I ask him. "It's not like I really go anywhere these days. Just between here and home. And Bri's." I don't tell him how much I abhor spending money on things that you can't see, like undergarments. Seems like such a waste, but then again, maybe that's because I'm broke.

"Street driving is harder on cars than most people think. Don't worry about it, though. She may still have some good years left in her. Hard to tell. I'll hold on to her a couple more days and let you know."

I swallow. An uncomfortable silence falls between us. And then I do the inexplicable. I hop forward and kiss Max on the cheek, startling both myself and him. I can tell by the purple cast streaking across his skin.

"Oh, Max! Sorry, it's just that I'm just so . . . so grateful for your help." He catches my hand and holds it longer than necessary. Still, he doesn't say a thing. Anyone who really knows me also knows that pregnant pauses and I cannot coexist. They seem to have a gravitational pull that yanks words right out of my mouth. "I-I mean, it's been a long week, you know? Well. A long month, really. And I'm trying to cope—really I am. And everyone's been so helpful, like Bri and Doug, and now Livi's helping me out." I point toward the shop. "I just can't thank you enough for stepping in to take care of my old wreck. What would I have done? Really. What?"

He's still staring at me. *Say something*, I want to shout. Oh, for a man wearing greasy jeans he's handsome! Finally, the right corner of his mouth lifts into a gentle smile. He lets go of my hand, leaving it warm from his touch.

"You're not a quitter, Gaby. You would've survived just fine. Glad I can help, though." He turns to leave. "Take care of yourself. I'll call and leave a message when she's ready for pickup."

"Yes. Okay. Fine." I take a step back and try not to watch him as he goes. Instead, I walk to the door of my shop, my dignity trailing behind.

Five

"DOUG'S RUNNING LATE."

I've been sitting at Bri's dinged-up kitchen island nibbling on slabs of French bread from the bakery while mulling over my earlier decision to ask her for a loan sometime after tonight's dinner. Doing so is moving far outside of my comfort level, and I'm still trying to get up my nerve. Her voice pulls me from my thoughts, and I sit up straight. "I thought Doug's long nights were a thing of the past," I say, referring to her and Doug's decision to work less and be together more.

Bri stirs the chowder, which—she assured me—Doug alone had made the day before. "He's trying to have less of them, but late nights come with a lawyer's job. I doubt he'll ever escape from them totally. This is weird though."

"How so?"

She shrugs. "Feels like something's up. Doug says there've been a lot of closed-door meetings between the big guns. Maybe they're going to ask him to manage the firm or something."

I jump up to pull her close with a hug. "I knew it! Doug's the best, and you . . . you're going to be the belle of the ball, the grand dame, the . . ."

Bri screws up her face and freezes in place, one hand wrapped around a ladle that's jabbing the air. She looks quite like a confused Statue of Liberty.

I continue. "I just mean that you'll be holding court next to that handsome husband of yours at all the company parties. You're both so beautiful—it'll be perfect!"

She drops her arm. "Oh, brother. Gaby, you're too much. That's the last thing that I want. But hey, maybe you could stand in for me. You're so much better at all that manners stuff. 'Pass the butter, *s'il vous plaît*' and all that."

I sit back down. Bri's my closest friend ever, although we are so different. She has little regard for appearances. Unlike me. My best friend keeps offering to help me get over this latest hill in my winding road, but I've turned her down every time. Mama never asks for help; never has, never will. Deep breath in. Start fresh. Swallowing my pride will be easier knowing that she and Doug are in a good place themselves—and Mama never has to know.

"What happened?"

I glance up, confused, and realize that Bri's not talking to me but to Doug. He just stepped into the kitchen, scowling. I've only seen Doug scowl one other time—the night he caught my date practically trampling Bri—and I'd prefer not to relive that moment ever again, if you don't mind. The way he's wresting his tie from around his neck makes me want to grab my chic suede bag and dash home to my lone can of Dinty Moore stew.

He opens his mouth, then sees me and stops, his fist still closed around the haphazard knot at his neck. "Oh . . . hi, Gaby." He glances at the bubbling chowder on the stove and I notice his cheek twitch.

Bri chimes in. "It's okay, Doug. Nathan's with Gibson tonight, and Gaby and I were just hanging out, eating too much bread. Max is late too."

I sink into my barstool. "Max?"

Bri slides me a casual look. "Max loves chowder. Didn't I mention he was coming?"

Doug unexpectedly stalks out of the kitchen.

Bri calls after him, "Doug, is something wrong?"

I finger my bag, but Bri pats my hand and whispers, "Stay." She follows Doug into the living room, leaving me alone to nibble too much and worry. Worry about my friends, about money, about . . . Max. I really don't understand why I'm nervous about Max. The other two issues, yes, but a longtime acquaintance showing up for a meal of chowder and hot bread? Been there, done that. Max has popped in unannounced to the Stone residence more times than Bri and I have baked up brownies for wallowing.

I'm just vulnerable these days. And I know it. Max hands me a lifeline in the form of free auto care, and I'm suddenly reading more into it than he ever meant. If anything romantic was going to happen between us, wouldn't it have happened long ago?

The chowder makes a bubbling noise, so I hop down and reach out to give it a couple of quick stirs. I also tear off another chunk of bread, and dip it into the pot. Yum. Nothing like warm comfort food to make everything all right. I hear a knock on the door and glance toward the doorway. Nothing from Bri or Doug, who headed up the stairs just moments ago. Last bite of bread in hand, I answer the door.

"You smell nice—it smells good in here," says Max, stepping into the foyer.

So which is it? "Hi, Max. Good to see you again." Although I had nothing to do with it.

We walk together toward the kitchen in silence. I've tucked my lips sharply beneath my teeth, determined not to drift into speech overdrive again.

I pry them open just to ask, "Can I get you something to drink, Max?"

He glances toward the doorway.

"They'll be out in a minute." My hand grips the handle of the open fridge door. "Let's see. Lots of Coke, Diet Coke, a jug of Arnold Palmer—that's for me, but I'll share."

"Coke's good."

I plop a couple of ice cubes into a glass before filling it with soda. "Here you go."

Max settles into one of the counter stools, and I realize that he's the same as always: an easygoing guy, someone to talk to about the day's forecast and last weekend's big box-office draw. He's just what I need. A guy friend, and nothing more.

I sense tension rolling away, and my body starts to relax until Max's chocolaty eyes catch mine. Great. A quiver surges through me, not unlike the sugar rush I'd felt when Max first offered me his unconditional help. I'm dying to splash myself with cold water. *Think straight, Gaby. Keep your head together.*

Max breaks the silence, his voice low. "You think Bri's up to something, Gaby?"

"Like what?"

"Don't know. That girl's a schemer, though."

"Excuse me?"

He smiles. "Don't take that the wrong way. Bri's a charmer all right, but you wouldn't believe how many women she's suggested I date."

"Actually, yes. Yes, I would." And that's what you think this is. "So. How many have you?"

"Dated? None. Well, one, but she just wanted a tune-up." He laughs heartily. "And a load of advice on whether to buy a Lexus or a Volvo."

"Stop it."

"I told her to get an AMC. Pretty much put an end to our romance right then and there."

I giggle and scoot my behind onto a stool. "Maximilian, did I know you were funny? I don't think so. You were holding out on me."

"I have my moments. You going to share that soup with me?"

"Chowder, Max. It's blasphemy to call chowder 'soup.' What am I going to do with you?" I shake my head at him and get up. "Doug got home just before you got here. He looked like he'd had a really terrible day. Bri dashed upstairs to talk to him, so we might as well help ourselves. It could be a while. Hope everything's okay."

"We could go someplace else."

I sneak a glance at him. That familiar ripple runs through me again. . . . Argh.

"Like the dining room."

That was just annoying.

I slide two bowls of steaming chowder onto the island and pass the napkins. "It's bad enough that I have the nerve to take over her kitchen this way—although Bri won't really care. Please pass the pepper." Our fingers brush as I take hold of the pepper mill. "Thank you."

"You like living near the harbor? Iris says you're her new neighbor."

I freeze. How does Max know Iris?

"What? Iris giving you a hard time already?"

"I don't really know her." No need to let on that my initial impression of Iris was less than remarkable.

"She's hard to know," he continues. "We served together for three years on an association board. Can be overwhelming when you first meet her, but she's harmless. I could cut her spark plug wires, though, if she's bothering you."

I cover my mouth. "Max, that's terrible! You wouldn't do that—would you?"

We both look up to see Bri, her face a blotchy red, stepping into the kitchen. "Do what?" she asks, clearly hoping to deflect our attention away from her.

"Oh, Bri," I say, stunned by the look on my friend's face.

She swipes her eyes with the back of her hand. "It'll be okay. Doug just had some hard news today." She turns to Max and cracks a smile. "Any openings at the shop, buddy? Oh, never mind. Maybe now's not the time."

Max and I look at each other, then to Bri. "What happened, Bri-Bri?"

She brushes one highlighted strand of hair away from her face and tucks it behind her ear. "The firm's . . . no more." She slaps the kitchen counter. "Oh, ugh! I don't want to talk about it. You guys want ketchup for your chowder?"

Just which atrocity do I address first? "What do you mean 'no more'?" I ask, aware of Doug's heavy footsteps descending the stairs.

Bri just groans.

Doug walks in and reaches out to shake Max's hand. "Max. Sorry I'm not much of a host tonight." He pulls a Coke from the fridge, pops the top, and takes a swig before continuing. "Long story, but my bosses have obviously been planning to walk for a while. Apparently they weren't happy having to share so much of the till."

We watch him stare out the window into the darkening night. "They took most everything—files, equipment, software—and left me with an office full of hungry employees." He grimaces. "I'm the low man, so this has left me scrambling. There's no way I can keep things going on what I bring in."

"What does that mean for your employees?" I ask.

Doug looks pensive. "I told them to dust off their resumés. I'm still analyzing things, but about the only one I'll be able to pay, at least for the short term, is me." He glances at Bri. "I hope."

Bri reaches up and touches his face. Her eyes, filled with compassion, stay unwavering on her husband. Instead of questioning Doug or demonstrating her angst with a few misdirected angry words, Bri's looking at her husband with an aching tenderness.

Man, I want that.

Max pipes up. "I've got some office space you could move into. No charge till you get on your feet."

All eyes turn to Max.

He continues. "Just off Main Street, not far from my shop. It's yours if you want it." He pauses. "Of course, if you don't mind moving into the industrial area, I've got a bigger place available over there. Your choice."

Bri and I stare silently.

"I'd like to take a look tomorrow, Max," Doug says. "Thanks for the offer."

Now see, this is where men and women differ. I'm sitting here, mystified that my longtime acquaintance and friendly neighborhood mechanic owns rental property at all. I'm also overwhelmed by his generous offer. I want to see some emotion here! Show me the love! If I were Doug, I'd grab Max and give him a big bear hug. Then again, hadn't I poured out my affection earlier in the day only to slink away in humiliation?

Max's offer has lightened Bri's mood, and she's actually donning an apron—the only one she owns—to dish up more of Doug's piping hot chowder. When she pads by, I notice Doug's hand reach over and touch the small of her back. Despite my friends' devastating news, the warmth in this room wraps me like my favorite wool coat—the one I lost in the fire—and my mind wanders off to ask the question: Will I ever know this kind of life?

Six

TWO ORDERS. IT'S EARLY AND I've just hung up the phone after listening to my shop's voice mail. *¡Gracias a Dios!*—Thank God!— I'd set up a voice mail system rather than using my old answering machine for the shop's messages. Sammy would've probably stolen that too. Two orders a day won't keep me in business, but considering I've been closed for days, it's a start.

My coffee mug's still warm in my hands as I sit by my open window, breathing in a salty breeze. In the last half hour two sailboats, one obnoxiously loud powerboat, and a couple of kayaks floated past, each taking with them a part of my soul. I've never been much of an adventurer, but I'm determined to change that. When I have the money. And the time.

I take three-and-a-half steps over to the kitchen sink and rinse out my mug. I've tried not to think about the red numbers bleeding through my checkbook, nor the fact that my plan to borrow from Bri ended with Doug's shocking announcement the night before. One thing I am pleased about: My reaction to their plight overshadowed my loss of a loan. Seriously, if I'd been more upset over their sudden inability to grant me a loan rather than feeling so sorry about the position Doug's been pushed into, I'd have questioned my own morals. Probably would've made myself pack up and run home to my mother for a good talking-to.

The doorbell rings and I hear a shout from outside. I can't make out the words, so I slide over to the other end of my narrow loft and peer out the window to find a delivery truck parked out front, its engine running.

I stick my head out the window. "I'll be right down."

The driver already wears a harried frown. He scrunches his brow in the morning sun. "You'll have to get someone to help you haul it in. It's a heavy one." He hops into his doorless truck and pulls away.

Unlike Bri, I'm an early bird. The way she chatters on into the night drives me crazy, just as my morning jabber causes her to hold her head in her hands and beg for another espresso. Sometimes even a brownie. So while she's probably still snuggled into sweats and a hoodie, I'm dressed and ready to tackle the early morning arrival.

I fling open the door to see two round eyeballs staring back at me.

"I'll help," Iris says, not waiting for a response. "Where do you want this?"

Considering Iris's already grabbed hold of the refrigerator-sized box, I grab its sides and shuffle backward. "We can just put it in the foyer until I figure out what to do with it." The foyer is the one common area of this old house. Double doors skirt the edge of the entryway on one side, with the stairs to my loft on the other.

Iris sets down her end. "Such a big package, Gaby. You must've spent a small fortune on something."

I search for the label and scan it quickly. "Actually, I didn't buy anything." The old Gaby would have offered her more info, maybe even a little speculation as to what the mighty package holds. Iris is bursting with curiosity, and it's killing me to keep quiet, but really, is this any of our business? "She's fishing, Gaby," I hear Bri say. So I don't tell her that the package has my landlord's name on it, nor do I mention the phone call I received saying that he'd be back in town soon.

"Thanks for your help, Iris." Let's just move along now.

Iris rests her hand atop the box. "Then somebody must really be fond of you. That's some gift. I'll help you get it upstairs. . . ."

"I don't want to bother you, Iris. I'll just leave it down here for now."

She peers over the box, her head reaching so far that I nearly stumble backward. "Oh, it's no troub . . . oh! How interesting. Looky there—it's something for Jake."

I peer at the label. "It is. But thank you again, Iris. It's such a nice day . . . are you headed out for a walk?" *And are you leaving soon?*

"It's large enough to contain an old-time trunk. Maybe that's what it is—Jake's things. This must mean that he's on his way back to civilization." Her mouth beams, but her eyes narrow slightly. "What brings him back?"

I blow out a nonchalant breath of air. "Who knows? I don't really know Jake, I'm just a renter. I can only speculate . . ." *No! Don't speculate!* I can't believe I said that.

"So you think he's got a reason for his return, then?" Iris folds her arms with a distinct smack. "I think you're right! I've always told him that he'd never be happy tramping around the world. Ventura is that man's home, and he's been running away from it long enough. Something tells me he's finally come around."

I have to hold my fingers still just to keep them from drumming along the side of the box. "We're all on a journey, I guess. Thanks again for your help, Iris. I have to head off to work now."

"In your fancy new car," she says. "Or should I say, in Max's car?" She smiles, her teeth hidden behind long, wide lips before they flap back open to yammer at me. "I just casually mentioned to Max that we had a new resident in our community, and it turns out you two already know each other. How precious! And then he loaned you his shiny car. Max would be a great catch for you, Gaby."

That's it. I move to the open door and stand beside it.

She doesn't get the hint—or at least ignores it—and continues on about Max. "Poor man. Lost his wife and has to raise that bedraggled child all by himself."

I nod listlessly.

"He really needs a woman to keep him warm at night—and to help him count all those stacks of money!" she says. Iris's laughter, the kind that trills on and on, fills the small entryway, and I know I'm stranded. Can't get any more awkward than this. Pretty soon, the forced smile on my face causes cheek fatigue.

She places both hands on her hips and rolls her globe-like eyes all over me. Like she's doing an inspection. "You and Max even look alike. Turn around."

"What?"

She doesn't wait and walks around me, nodding her head. "You're the same height, same coloring. Well, can you believe this? Your babies would be very symmetrical!"

My mind wanders. I'm dressed in the negligee I packed just for the hospital, waiting to receive my first guests after giving birth to my bundle of joy. My first guest enters, her face bright with awe and joy over the miracle of birth. She sucks in a wondrous breath, and with a gushing smile says, "Gaby, your baby is amazingly symmetrical!"

A voice calls from outside. "Mom?"

I peer around the door to see a twiggy girl in a tattered red robe standing on the sidewalk. Dark gray splotches encircle her eyes, and her skin looks much too light against the straggly blackness of her hair.

"Kit? What's the matter, sweetheart?" Iris's face etches in motherly concern.

Other than a slight eye roll, the girl's face barely registers any emotion. "Dad's on the phone." She tightens the threadbare robe around her narrow waist and begins to walk away, then stops and turns back. "Where's your Advil?" she calls out. "I need some Advil."

"I'm on my way," Iris sings out as she scurries along the path toward my gate. "That gorgeous new robe of yours is hanging in the closet, sweetie. When you get home, why don't you put that on?" She stops then to point at Sarah's second-story window, and in a stage whisper adds, "Perhaps I should keep my voice down. Wouldn't want to wake up your rather mystifying neighbor."

And she's off. Thankfully. Before I shut the door, though, Kit peeks over her shoulder, her gaze assessing me from behind those oily bangs. I'm drawn to those searching eyes and send the young girl a deliberate smile.

I tear my eyes away from hers when Max pulls up to the curb in my Volvo. He steps from my car, and my heart jolts. Ooh, he's hot when he's all cleaned up. I turn back briefly to see Kit scurrying away in her tattered robe.

Max moves up the walk. "Hi," he says, eyes crinkling.

"Hi," I say back. "Again."

A boom behind Max catches our attention. A guy in neon yellow shorts and a ripped, paint-splattered tank bends down and picks up the ginormous skim board he'd just dropped onto the sidewalk. "Sorry 'bout that!"

Isn't he the loony neighbor Iris warned me about? And, oh my . . . tell me neon shorts aren't coming back. He grabs up his board again and slides it into the bed of his truck before swinging a wave at us. "Live it good today!" he hollers, taking off just as Barbie Runnergirl jogs by.

Max peers around me. "Can I help you carry something?"

I remember the love-seat-sized box in the foyer. "No, that's just something for my landlord. So. Couldn't get enough of me last night?"

Those crinkled eyes of his widen, and he stays silent, like he's lost all ability to speak.

What was I thinking? I clear my throat. "Come on up, Max. For coffee. It's the least I can do for all your hard work. Besides, my new loft has a gorgeous view. I want you to see it." *Don't talk so much.*

He hesitates, but those eyes are smiling. "Sure."

I'm getting a mixed message here. First he offers to fix my car, gratis, and tells me that he's here for me, if I ever need him. He makes me laugh over chowder at Bri's, and then he shows up here this morning looking finer than a bachelor up for auction, all cleaned and pressed. But when I ask him up, he hesitates. Like I'm *that* kind of woman. Maybe if I didn't open my mouth so much.

Upstairs, he looks at the view of water and upscale homes from my one and only west-facing, yet substantially large, window. "Yeah, that's a nice one," he says.

"Cream and sugar?"

He glances at the carafe on my narrow counter, the one wedged between my old jar of coins and the paper-towel rack, and then at my face. "Thanks, Gaby. I'll take it black, if you don't mind."

"Not at all. I saved you a seat by the window. I love sitting there. So much to see, you know?" I pour his coffee into a mug. "Will you be meeting with Doug soon?"

"He called this morning. Sounded better than he did last night."

I plunk onto the window seat next to him and curl my legs beneath me. "God must've put you there at the right time, Max. Your offer was so sweet, and timely too." I sip my coffee and lean against the glass. "I had no idea you were such a tycoon."

He laughs, and I feel giddy.

"I mean, really. You're usually so, so, um, so quiet and all. I thought you were . . ."

He watches me.

He smiles.

He's amused!

"Just a loner. A nice loner, mind you. But, you know, well, someone who works all day at his shop and spends the rest of his time with his son, and . . ." I trail off this path that leads to nowhere.

He gulps his coffee. "Appearances can trick you, can't they?"

I think he's annoyed until I notice the twitch at the corner of his mouth.

"You're laughing at me."

"Am not."

I squint at him and purse my lips, trying to hide my own laughter. "Are. So."

He laughs out loud. When his laughter subsides, he looks me squarely in the face. "What about you, Gaby? You're not exactly what you seem either."

Excuse me?

"Things are pretty tough right now for you. I'm right about that, aren't I?"

I shake my head and glance out the window. A woman has just fallen from her dock. A tiny woman is trying to haul her out and looks to be losing that battle. They're both shaking from laughter. I pull my gaze away.

"Max, I'm doing fine. I mean, seriously, look at this great view."

He glances away from the window and down my narrow loft.

"At least I'm not dead!" I blurt.

Max blinks, hard.

Oh. No. Max's wife died. "I-I'm sorry. I didn't mean that . . ."

"I know you didn't."

I set down my mug and fold my hands in my lap, as if this will help me control my mouth. "I'm trying to have a good, no a *better*, attitude about all that's happened lately. I thank God every day that I still have a roof over my head . . . and one with such a pretty view too."

"Why didn't you just move in with Bri and Doug? I'm sure that was an option."

I sense my eyes narrowing. "And walk around defeated? Maybe I've done things wrong in the past, maybe I haven't worked hard enough to accomplish what I need to survive, but giving up and moving back home or into Bri's place—that looks too much like failure to me. Not an option."

He holds both palms up in surrender. "Okay, okay. Not trying to start a fight—although you are a pretty gal when you're angry."

Don't even start.

He chuckles. "We're a lot alike, you and me, Gaby. We're both fighters, aren't we?"

I ponder this. Max has always seemed soft and gentle to me, yet he's right, in a way. Despite losing his wife, he's raising a great kid, running a respectable auto repair shop, and from what I'm learning, is quite the local real-estate investor. He's generous too. Our eyes meet, and I feel like folding myself into him. It's a startling reality for me.

"We're both survivors, Max," I finally say. "I'd have to agree with you on that."

He reaches for my hand and opens it up. "That's what I thought." With his other hand he places the key to my Volvo into my palm. "How about a ride back to my shop?"

Seven

I T'S BEEN A LONG, HARD, tiring day.

I've slipped myself into a pair of midnight-black yoga pants, a blouse milled from satin-finished cotton, and golden slippers. Not because I plan on twisting myself up like a pretzel anytime soon; I just like the sensation of soft fabric clinging to my body. It's like comfort food for the skin. And since I lost most of my things in the infamous apartment fire, favorite nighties included, my rarely used workout clothing has been reassigned as sleepwear. And I need sleep.

Sundown for me has always been synonymous with bedtime. This is probably because of my mother, who to this day runs a roadside flower stand along the highway east of here. During the summer I rose early to help her choose and bundle fresh-cut flowers and then set them up at her own stand, the one we painted yearly with the same leftover drum of Navajo White used throughout our side of our small duplex. When I wasn't in school, I stayed by her side all day. Sometimes I'd prop myself behind her handcrafted table and wrap carefree bouquets in thick stacks of old newspaper. I'm not sure which smell takes me back more—pulpy newsprint or woody branches, like the ones we used as filler. By the time daylight slipped away in those days, both Mama and I could do little else but eat and sleep.

I sink into Bri's old couch, rolling up a pillow and placing it against my lower back, trying to relax. But a plethora of words fling themselves around inside my head like errant acrobat artists. I shut my eyes and try to visualize my young hands picking words like flowers and bundling them together, all neat and tidy. You'd think that the quiet of my loft would help, but it's actually a little too. Too quiet, that is. Restlessly I stand and raise my waterside window just enough to allow the sea air and accompanying sounds to drift in. Satisfied, I settle back into the couch and relive my day.

Up at dawn, I began the morning eager as those seagulls posted on my rooftop watching for the first fish of the day to launch itself out of the water and into their waiting chops.

After dropping dreamy Max off at his shop and feeling the purr of my Volvo beneath my body, I dove headfirst into my first official "open" hours at the shop. Livi arrived in the early afternoon and—¡Gracias a Dios!—two brides called for appointments.

Two! The fire had chased many of my previous appointments away, but God was good and found me some replacement business.

My eyelids now droop to the sounds of water lapping against the dock below, persistent like a puppy nudging against a closed hand. Sleep nuzzles my ear. I need to flop open this sofa sleeper, but I'm tired. So tired. I'm lounging on a skiff, drifting into the open sea . . .

Whomp!

My eyes pop open.

Whomp!

With reluctance and a stroke of fear, I pull myself from slumber, pad to the top of the stairway, and lean my ear against the glass-paneled French door leading to the lower floors. A distant rattle begins, as if wind has kicked up, yet it continues long after most gusts have died down.

Whomp! Whomp!

I jump back and glance around. Until this moment, both east and west facing windows of my loft had provided a way for me to say hello and, later, so long to the day's sun. At three stories up, though, I realize now that they offer me little protection . . . or escape.

I grab my cell phone—my only phone—and punch in Bri's number. It answers on the second ring. "Hey there, you've reached Bri's beach pad. . . ."

Laughter boils up from the street below. I slide shut my phone and tiptoe to the lone east-facing window, which I had left ajar this morning.

My neon-shorts-wearing neighbor guy, the one who blinded me with his retro garb and annoyed me with his glib remark this morning, jerks his head upward, and waves vigorously at me as I peer at him from the shadows. Apparently that was enough of an introduction. "Hey there," he hollers from below. "Live it good tonight!"

See what I mean?

A beefy man, his head a swirling tangle of blond and copper hair, stands next to him. His arms crossed and grin wide, his eyes search for mine through the darkness. "Hey, Gaby," he finally calls out.

I blink. For one, I'm three floors up and not wild about shouting to carry on a conversation. Second, except for the Pollyannaish wave from neon-shorts guy this morning, I know neither of these men. As I move away from the window and search for my sweater, I hear the continuation of laughter below.

Downstairs, I step into the light on the path. Beefy man watches me with raised eyebrows and then steps forward. "I'm Jake."

I knew that. Somehow, I knew that.

He turns to neon-shorts guy. "And this strange fellow over here is Andy."

Andy smiles at me. "Beautiful night, isn't it?"

I glance at Jake. Man, he's tall. Tall like Doug, but thicker and rogue, like the Brawny Man. Only with messier hair, and younger too. Doesn't he have a grown daughter? Must've been a teenaged father.

"Andy's a happy guy," Jake says, his skin flecked with stubbly new growth. "Tell 'im it's going to rain and he'll tell you that's just what the grass needs."

Andy nods. "Gotta appreciate every day on earth."

They part to invite me into their conversation, and with reluctance, I step closer, drawing in the scent of cardamom and citrus and. . . pineapples? There's something about a man who wears his cologne well. "Nice to meet you both."

Jake slides closer and runs an animated glance down my comfy clothes. He reaches out to shake my hand, and my mouth turns to cotton. *Please, God, don't let him feel that sudden blood surge.*

I swallow some saliva, lick my lips, and glance back at the house. "So you found your delivery, I see."

His arms still wrap themselves around his solid chest. "It beat me by hours." He gives me a questioning look, his eyes peering down beneath heavy eyelids, but then he turns to Andy. "How'd a little thing like her drag it in?"

Andy laughs. "I saw Iris helping her this morning. Hilarious."

Jake hoots into the air.

Really. Okay, niceties over. Maybe I'll just step back and let these two old pals talk about me behind my back. It'd be more polite that way.

I clear my throat.

Jake nods at me, reminding me of a rancher appraising a side of beef.

Andy turns to Jake, and I'm suddenly invisible. "Check it out, man. Saw our old friend lying next to the railroad tracks the other day. Not good. I'd seen him bad before, when we hung out, but, Jake, he didn't even recognize me."

Jake nods quietly and his eyes shift to me.

Guess this is a private conversation. I step back. "Well. A pleasure meeting you, gentlemen."

Movement near the lighted window next door catches my eye as I move back up the path. It seems we've attracted the attention of our curious neighbor, Sarah.

Jake's booming voice breaks into my thoughts. "What?" he calls out. "To bed so soon?"

Andy chimes in. "Yeah, it's just the shank of the evening, Gaby! Jake will make a night owl out of you yet, cuz no one can throw a bash like him."

"Well, not tonight. Good evening, gentlemen."

Andy slaps Jake on one broad shoulder as I slip away. "Man, this neighborhood missed you, buddy."

Upstairs, I slide my window closed, shutting out the deep voices still punctuating the crisp air from down below. Cleansing breath in. It was too good to be true. I should have known. I told myself not to be gullible, and well, there you go.

I move to call Bri, see that I've missed a call, and punch in her number.

"It's me," I say when she answers.

"Hey, Gaby-girl. How's life in Snoot-ville?"

"Oh, Bri."

"Yeah, yeah, I know. Lots of your neighbors are regular folk, like you." She laughs. "So what's up?"

"My landlord's back in town."

"You're kidding."

"He . . . he just showed up here, without any warning."

Bri hesitates. "Is that okay with you? I mean, does it feel weird? Do you want me to come stay with you tonight?"

I glance at the French door that separates my loft from the stair-case to the main house. Those pretty little glass panels all flimsy and thinning have suddenly lost their charm. But I left my mother's home fifteen years ago, and although my decisions may not have always been stellar, I've managed just fine. On my own.

"No, no. I'm just going to bed anyway, chica. I'm just too tired to think straight right now."

"What's he like?"

I plop myself into the cushions of my window seat. "Let's see, he's blunt and kind of abrupt. And he's got a voice that could cut through the fog. But he smelled great."

"Uh-huh. What's he look like?"

"Well, it was dark . . ."

"That good, huh?"

A light pops on from the neighbor's deck, illuminating the waters beyond the dock. I squint into the murkiness. I think I've just spotted a dolphin or maybe a sea lion out there.

Bri cuts into the silence. "That's what I thought."

I shake up my wandering mind. "What do you mean?" I ask her.

"Gaby, my friend, it sounds like your landlord is a distraction of the best kind. . . ."

"Not."

Bri laughs. "Whatever you say."

I twist the toe of my shoe into the bare wood flooring. "What's up with you? He's my *landlord*, crazy girl. Besides, he and this strange neighbor guy were talking about me right in front of me! Have I mentioned him? He could've been an extra in *Saturday Night Fever*, I tell you. Very retro and . . . I hate to say this, but a little creepy."

"Like dangerous creepy?"

Sigh. "I won't go that far, but he does live in that house across the street that Iris pointed out the other day. I shouldn't be saying anything. There's definitely a story there, but he's nice enough, although still odd in my opinion. And oh! Did I tell you that Max stopped by this morning?"

"Uh, whoa. No, you didn't mention that! Tell me, tell me."

"Well, you know he fixed my car. Anyway, I invited him up for coffee and, I've just got to say, he's dreamy. Don't know why I never noticed that before."

"Well, I'd thought about it. But, Gaby, you always go for the, you know, the white-collar type."

"Seriously?"

"Yeah, seriously."

I feel a pout coming on. "That didn't stop you from inviting us both to chowder last night."

Bri laughs. "Matchmaking for you has become like decorating: Sometimes I just have to throw together colors that I'd never have thought of before to see if they complement one another."

"So now I'm fabric?"

Bri sighs. "Listen, Gabrielle. Can I help it if I want everyone—especially my best friend—to be as happy as I am with Doug? I know I've picked some duds—"

"That's for sure!" Her old boss springs to mind.

"But Max is true blue. He's kind and generous—in fact, he just met with Doug today and offered him a great office if he needs it. I guess I was just testing the waters with you two. Anyway, if you want to date Max, I'm all for it. And if your landlord turns out to be a looker . . ."

"Oh, please, Bri-Bri! Would you stop that already?"

"Ha, ha. Just kidding. Seriously, if he upsets you that much, maybe you should think of moving out before you get too settled. You know I'm totally willing to convert our messy office for you."

I cautiously shake my head. Fatigue has suddenly landed on my shoulders like a pigeon on a line. I take a slow breath in. "I'll be okay," I say. "I won't bother him, so I'm sure he won't bother me."

"'Kay. Call me if you need anything. Promise?"

I promise her that, and we hang up. What did I think anyway? That I'd have this mini-mansion to myself? I'm broke, and my business has taken a major hit. So this loft is tiny? So it's somewhat unkept? I'm surrounded by an eclectic mix of high-end properties, so I should be pinching myself at my good fortune. The mortgage of the loft's square footage alone is more than I could ever afford to own myself.

I crawl into my couch bed, pull the covers up to my chin, and breathe in their fragrance. *They smell like my old apartment.* My throat clutches at the thought. And as laughter ruptures from down below, I realize it's going to be a long night.

Eight

.

R*YAN* S*EACREST'S DAZZLING SMILE CARESSES* me as American Idol *plays across my fifty-two inch screen. Through the magic of high-def television, his eyes, ever-changing in color, rivet on mine, drawing me like a mythical goddess through the air and onto the stage. He turns to the audience, and in his winsome way introduces me to the panting crowd, using adjectives such as* "Inspired!" "Electrifying!" "Hideous!"

Huh?

Whomp!

My eyes pop open, and a spear of light assures me that morning has arrived.

Whomp!

Again with the whomp! Doesn't that man ever sleep? A quick glance at the clock, and I jerk upright. It's after eight. Way after. Mama's been at the flower stand since five, prepping bunches, trimming deadwood, watching carefully. . . .

I lunge for the robe Bri gave me and dart several glances at my French door, making a mental note to tack up a towel over the see-through panes. The space between my brows throbs, and I reach to turn on the coffeemaker, knowing a tall shot of caffeine can drive away menacing headaches. With the coffeepot sizzling away, I grab a quick shower.

As I lather up amidst the steam, I inhale the fragrance of honeysuckle bath foam. Oh my. If it weren't for a little thing like making enough money to keep me eating, I could stay in here all morning, because what this loft apartment lacks in space, it makes up for in bathroom amenities. The shower in here just rocks! It's roomy, all done up in fancy Spanish tile, and even has a porthole window that opens to let the steam escape. Ahhh . . .

"Mornin', Gaby!"

The disembodied voice fills the bathroom, and my scream ricochets against the ceramic tiles. I slouch against the cold wall, my eyes darting for a place to land, my hair gushing water down my shoulders.

The Voice continues to blow in through my shower porthole. "Coffee's on down on the back deck. You're welcome to it!"

I switch off the water slowly to avoid the squeak in each turn. On tiptoes, I strain to peek out. I don't see a thing, but I can hear shuffling on the second-floor deck, and then a screen door slides shut with a clank. I push out the breath that I'd been holding. He's got to be kidding.

If that man thinks he can just disturb my sleep and interrupt my shower, then he's . . . he's . . . well, he's just not right about that! I don't even know him! Wrapped in my terry-cloth robe, yet hardly dry, I grab my coffeepot in a huff, but it nearly hits the ceiling. I realize that it's empty. Empty?! My heart races, and the question of whether I really need more caffeine glides through me. Then it hits me: I forgot to fill the reservoir with water.

Oh!

And there's the rub. I need coffee before I can make coffee, caffeine in order to think well enough to make more. I miss my expensive, state-of-the-art programmable coffeepot. And my privacy! Glancing out my harborside window, I see my landlord on the deck with a coffee mug the size of a small boat. He's kicking back on a lounger like a "parrot head," one of those Jimmy Buffet fans who wear slip-ons, denim shorts, and a Hawaiian shirt all the livelong day. Even from three floors up, though, I can appreciate the plate on his lap piled high with eggs, muffins, fruit— Is that bacon?

Forget that, girlfriend!

I throw back a handful of granola, crunching down on it while pulling on my boots, white knit sweater, and just to cheer myself up, the tropical A-line skirt Bri gave me. The print reminds me of an island garden gone wild. Slipping it on tells the world that I'm not about to let my recent misfortunes (and current lack of fortune) affect my countenance. I'm okay! I really am!

At least I look as if I am.

I grab a handful of coins from my rainy-day jar—that's what my mother used to call Grandma's old peanut jar—and hurry downstairs, trying not to clomp too loud. I'll just slip out and forget—or at least try to forget—about my shower from the dark side. I shiver.

As I pass through the foyer, I see that the door to the main house is open. I step toward the opening, expecting to see . . . Well, I'm not sure what I expect to see, but from what I gather, Jake must be independently wealthy. A world traveler with nothing but time and money to burn—*¡Qué bueno para el!* Surely the inside of this place is in better shape than its weathered exterior. I bet it's filled with collectibles from faraway lands and exotic antiques. I turn my head ever so slightly, and blink.

Wow.

The smell of old cigarettes floats in from behind, and along with it a voice laced with familiar optimism. "Great space, isn't it?"

I shrink back but straighten and turn to see Andy, his hands tucked squarely into his pockets, his head rocking forward and back on his neck.

I, on the other hand, am nonplussed. "*¿Que?*—what did you say?"

"I heard you gasp."

I screw up my face. "That was shock you heard."

He shrugs. "Sounded like you said 'Wow.' I wouldn't blame you. This place is paradise."

I suppose that would explain my landlord's Jimmy Buffet attire. As for the house being paradise? Not so much. Velour couches, shaggy throw rugs, a doily draped over the top of a leather recliner, and what's that musty odor? Not at all what I expected, considering the grandness of most of the other homes that perch along the waterways in this town.

Andy opens the door a little wider. "Go on in. Check it out."

I halt. "No . . . no. . . . My flowers need me." I am still reeling from my shower gone wrong but am not about to let on. I'll just politely decline and get on with it.

"Well, then, live it good today."

Right.

Just as the toe of my gray leather boot catches on the cockeyed entry mat, and as I stumble out the door as if I'm part of a slapstick comedy routine, I hear Jake's unmistakable voice slicing through the quiet. "I'll leave the light on," he calls out.

I hurry to my car, noting that the damp ends of my hair have soaked a spot into the front of my blouse.

"*This* is not what I signed up for."

Livi, dressed in running tights and an itty-bitty tank, rubs her eyes. "You mean resort-style living? Free breakfast? A man at your beck and call? Why, Gaby, would anyone want to sign up for that?" She giggles.

"All I'm saying is that my privacy is important to me. And besides, I'm a member of the early to bed, early to rise club. Andy says Jake's a night owl, but this morning he practically barged into my shower, he was up so early."

Livi's eyes widen. "Tell me more."

"Stop it. The whole morning was distressing, Livi. And last night. Oh, last night . . ."

"Yes . . . what about last night?"

"Cute." I wrap my arms around my sides. "You remember how tired I was last night? I dragged myself home, slipped on some stretchy pants and thought I'd curl up with my latest issue of *Today's Christian Woman* or something. But Jake and Andy, my other cheery neighbor, kept me awake."

"What, serving you a late-night snack? Offering you a glass of wine and some warm conversation?"

"Chatter, Livi. Those two men were snorting and chattering all night long. *Ay,* they're worse than women!" I drop my head onto the counter, only to jerk up when the phone rings. "Florally Yours," I sing out.

It's Agnes Trilly, asking if I have any sweet peas available so she can create nosegays for the ladies in her bridge club. I ask you, is there any dearer woman on earth than Agnes? She gives church ladies everywhere a good name. I glance around, knowing full well there's not a pea in a pod around here. Not that we carry all that many of them. They grow in such abundance in Ventura, that it's hardly worth the money and effort to carry them. But for Agnes?

Her soft, earnest voice continues through the receiver, "And, oh, I do love the fragrance of the Painted Lady variety. Do you have any, dear?"

I don't, but that won't stop me from scouring every flower stand from Olivas Park Drive to Gonzales for a batch that'll make her bridge club heady over their perfumed scent. "When does your club meet, Agnes?"

"Friday at nine a.m. sharp."

"I'll have them to you by three o'clock Thursday. Will that give you enough time?"

"Oh my, yes. Thank you, dear. That will be so lovely."

I hang up, and Livi keeps her eyes on the Excel spreadsheet in front of her.

"What?" I ask.

She shrugs. "I didn't say anything."

"You didn't have to. How many deposits do I have?"

"Those are for particular orders. You know that."

"Yes, I have a particular sweet pea order to fill. How much?"

Livi grimaces at me. She spins her file around for me to see, and the number sends an instant stress dart through my head. I reach for my purse and pull out a couple of Tylenol. "That'll be enough." I guess. "I have plenty of favors to call in, so now is as good a time as any for that."

"I know you want to hang on to this business, Gaby."

"And?"

She taps her chin with a pencil. "I think you should move in with Bri. You know I'd invite you to stay with me in a minute, but . . . my roommate and all."

Double stress dart to the temple. A sigh escapes me. "Okay, Livi," I say. "You didn't hear this from me, but Doug's firm fell apart the other day. I don't think they need the pressure of another mouth to feed."

"Pffst! You and Bri are practically joined at the hip. Well, when she's not entertaining tourists or acting like Nathan's personal taxi service. You know what I mean; she'd love having you around."

But could *I* handle it?

Livi's digging a fist into her side now. "Of course, maybe things will work out for you and Max and he'll whisk you away from all this." She sweeps one hand through the air.

Max. A little ripple runs through me and my face heats at the sound of the name. How cute is that? Maybe there is something there. Livi apparently sees it. And the way he sat across from me in my loft the other morning, telling me how much we're alike, how we're both survivors . . . Well, talk about peas in a pod!

Livi hands me her cell. "I keyed in Max's number the last time I had my car repaired. Why not call him?"

"For what?"

She is undeterred. "It's the twenty-first century, girlfriend. Ask the man out for a date."

So unladylike, Mama would say. Despite my attempts to focus on the bright side, though, to just be satisfied and glad I'm still alive, I'm wearing down. My apparently party-loving landlord's sudden appearance hasn't helped either. I glance again at the phone in Livi's hand, and decide that maybe you have to make your own luck happen, you know?

I find Max's name in the list of contacts and press Call.

Nine

I LEARNED SOMETHING NEW TODAY: how to give myself a stellar manicure on a puny budget. I flex my hands in front of me and admire the flash of Robust Red that I managed to paint on fairly well during my quick lunch break. Not bad.

Not that Max will care much. As the owner of his own car repair shop, he's certainly seen his share of grimy fingernails, among other things. Although I have noticed lately that his hands have been rather grease-free for someone who works on cars. Who knows? Maybe he's been spending more time signing tenant agreements than draining oil pans.

My cell rings, and I answer gingerly, showing a sudden lack of confidence over my do-it-yourself manicure.

"Hey, Gaby-girl."

"Bri-Bri!"

"Whatcha doin'?"

I turn the bolt lock on my shop door. "Just closing up." Maybe Murphy's Law will kick in and my Closed sign will actually draw customers—as opposed to the Open sign that seems to

repel them much of the day. I push aside my temptation to unload my frustrations on Bri and focus on the knowledge that I have a date this evening with handsome Max. That fact alone has cooled my worry over my shop's lack of business.

I straighten my stack of business cards for the umpteenth time today. "Thing's getting settled for Doug?"

Bri clears her throat. "Sort of. Listen, I have to tell you something."

I lean against the counter. Bri sounds serious, and that's a funny statement in itself. "What's wrong?"

"Nothing, Gaby. Nothing's wrong. It's just that, ugh, I was talking to Max today, and he said that some woman he knows in your neighborhood told him that your landlord's kind of a jerk. Guess he's a slick one with the ladies, if you get my drift."

"You mean Iris? And yes, I get it."

"No! Well, I don't know. He didn't say her name. Does he know Iris?"

"Apparently. They served on some board together."

"Hmm. Sorry, Gaby, it's just that I'm a little gun-shy after leading you astray with that good-for-nuthin' ex-boss of mine." She says that with a growl. "Anyway, I know Iris's an odd one, but she has lived in the neighborhood a long time, right? I don't know . . . maybe you ought to listen to her. Just this once. Even though I can't believe I'm saying that!"

I grab my black vinyl clutch and slide a finger over the small tear near its clasp. "Doesn't matter anyway, Bri-Bri. I'm over it, and besides, he's just my landlord. So what if he's jerkish? It really shouldn't affect me."

After a pause, Bri asks, "You okay, Gaby?"

Well, I'm broke, my business is barely making it, and my quiet loft has become the icing on one big party cake. I shake it off. "I'm good, I'm good," I tell her. "Did you know I'm meeting Max tonight?"

"Oh? Really?"

"You knew."

"No, really. I had no idea. . . ."

"Hah! You could never lie to me."

Bri giggles. "Yeah, yeah, I knew. He said you were going to the pier. Make sure to forget your coat, so Max can keep you warm."

"That would be naughty, but I'll think about it."

"When's he picking you up?"

"What? You don't have my schedule committed to memory yet? You're slipping, Bri-Bri."

"Silly me. Guess I've got other things crowding out such thoughts. I did tell you that Aunt Dot called yesterday?"

"I don't think you mentioned that." Aunt Dot practically raised her niece while Bri's parents were off saving the world in one way or another—you know, building orphanages and caring for endangered monkeys. That kind of thing. She showed up last month, and unfortunately, got to witness that disastrous encounter between Ty—my ex-boyfriend—and Bri.

"Where did she fly off to anyway?" I ask.

"That's the thing. She never really made it out of the country. She was supposed to go back to Africa, but get this—she decided to stop off in Florida to try kite boarding."

"At her age?"

"Yeah, she did. Tore a ligament in her knee."

"No!"

"I wanted to fly right out there, but you know Aunt Dot—wouldn't hear of that. Thankfully I was able to talk with her surgeon." She laughs. "I got him to tell Auntie that he'd only release her from the hospital if he could put her on a plane to LAX so she could stay with me."

"You're in cahoots with a surgeon?"

"Yeah. I'm making him some brownies as we speak."

"Well, that's payment enough!"

"So, yeah, I'm glad that the loft's working for you. Looks like we'll be needing the office for a bedroom after all."

Her words startle me. My backup plan just fizzled. I gulp and stare down at the counter, noticing that the laptop's still on. "Yes," I finally say. "The loft is working out just fine. Just fine. No worries, Bri. Besides, having your aunt around will be so good for you. I am sorry that she's hurt, but it'll be like old times. Won't it?"

Bri cackles. "I hope not! She might have me climbing out of bed at the crack of dawn, just to wheel her down to the beach. Sheesh. I better keep plenty of strong coffee around here so I can keep up with her."

"Yes, yes. Coffee." I shut down the laptop and close its lid.

"You sound distracted, Gaby, but I get it. Go get ready for your date and make sure you call me tomorrow and give me the scoop."

"Okay, Bri."

My Volvo starts right up, and as I roll along toward home, my mind whirs with the important things in life, like will I have a roof over my head next month? And, of course, what to wear on my date with Max.

Max. Again, the thought of my old friend turned potential dream guy blows away the steam of worry that's been rising in me all day. There's so much I want to know about him, you know? Where did he grow up? What schools did he attend? Does he prefer action films or will he smile and sit through a chick flick just for me?

As I turn down on my street, the lights from Jake's house seem to illuminate the rest of my drive home. Is he expecting a crowd? I park my car, step lightly up the walk, and notice the front door ajar. I give it a light shove and step inside.

The door to the main living area stands open. A pine-laden scent flows into my nostrils, and I sneeze.

"Bless you!" Jake rises from the leather "man" chair positioned awkwardly in the center of the great room. He nearly topples the large, curved reading lamp at his elbow before catching it with one meaty hand. He moves toward me with an expectant look, like he's been waiting for me all afternoon. "Sorry about the smell. Cleaned up the kitchen earlier. Anyway," he asks, "how was your day?"

"I . . . I . . ." A million thoughts crowd my mind, but I can't seem to retrieve even one cohesive phrase.

He stands at the threshold of our common area. "Business picking up for you?"

I open and shut my mouth in one slow but deliberate action. How does he know about . . . never mind. Words have rarely been lacking for me, and that hasn't always been a good thing. I remember Doug telling me about a case where a loose-lipped lawyer almost won his argument in front of a judge—until he said just one word too much. Doug said it was like watching the proverbial domino tower topple under the weight of that last white-spotted black rectangle.

"Business is lovely," I lie.

His eyes never leave my face, as if he's waiting for something else to be revealed. Maybe like the truth.

He chuckles. "Glad to hear it. So, any plans tonight?"

My head snaps up. "Well, Dad," I say. "It just so happens that, yes, I have plans. I'm meeting a . . . a friend for dinner and a walk along the pier."

Jake presses his lips together and nods his head several times, as if considering my plans for the evening. It's like I'm standing in front of my father—not like I really know what that would feel like—waiting for the green light. Just why did I feel the need to fill Jake in on my plans?

He looks past me. "Looks like a nice night for it."

I glance over my shoulder. "You're right about that. I'm so glad there's none of that bothersome wind tonight."

He smiles.

"It does a number on my hair." Not like he needed to know that. He peers at me with animated eyes, as if we're old friends, which I find oddly comforting. Then again, maybe this is his *modus operandi*. From what Iris let "slip," he's got quite the harem. I get a whiff of his tropical cologne and glance again at those smiling eyes of his and admit it—if I hadn't become reacquainted with Max, and if all the other details of my life were not so precarious, I too might have succumbed to his charms.

With a hastily muttered excuse, given before I have another chance to divulge any more details of my life, I dart up the two flights of stairs. Once inside my loft, my eyes settle on the bubble-wrapped package still propped against my solitary kitchen cabinet. In one hasty movement, I swoop down on it and tear into it.

The sight stops my breath. I run my fingers along the raised intricacies of the frame's gilded edge, staying careful not to touch the painting itself. It's just a copy, but like they always have, the colors, the mood, the people—as I imagine them to be—transport me away from anything resembling heartache.

A tap on my door pulls me away from my dream, and I slide the picture back into its paper sleeve.

I open the door. "Hi, Max."

He gives me that long, crooked grin of his, and I think my heart's about done looking. Why did I not see you all these years, my friend? "Hello, Gaby. I'm hungry, are you?"

You could say that. I giggle, and Max looks confused. "Actually, Max, I'm starved. Would you wait while I change? I just got in from work."

He shrugs. "You look good to me, as always, but I'll wait."

"Thanks."

I dash into the bathroom to freshen up, and when I return, Max is standing at the back window. For an instant, I imagine what it would be like to have a partner in life, someone sharing my home and harbor view with me. I want that. I know I do.

"So," I say. "What's so interesting over there?"

"Dunno exactly. Something's swimming around down there. Probably just a big sea lion."

"Or the Loch Ness monster."

He grunts out a knowing gust of a sigh. "As if this neighborhood needs more to talk about."

"Yes, well." I want to say that I'd love to know more about the rumors surrounding my landlord, but I'm trying to stay true to myself here and stay out of that fray. I catch Max's eye. "I'm ready."

Out on the pier, we fight over the last slice of garlic cheese bread until a fat seagull lands on the empty table next to ours, apparently hoping to get into the act. Max sits back. "I give up! For a girl, you can *eat*, Gaby."

I dart him a look. "What're you saying? That I'm pudgy?"

He snorts. "Babies are pudgy. You, Gaby, are anything but."

I bite into the bread, satisfied by its delicious flavor and by how wonderfully comfortable I'm feeling right now. This is how life with a handsome man should be. Warm, comforting, playful. I could get used to this.

After paying the bill, Max holds out his hand. "Up for a walk?"

I slide my hand into his, vaguely conscious of the roughness of his fingers beneath my homemade manicure. And as we stroll along in the twilight, seagulls scattering out of our path, I abandon my heart's deepest worries and look with hope upon the darkening horizon.

Ten

"Spill."

I try not to laugh at Bri. "A lady doesn't tell of her secret intimacies."

"Pffst! You've been watching Jane Austen movies again, haven't you?"

Phone in hand, I glance out the front door of my shop. "Something like that."

Bri's growl hits my ear. "You know that I've given up my matchmaking ways, but I'm a curious creature. So. You and Max . . . ?"

" . . . had a very nice dinner."

"And?"

" . . . and a walk along the pier."

"Real-ly." Bri's voice sounds an awful lot like a cat's meow. "Any funny business?"

It's my turn to growl, but it comes out more like a high-pitched giggle. "Oh, there was nothing funny about it."

"You're such a tease!"

"He said that too!"

"He did?"

"No. I'm just messing with you. Bri-Bri, there's not a whole lot to tell. Well, maybe there is, but I'm being more careful this time around. You know? Oh, I just don't want to see my heart smashed into a million bits again."

Bri sighs into the phone. "I know, Gaby. I know."

I peek out the window toward the empty sidewalk. "I will say one thing, though, Max is an easygoing date. We talked and laughed the entire time. I never felt . . . felt . . . What am I trying to say here . . . ?"

"Ill at ease?"

"That's it! It was as if we've known each other in a forever kind of way. We even talked about you and Doug. Max told me that Doug's all moved into new office space, by the way. Congratulations."

"Thanks. Yes, he and Darla moved in there yesterday. Actually, they ended up getting an extra office in the deal because some tenant abruptly moved out. A real blessing." She starts cackling. "Between us, I wasn't sure how Doug would handle sharing one office with Darla. She can be a bit, um, tedious."

A shadow passes by. "Listen, Bri, I've got to run. Customers you know."

"Gotcha. I'm off to the airport to pick up Aunt Dot. Then I'll be running harbor tours for the rest of the week. Leave me a voice mail, though, 'kay? And let me know what's up."

The doorbell jangles, and I make a mental note to change to a more soothing welcome chime. When my ship comes in, anyway.

"Gabrielle Flores?"

"Yes?"

An older gentleman shuffles over to the counter, a drab white shirt tucked into pants hiked up far above his midsection.

Dear old fella—probably looking for a small arrangement for the love of his life. "May I help you?"

He hands me an envelope, plain and fat. "This here's for you. Thank you for your time." I watch him shuffle back out the door without a word. I turn the envelope over and search for a name. The only one on it is mine.

Livi breezes in wearing vibrant blue running pants and a stretchy black top that I'd never fit into. Her fine blond hair droops out of a pink scrunchy. She plops a stack of files on top of the counter and begins to name and point to each one. "Profit and Loss . . . Business Plan . . . This one's got your blog password and username along with a few articles that might interest you . . . and bank statements." That last file is the emptiest of the bunch.

"Hi, Livi."

My greeting shakes her from her all-business face. "Ah. Hi, Gaby. Sorry, I've been swamped today. Haven't even found an hour yet to work out."

"That would explain your outfit."

She drops her chin to examine herself. "I figured if I dressed the part I might actually be motivated to find the time to run or cycle up the coast."

"I've never known you to need much motivation in that regard. Your friends are all insanely jealous, you know."

"Right." She flips her ponytail from side to side. "Anyhoo, I worked on this stuff all night, Gaby, and . . . I'm really worried about you."

I swallow. "That bad?"

"I think you need to face it. Gaby . . . how exactly are you eating?"

I shrug, wiping away the image of grandma's coin jar on my counter at home. "I manage okay."

"Maybe I've just been a poor excuse for a friend not to notice this, but has business always been this slow?"

I paste on a smile and prevent my shoulders from offering up another shrug. "It's not all that unusual to experience a lull during this time of year." Although where are my usual June wedding orders? Oh. Right. Probably at that new emporium down the street.

"Well. All right. All the more reason to move you technologically into the twenty-first century." She taps the file marked *Blog*. "Maybe now would be the perfect time for you to study up on marketing via the Internet. Don't forget to take these files home with you."

"Yes, ma'am." I give her a winning smile as she heads off to sweat.

For the next three hours, I manage to stay busy cleaning the cooler and selling several arrangements that I'd copied from the pages of an FTD catalog—people always seem to want them to be exact. Although the phone rings a handful of times, only two new orders come in. At least I have my regular business customers who bring in seasonal orders every two weeks.

Just as I'm ready to shut it down for the night, the familiar front doorbell rings, telling me that perhaps I'll be closing up in the black tonight. Although it would have to be one giant order for that to happen.

"Hi."

I swivel around. "Max!"

He takes a tentative step through the doorway. "Busy?"

Did he just get better looking overnight or what? "Just closing up. Come on in. What're you up to?"

"Thought we could grab a bite . . . if you don't already have other plans."

Other plans? You mean like rooting around in my pantry for something healthy to eat that's stored in a box or can? You mean like climbing into sweats and scrubbing my loft while my landlord rocks out just beneath my floor?

I try not to gush at him. "Actually, I don't have any plans for tonight, Max, and I'd love to grab a bite with you." I lean my waist against the counter so he can't hear the celebratory leap my stomach just made.

"Great. We can take my car."

Stepping inside Fat Gregory's Italian Eatery is like being basted with garlic butter and warmed from the inside out. We cozy ourselves into a booth secluded behind a trellis of plastic grape leaves and vines. Candle wax oozes from an old Chianti bottle on our table, and music pops and crackles as if it's flowing from an antique Victrola.

Max smiles at me. "Red or white?"

The stack of files waiting for me tonight pops into my mind. "Actually, I'd love an espresso."

While Max orders our drinks, I study the menu. Would asking for one of everything be too transparent? I make up my mind and shut my menu, hoping I don't look too obvious.

"Where's Gib tonight?" Gibson is Max's son, a kid who'd seem naked without his sun-streaked locks and a surfboard under one arm.

Max sits back. "Nathan dragged him to the youth group at your church."

"Oh! I love it. Is this Gib's first visit?"

"In a long time." Max sits upright again. "He's not been that interested in church for a while."

"That's rough. I'm sorry."

Max blinks but doesn't say anything.

"I just meant that, you know, maybe he's been having a hard time lately. He's a great kid and I know what a good dad you are, Max, when you're home." Open mouth, insert pointy-toed shoe. "I . . . I didn't mean it like that. I just meant . . ."

Max reaches for my hand. "I understand, Gaby. And you're right. I work a lot, and Gib, well, he's got a lot of time on his hands. Not a bad thing for a boy. Builds independence. He has been acting like a mope, though, lately." He takes a deep breath, then exhales. "I just don't know."

"Again, I'm sorry." Max's hand still rests on mine. I try to fill the lull. "I know what it's like to grow up without both parents, Max. My mother worked long days too, but I did okay. I'm sure Gibson will get through it and come out a stronger man for it."

"What happened to your father?"

A tiny laugh escapes me. "That's the million-dollar question, now, isn't it? No one seems to know what happened to him."

The waitress serves our drinks. Max releases my hand and gulps his Lambrusco. "You ever try to find him?"

I shake my head and wrap my hands around the warmth of my coffee cup. "I don't even know his last name. My mother gave me hers. All I know is he was a big Czech man." The memory stirs up a giggle in me. "When Bri heard that, she called me a 'Chex-Mex.'"

Max bursts into laughter. "That sounds like Bri. What a character." He shakes his head. "Did Bri mention what Iris said about your landlord?"

I inspect the red-checked cloth covering our table and brush away some left-behind crumbs. "She mentioned it."

"You don't think it's worth knowing about."

I shrug and look directly at him. "I just don't consider Iris's word very reliable."

"Oh, so have you two ladies had words?"

I giggle. "Who says that? You're too cute. No, we haven't exactly 'had words.'" I giggle again before pushing out a sigh. "Oh, Max. It's just that Iris's kind of nosey. She keeps dropping hints about the neighbors and making assumptions about me. And this is all to my face. I . . . I don't think I trust her."

Max sets his glass down. "Fair enough."

"You won't tell her what I said, I hope?"

"Nah. I know you don't want to offend her."

My mouth drops open, and I laugh. "It's not that. I'm just scared of her!"

He shakes his head, smiling, and I take the opportunity to move on. "May I ask, Max, how you got into the landlord business?"

He grabs a hunk of bread from the basket on the table and tears it up. "My wife was never too keen on it, but after she died, I thought I'd better invest for Gib's future and for my own. The shop's almost running itself these days, but I'm not getting rich from it. Lots of overhead." He catches my eyes with his own. "It's probably the same for you."

"Not really. I was down to one employee, and he's long gone now—as you know. Anyway, I've been doing this awhile so I can get by just fine."

"Getting by 'just fine' and actually finding success aren't necessarily the same thing."

"I never actually planned to become a florist, but when my other prospects fizzled, I figured 'do what you know.' Truly, Max, I've found that I don't really need all that much." *Tell me that didn't sound pathetic. What am I doing? Trying to sell him on my frugalness? Pick me! Pick me! I won't cost you much!*

"I can see that. You're a natural beauty, Gaby."

Oh. My. If he reached out to caress my cheek right now, the rising heat would burn his hand.

He laughs. "I've always thought you were a looker, Gaby. Only you weren't looking at me. Maybe until now, I guess."

He gives me a suggestive wink, and I relax into a fit of giggles.

I'm replaying the entire, scrumptious dinner, lingering over every word, as I climb the stairs to my loft. My heart has grown two sizes, at least, and I can't stop savoring the moments I've spent with Max. I still can't believe that the man I've breezed by for the past few years at Bri's just might be the man God had for me all along.

And just in the nick of time.

Still, duty calls. Snuggled into the couch, I spread out the files Livi brought me earlier. A plain envelope slips out of the pile, and I remember the elderly man who shuffled in and dropped it off. I slide a nail under the flap, tear it open, and read:

SUMMONS. Notice To Defendant: You Are Being Sued

Eleven

"GABY, STAY CALM. JUST READ me what it says."

"None of this is true, Doug! I may run a shoestring operation, but my flowers are not ugly. How could she say that? She never told me that to my face."

"Gaby?"

"She's the one who insisted on the red, white, and blue theme for her wedding! I told her that was highly unusual—even for a military wedding like hers, but *no*. She had to have the colors of the flag."

"Well . . ."

"And you know what? I gave her extra! She kept adding guests and tables up to the very last minute, and I made her several more centerpieces and didn't charge her a thing for them. And then when her mother went ballistic over having a pinned corsage—even though that's exactly what she ordered—I converted it to a wrist corsage with a hair band and some hot glue! *¡Basta!* My mother would never have let that happen, but I'm so gullible. Oh, I've got to stop that, Doug."

"Listen, Gaby. I'm here to help you. Let me tell you what to expect." He pauses. "First, are you going to be all right?"

Bri's husband rocks. The man's a lawyer with a heart of gold, and that's no oxymoron. At least not with Doug. What would I do without him in my corner? What would I do, what would I do . . . ?

"You there, Gaby?"

"Yes, yes. I'm here. Please! Tell me what to do, Doug."

"First, don't worry. I'll check with your insurance company for you, to see who they assigned to your case."

"My case!"

"Then we have thirty days to file a response to the complaint with the court. You will have a chance to either file an answer to the complaint, which will lay out all of your defenses, or—"

"Defenses!"

"Or we can ask the court to throw out the lawsuit altogether. It's called a demurrer."

"Yes, do that. Oh, do that, Doug."

He chuckles. "Hold on. I need to see the complaint, and then I can better advise you on which way to go. Of course, your insurance carrier will have a say in this as well."

I sigh into the receiver. This would be the same insurance carrier that sent me a mere pittance after Sammy stole from me. Their name, Fly By Night, Inc., is rather appropriate, don't you think? "Thank you so much, Doug. You just send me the bill, and I'll handle it."

"And have Bri lock me out on the back deck in the fog? Not a chance."

"Oh, Doug. But there's got to be some kind of cost involved, right?"

I hear Doug sigh now. "There is the matter of the filing fee, Gaby. But if you've got insurance, they'll most likely handle that. We can talk about all that later, after I've had the chance to look over those documents. I'll be out of the office tomorrow morning, but Darla will be here to receive them. Can you drop them by my office?"

"Absolutely, Doug. I'll have them to you first thing."

"Not to worry. Listen, I know you probably need to talk with Bri, but . . ."

"How're things going with Aunt Dot?"

Doug lowers his voice. "The woman has more energy than Bri after a double-espresso. I see where my wife gets all her attitude from now. Despite Aunt Dot's major surgery, those two women spent the evening redecorating that whole office."

"Any shot glasses on the wall?"

Doug hesitates, then laughs hard. Recently, Bri went through a phase where she felt compelled to turn her life upside down and redo herself and her living room. It didn't go over very well. Especially the cheesy barware that her mother-in-law talked her into displaying near the fireplace.

"No, Gaby," Doug finally says. "I think those shot glasses have been retired to a landfill somewhere by now. But I will tell you this: I just checked in there a few minutes ago and found Bri passed out on the sofa next to her aunt's bed."

I glance at the clock. "Already? Sounds like our night owl has met her match."

"You get some rest, Gaby. Please call Bri in the morning. She'll want to talk with you."

I hang up the phone and let the news that I'm being sued sink into my mind. Part of me wanted to reach through the phone line and shove Doug over to get to Bri. I wanted him to shake her awake so she could get on the other end and tell me it's all going to be fine. But how selfish would that be? She's running a new business, taking care of her aunt, mothering Nathan, and cheering on her husband, who's been forced to move his law firm and start over. She doesn't need me to wear her down with my problems.

As if on cue, violins start. With a heavy sigh, I step toward my open harborside windows and take in the soft breeze, and with it, Jake's choice of music for the evening. At least it's not something harsh or jarring. More than music drifts in. I peer onto the deck, and see Jake carefully flip something on the grill. He stops and looks toward my window.

Only this time he doesn't call out to me, and he doesn't invite me for a late-night snack. He just grins and turns back to his grilling.

Beyond the rooftops on the other side of the channel, a crashing wave echoes into the night, and I shut my eyes to the sound. Now I know why business has dropped off so much lately. Summer, the disgruntled bride, must've spread the word that my flowers were ugly. I never should have accepted her as a client in the first place. She turned up her nose at my tiny shop the minute she walked through my doors. But she married an enlisted man, a man destined to become "captain," as she put it, but a seaman just the same.

Hmm. It's been just a few months since their wedding. Something tells me their credit card bills have begun their attack. Like mine. I pull the windows shut, muffling the orchestra of the sea mixed with Jake's stereo selection, and collapse into bed.

"I am my beloved's and my beloved is mine."
"Be still and know that I am God."
"Strike all my enemies on the jaw."

My attempts to meditate on uplifting Scripture this morning keep being invaded by the dark side. God must have known this would happen when He allowed David to be chased into a cave where he could pour out his anguish into the Psalms. I've been stumbling across his angst-ridden words all morning, and frankly, I can relate. Maybe too well.

Resigned, I head out the door, my pockets filled with change and my armpits clutching all sorts of reading material aimed at brightening my day: a devotional, my Bible, a copy of a screamingly funny chick-lit book from my favorite author, and oh yes, the missile that the old man with high waters dropped off yesterday. Not nice of me, but he chose his profession; he gets to live with my ridicule.

"Good morning, Gaby. How are you?"

It's Iris. *God, didn't that time of prayer this morning achieve anything?*

"I'm fine, Iris. Thanks." I want to add that I need to dash off now, so please step away from my car, but her yappy dog appears ready to tear into my skirt.

"How are you and Jake getting along? Does he feed you well? Are you enjoying your nights together?"

I've got this one eyebrow that does amazing things, often on its own, so I've learned to control it, to use it only for those occasions when its subtly arched presence is warranted. This is one of those times, and my eyebrow shoots up.

Iris laughs in the silence. "You know, Gaby, I hadn't wanted to say anything to you about this, being that you're new to our neighborhood family and all, but that landlord of yours can be quite the . . . charmer." She glances at the house. "I'm only saying this as one who sincerely cares about your well-being. Between Sarah next door—if that's truly her name—and Jake's often wild ways, you might want to take steps to protect your privacy. From one wise person to another."

The puff ball on the end of her leash keeps tugging and spinning. Iris doesn't budge.

"Well, thanks for your, hmm, your concern," I say, failing at my attempt to keep the sarcasm out of my voice. So what if the attempt was weak at best? Trying counts, doesn't it?

Still hugging my load, I make a move toward my car and drop the summons and complaint, which I'd neglected to put back into its envelope. When I squat down to pick it up, the devotional slips from the pile, taking with it my Bible, and a stack of notes I'd made over the past few months. I'm left scrambling for my things with nothing but a fluorescent-covered chick-lit novel in one hand.

Iris plucks the summons from the pile (leaving all the heavy things spread on the ground, mind you), and makes no attempt to hide her fascination with what the document so boldly proclaims in black and white.

I reach for the pages in her hand.

"You know, Gaby, if you're in need of a good lawyer," Iris says. "I can provide you with the best. My cousin's husband works for a big LA firm."

Fabulous. "Thanks, but no." I squeeze past her, swing open my car door, and plop the books onto the seat before stepping in.

Iris glances at Jake's house, then back at me, her brow more furrowed than her puffy dog's face. "Well, then. I see."

That's it. I climb back out of the car. "Really, Iris? Do you really see?" *¡Basta! Gabrielle, stop!* I hear my mother tell me.

"Jake's got a soft spot for pretty women in a bind." She shrugs. "You're lucky to have someone like him looking after you, I suppose."

"What an imagination."

"I've tried to warn you, Gaby, but you don't seem to want to take my advice. Believe me, I have been in this neighborhood a long time and could really be of help to you, but . . ." The word hangs in the sea air, a little dramatic show. She continues. "You just don't seem to be listening."

I know it's the lawsuit that's got me wound tighter than a coiled spring. It would be much better for me to walk away right now and let Iris be her weird self. But her nosiness has overruled my good sense, and I long to get to the bottom of her incessant comments. "Iris, what's the beef you have with Jake? And with me, for that matter?"

"I have no trouble with you, Gaby. As for Jake? He and I go way back, and I just need you to trust me on this one—the man's trouble. He took—he'll take full advantage of you if you let him."

"What's your story, Iris? You seem to have one on everybody, so what is yours?"

Iris pauses. She blinks away a shimmer of mist and suddenly her eyes harden. "You're obviously emotional over being the subject of a lawsuit, Gaby. I can't dabble with you any longer." She turns to her neglected pooch and puts on an adoring glance. "Poor Ivanna needs her walk, so I must go. This is a family-friendly neighborhood, Gaby, so a word to the wise: You might want to work on that temper of yours. Ta-ta."

I shut my car door with a little too much oomph and head to Doug's office, seething inside for the entire two-mile drive south on the 101. I check the address and pull into the parking lot. In the quiet, I let my eyes drop closed, reminding myself of my efforts to avoid conflict. Deep breath in. Start fresh. My mantra of late helps, but only a little.

Still at a fast clip, I stride down the hall toward Doug's new office, vaguely aware of a heated voice drifting from a doorway that I'm approaching.

" . . . but that's not the deal you promised me."

Someone responds, but the tone is too quiet for me to decipher.

The other voice cuts back in. "Then you can just forget it. I'll fight you for my deposit, though. You can just bet on that!"

A middle-aged man wearing a light gray suit—and, oh my, a politician's skilled hairstyle—charges from the office and right into my path. He pushes past me with a mutter.

Tell me that wasn't one of Doug's clients. I walk toward the open office door and peer in.

"Gaby?"

"Max?"

We both blink a couple of times before Max responds. "What brings you here, Beautiful?"

Troubles? What troubles? "I'm just here to drop off some paper work for Doug." I hold the summons against my torso. "So," I say, with a glance back down the hall. "Problems in the landlord business?"

Max shakes it off. "Dealing with the slick ones is all part of the business. Unfortunately."

"I'm sorry."

He steps closer. "Don't be. It's good to see you again so soon. I think things'll be looking up for me today after all."

While I may be able to somewhat control the dramatic arch of one eyebrow, blushing happens on its own. And at the moment I'm quite sure that I resemble a cherry tree in full bloom. I slump against the doorjamb, knowing of no way to wipe the I'm-suddenly-at-peace-with-the-world smile off my face.

"So you have something for Doug? Brownies or . . . ?"

An alarm shrieks in my brain. Oh! I want to hit the snooze button and drift off to dreamland again, but it's not to be. I straighten. "Just some paper work regarding the shop." It's not like we've reached that point in our relationship where I'll have to tell him everything—the point we'll be at, like say, after reciting our vows.

"I'll walk you over to his office."

He takes my hand in his, the gesture warm and affectionate, and as I glance down at our intertwined fingers, the word *symmetrical* pops into my head.

Twelve

MY VOLVO NEEDS A DECAL. It's positively naked without one. I decide this while driving home after another dismal day at the shop, a day in which I gave up and closed early. The one bright spot came when Livi unveiled my new Web site and blog design. She's got the gift, I tell you. Other than that, I sold a few sprigs of baby's breath, some stargazers, and other floral randomness, but not much. Instead, I spent the afternoon doing something I detest: calling old clients to ask for endorsements. Livi's idea. She thought that some personal recommendations would help my Web presence, as she put it.

So anyway, back to my car. I think it's a rule that if you live in California, especially in a coastal town, then you've got to show your allegiance to the sea in some way. You just have to. So I'm imagining a pretty seashell would perk up my rather weary mode of transportation. I mentally add that to my list of virtual purchases. (You know, the kind you can buy with virtual money.)

Jake's house appears deserted, but it wouldn't matter if he was home anyway. I'm tired of hiding out from my landlord. I am paying for access to the water, after all. There's no reason I can't sit in the afternoon sun and mind my own business while he minds his. Whatever Iris's issues with Jake are, I'm committed to keeping myself out of that web.

I dash upstairs for a quick change and a towel, and then tiptoe past the doors to the main house. Still no sign of Jake, but like I said, it wouldn't matter anyway. Out on the deck, the sun coats me with light. I ease into a lounger and close my eyes to better take in the slosh of the sea just steps away.

I'm not sure just how long I slept, but as my mind pulls itself out of the most blissful slumber it's had in weeks, I'm drawn to an aroma more decadent than the surroundings in which I now live.

"Hungry?"

My eyes snap open. My stomach grumbles.

It's Jake, standing over me. "Fresh tuna. Just caught today off Anacapa Island. I've made enough for the both of us."

Wearily, I sit up. My hand wanders to my face and brushes away any imaginary thing that might cause me acute embarrassment.

"Did I wake you?"

"I . . . I . . ." He's standing there, tanned and relaxed like a beachcomber, only cleaner and smelling musky, like papaya and nutmeg. "Yes, I think you did."

He chuckles, obviously unapologetic. "Sorry, I thought it was the snoring."

What did Iris say about Jake being a jerk? I clear my throat. "Oh? Did you take a nap too?"

"Nope, not me. I've been right here next to you, though, cooking up this fresh catch. Do you like dill?"

"I don't snore."

He's smiling and whistling now. I stare at him, but he just keeps bouncing to some unperceivable beat. He stops suddenly and gives me a feigned look of surprise. "Sorry. Did you say something?"

"I want you to know, that I know that I don't snore. That's all."

Broad smile now. "Right-o."

I know in my gut that I don't. Wouldn't I feel it? Wouldn't I hear it? And wouldn't I wake up with a sore nose if all that scraping and grinding were going on? Besides, everybody knows that snoring is bad manners. Sigh. Relaxing afternoon? Not so much.

I stand and throw my towel over my arm. *I'm not harem material. I'm not. I'm not.* I think back to the warmth of Max's hand holding mine and glance over at Jake. "Thank you for the invitation, Jake, but I've got other plans tonight." A little bit of haughtiness in my reply, I know. But some people just don't get the hint. On the way upstairs, my stomach makes another plea for me to reconsider, but I shush it like a mother cross with her young.

Since when do I look like some poor waif who needs fattening up? I only wish! (Not to be hungry—just to have one of those model-like figures. You know, the ones that scream "Give this chick a burger.") My fridge isn't exactly bare, but it's not pretty inside: half a loaf of bread, two yogurts, and more peanut butter than I'll eat in a year. A good thing too, since I might just have to.

Maybe he was just being friendly.

Now there's a thought for you. I bat it away, remembering that Iris seemed friendly at the start too. And a little neurotic.

My cell phone rings.

"Gaby, I'm so sorry. I've been gone all day. But Doug told me about the lawsuit, and all I can say is, that stinks!"

All day long, I've been like a dam with a microscopic hole punched in its side, just waiting to talk to Bri and let the torrent of emotion rush out. Now that the moment has presented itself to me, nothing's coming. I'm not sure why. Maybe it's because a day has nearly passed since I received the news. Or maybe it's because of my relaxing, albeit interrupted, nap by the water's edge.

Or maybe you're just too tired and hungry to care.

Yes, maybe that's it.

"I'm so glad Doug's looking into this for me, Bri-Bri. Has he . . . has he told you anything more?"

"Not really. He's been down in LA most of the day, but don't worry. He'll stay on top of it." She blows a sigh into the phone. "Ugh! The legal business can take so long, Gaby. I'm thinking of driving by that sue-happy bride's house and . . ."

"No! Don't do that."

"I just said I was *thinking* about it. Sheesh. She must be a real loser. Did you have any idea that she'd pull something like this?"

"None. Although she was very difficult to please. Ones like that usually inspire me to do my best, to really come up with something fabulous that will shock them into awe over my striking designs." I laugh at my own naïveté. "Guess I handled the shock part all right."

"Oh, shush. There's no basis for that lawsuit; we both know it. No, I think there's something else. Like maybe she spent too much and is taking it out on you. Could that be it?"

"I thought the same thing. Her husband's a chopped-steak kind of a guy, while she's . . . she's more of an oysters-on-the-half-shell kind, you know? I'm aware that opposites attract, but . . ."

Bri laughs. "Yeah, like Doug and me."

"Exactly! But I watched those two, and they seemed like a train wreck in progress."

"Hmm."

"Hmm, what?"

"Nothing. It's just that the train-wreck reference could refer to my homelife right now."

"Is it the business? Or your auntie?"

"It's both." She sighs. "I don't know. Both Doug and I starting businesses at the same time . . . well, the timing could have been better. Neither of us has any regular income to lean on at the moment."

"I guess there's always your in-laws . . ."

"Don't!"

"Sorry. Of course not." I wouldn't do it either.

"We'll be fine. We've got great credit." She cackles. "But seriously, Aunt Dot's condition has me even more worried. She's as feisty as always but also kind of erratic, like she's not always completely sure of what's going on. Just the other day she asked me if I remembered to put pecans in my brownies. Pecans!"

"What did the doctor say?"

"Nothing. I guess she seemed fine to him, but that's only because he really didn't know her. It's not like he was her regular doc or anything. Anyway, I'll be keeping a close eye on her. Maybe it's just all the meds."

"You're probably right. Hang in there."

"Yeah, you too." Bri sounds wistful, and she never sounds wistful. As much as she denies it, it's true that she inherited her Aunt Dot's spunk. She really did. Only I can tell by her voice that her usual zest for the day to day has dulled somehow. I wish I could be there for her. But what I really wish is that she could be there for me.

The sun's setting as I finish up my peanut butter on whole grains sandwich. I down a long glass of cold water and watch the sky turn pink. I'm full but not satisfied. I lean forward and watch Jake close the lid of his grill after scrubbing it down.

I could have enjoyed a delicious dinner by the water tonight.

But I'm not some damsel in distress. Mama used that term a lot, saying the whole idea was an American fabrication. I try to smile, remembering how she would scold me when she'd catch me reading *Cinderella* or *Snow White*. She always pushed me toward Nancy Drew, saying, "Now, there's a girl who can think on her own, *Mijita!*"

Yes, but I always imagined that the Hardy Boys would come running the minute Nancy picked up her vintage wall phone.

I wipe the crumbs from my plate into the trash can, along with those old memories. I consider giving my mother a call, but for what? She refuses to move into the twenty-first century and get a cell phone,

and heaven knows she'll be at the flower stand until far past my bedtime. As usual.

And yet, I'm not tired. I'm wide awake, in fact; the inkling of sleep
as unattractive as my recent homemade manicure has become. My
dinner sits lump-like in my stomach, and I'm uncomfortable. Restless. Cheerless.

I pad downstairs, careful to make sure that the back deck is quiet.
Water laps against the dock, both its song and gentle ripple attempting to soothe against a sleepless night. I lean against the handrail, and
a tendril of aroma from Jake's blackened fresh tuna taunts me. My
mouth salivates, and I swallow my lingering hunger.

The slide and snap of a window shutting alerts me that I'm not
completely alone. Living in a home backed up to a channel filled with
ocean water can give a person that illusion, but it's really more like living
in a fishbowl, you know? Glug, glug. I glance at the Mediterranean-
style home to my left, and see Sarah's silhouette in the lit window.

"A fellow night owl."

I yelp.

Jake steadies me with a quick hand. "Sorry. I didn't mean to scare
you."

My heart pounds in my ears. "Well, you did a pretty good job of
it anyway."

He releases me, and I avert my eyes from him and those Brawny
Man shoulders of his. Jake follows the path of my gaze to Sarah's
house. "Like I said, she's a fellow night owl. Have you met Sarah?
Nice gal, although kind of shy. She usually opens her window when
I've got the music going out here at night. I've always taken that to
mean that she enjoys it."

My stomach grumbles, and I try to smother it.

Jake peers down at me. "Plans cancel?"

No, I lied about them in the first place. "Yes. They did."

"Sorry to hear that."

The phone trills from inside, and Jake begs off to answer it. I glance again at Sarah's window, and see it's now dark. I shiver beneath a breeze from off the top of the water but stand against the railing anyway, waiting for sleep to float in on the wind. Time passes and more lights dim from the houses across the channel before I head back upstairs, more awake—and hungry—than ever.

I walk through my narrow loft, closing windows and switching off lights, and then stop. A foil-wrapped plate and a note sit on my counter. I grab the note.

> *Thought you could use some leftovers, since your plans changed and all. Jake*

The tears that I had been so careful to control begin as a trickle, then proceed to tumble their way out with no end in view. And I don't know what caused them more: relief over having a decent meal today, or the fact that I am not the only one with a key to my apartment.

Thirteen

"Punitive damages?"

Bri often jokes about the way Doug can switch on that lawyerly voice of his when times warrant it. Funny stuff, until he starts to use it on me. "What's that?"

"You're being sued for intentional affliction of severe emotional distress."

Livi's in the shop with me when I hear the news, and my zombie-like stance causes her to frantically wave a hand in front of my face.

I snap out of it. "You're kidding me, Doug, right?" The only one I inflict that kind of distress on is myself!

"I wish I were, Gaby. I wish I were."

"Well . . . well . . . Doug, have you talked with my insurance people?"

Doug clears his throat. "I hate to tell you, but insurance won't cover punitive damages—only negligence. And it seems they're only suing on the former. Strange case."

I'll say. Doug proceeds to map out a plan of action—blah, blah, blah and yada, yada, yada—his carefully laid-out words falling on me like so much vapid smoke. My conversation with Doug ends, and although Livi's showing a house at three, she promised to help me out until then. Not that Florally Yours is suddenly overrun with customers, but even if it were, how could I pretend to care as I should? I'm being sued! By a nutso bride! And I didn't even charge her full price!

Deep breath in. Start fresh.

"Anyhow, Gaby, so I thought today would be a great day for you to give the public your thoughts on ways to make their spring bouquets last longer." Livi, God bless her, tries to keep me occupied, but she's lost me. "Just write it out and I'll post it for you, okay?"

I blink. "Did you say something?"

Her eyes watch me as she slides the laptop in my direction. "Do you want me to explain it again?" She talks to me as if I'm two.

And the answer is no, not really, but I cooperate anyway because that's the polite thing to do. It's the right thing. Isn't that right, Mama? Her voice fills my mind. *Be responsible, Gabrielle! Stay quiet and nod, and you will have a good life.*

Livi's still talking, but I don't hear her words clearly because there's another conversation going on inside my head at the moment. *And just how will staying quiet make my life better, Mama?*

Livi asks me again. "You okay, Gaby?"

I nod. "I've got to go."

"Okay, but remember that I have a showing at three."

"Yes, yes, I know."

"Will you be back . . . by then?"

I shrug. "Just lock up if I'm not."

I swing my car onto Highway 101 and follow its curves until the 126 East. Twenty-five minutes later I pull off the road onto a dry patch of hard dirt in an area hardly touched by progress. Outside the car, the air wears a perfume of citrus, and I walk past a row of orange trees toward the rectangular box that I once considered home. I never actually lived there—we weren't homeless or anything—but I spent many hours within its splintered limbs. I had to if I wanted to see my mother.

"Gabrielle." She states my name with affection yet no surprise.

"Hello, Mama." I watch her make change for a woman in overalls and scuffed work boots. Behind her, an elegant woman wearing tweed and heels patiently waits for her turn to witness my mother's artistry. In the distance, I see Rudy heading away in his cart, kicking up dust behind him. He's worked for my mama for years.

The stand has cleared. My mother's perfectly formed eyebrow, painted thin and dark, arches like an arrow. I got that from her.

"You really should get a cell phone," I tell her.

She waves me away. "This old talk again? Why do you bother me?"

I laugh. "I bother you because I care."

"Aww-ah! Tell me about your new life as a beach girl."

"You know better."

"Yes, of course I do. No daughter of mine will waste her life on the sand. No offense to Brianna. I like her. But you, you work hard at that shop of yours."

She makes me laugh.

"They catch that boy yet?"

"No, Mama."

She punches her palm with her fist. "If I ever get my hands on that *malvado muchacho*. Aww-ah!"

I look away.

"Why are you here, Mijita?"

"Just to see you, of course." Even more than my own shop, Mama's dense supply of flowers gives off a heady, sweet aroma. I gaze around at the same weathered plywood, the same dried twigs hanging upside down, like bats, Mama in her same crisp white blouse, worn sweater, polyester slacks, and black ballet slippers. She still makes three loops with the bows.

"It's a work day. You should be caring for your customers." She smiles at a couple of women when she says that, one elderly and gripping the arm of a younger girl.

If I had any customers.

"Your flowers are fresh and beautiful as always, Mama."

"*Gracias.*"

"You know, you could always come work for me. Then you wouldn't have to be outside when it's cold."

"This again?" She pulls her sweater closed. "I like the weather. This is California, Mijita."

"I know, I know—where the weather's always fine."

She nods her head with that familiar firmness, and I want to laugh but nothing comes out. What was I thinking? That my mother had suddenly changed? That something in the oddly comforting dwelling would be different, even after all these years? *What are you waiting for, Mama?*

It's then I notice it. A brief twitch of one of her hands. I'm wondering if it's all in my head when it starts again, a steady yet nearly invisible tremble. I swallow the words that come to mind.

"Well, you know that my door is always open to you, Mama—if you ever want or need me." Even if I were bankrupt and homeless, that would be true.

"You are a good girl, Gabrielle. You know where to find me."

Our standard conversation done, I climb back into my Volvo and aim it westward. White clouds shine brilliantly against the afternoon sun, and I long to go home. Livi left me a message about closing the shop, then reopening it later after her showing, so I guess that means I'm free to throw myself a pity party back at my loft. Woo-hoo.

Unfortunately, Iris and another woman block my front gate.

"Hello, Iris."

"Gaby." She nods, and her eyes run down the length of me.

Neither woman makes any attempt to give me room to pass, so I make my own. Iris pipes up. "Have you met Shonda? She lives a few houses down from you, on the same side of the street."

"Hi, Shonda. Nice to meet you."

I keep moving past the gate, and up the path when I hear Iris stage-whisper, "She's the one I told you about." She clears her throat. "So how are you, Gaby?"

I glance back to see Iris scrunching her face.

"I'm fabulous, Iris. Thank you for asking."

"And how are things going with Max, Gaby?"

I pause.

"Like I told you before," she says loudly, "he is just perfect for you. Don't you agree?"

Shonda's nodding like she has an idea of what Iris's talking about.

"Max is a great friend, Iris. Things are going well. Thank you for asking." Yada, yada, yada.

"I'm glad to hear it, Gaby. I hope you're not still angry with me. I really could not stand it if you were. You aren't, are you?"

I glance from Iris to Shonda and back again. I wish I could visualize the chaos behind those two pairs of shifty eyes. Iris almost acts jealous, but why? She's got a family, a fourplex by the sea, and from what I hear, a lively blog. And what have I got? A dying business, a pending lawsuit, and okay, maybe a new romance—but I'm trying to protect myself from another heartache, so even that sits precariously on the edge at the moment.

I'm tired of forgiving and forgetting. I'm tired of looking to the positive side of things. Standing here in front of these two gossips, after the month I've had, makes my simmering blood long to boil over and spill out onto the sidewalk in front of them.

"Tell me again why I shouldn't be angry with you, Iris?"

Iris gives her head and shoulders a shake. "I was only trying to warn you, Gaby—to protect you."

Shonda nods. "Oh yes. She's protecting you. That's right."

The heat rises in my veins. "How so?"

Iris drops her mouth open in a dramatic gasp and looks wide-eyed toward Shonda before turning back to me. "Well, word in the 'hood has you paired with your landlord, but I just keep telling everyone how silly that is."

.I cock my chin. "Really? Why's that?"

Iris makes a garbled sound, like she's laughing with rocks in her mouth. "I keep telling you! Everybody knows what a womanizer Jake is. You have enough problems right now, so I'm sure you have better sense than to get yourself mixed up with someone like that."

Shonda chimes in. "Amen. That's right. He's no good."

I keep eye contact with her. "I like him."

Iris stops. Shonda glances at her.

"He treats me well," I continue. It's the least I could say after he surprised me with dinner last night. Either that or lay into him for breaking and entering.

Iris whips me a Mommie Dearest look. "What about Max?"

A wave of rebellion washes over me. With one hand on the front door, I wiggle my eyebrows and give her a goofy grin. "I like him too." I swing the door behind me with panache.

Jake stands in the entryway, his smile large and lopsided. "You like me. You really like me!" He's rubbing those rather large hands together, like he's just mastered his first chocolate soufflé.

"Heard that, did you?"

"Yes, ma'am."

I shrug. "It wasn't for your benefit."

Jake watches me walk up the stairs, grinning. "I appreciate it just the same."

I stop midflight. "Yes, well. You might want to watch out for that neighbor of ours. She's watching you, you know."

His face freezes.

"So what is it with you and Iris anyway?"

His gaze flits away from mine, eventually landing on the lone, dusty window in the foyer. "Iris is . . . well, she's one of a kind. I've known her since we were kids, and I've made some mistakes where she's concerned."

You mean something other than posting a No Trespassing sign on the neighborhood tree house when you were twelve? That kind of mistake?

He continues. "Anyway, apologies aren't enough for her—her reputation means everything. Don't let her bully you or fill your head with her observations about the good people of this neighborhood, though, because believe me"—his eyes find mine—"she'll try."

Now I'm the one trying to steady my gaze. "I make my own decisions about people, Jake." And at the moment, I'm spending an extraordinary amount of energy trying to figure him and Iris out—and to understand why I care so much.

"Gotcha." He pauses. "By the way, Gaby, I noticed you don't have a TV up in the loft . . ."

I snap out of my meandering thoughts. "About that. Thanks for dinner . . ."

"You're welcome."

"But I'd rather you knock first."

"Sure thing," he says with a wink. "Just trying to be neighborly."

And that's when I see what my nosey neighbor has been trying to tell me about Jake. Beneath the day's whiskers, the man's smile beams. His eyes dance, and his shoulders loom. And has that luscious dimple been there all along? Just trying to be neighborly? Sure, I get that. Iris, despite Jake's claims, just might be right about him. And how annoying would that be?

"So I'll be taking off in the morning. I've signed on to help open a new restaurant, La Cofradía, in the Pasadena area soon, and I'll be staying down there until it's up and running. But I wanted to offer you access to my TV while I'm gone. HDTV—at your service." He dangles a key in front of me.

I raise a questioning eyebrow.

His eyes snag me. "You'll need this to get in."

I reach for the key and he grabs my hand. "C'mere. I'll need to show you how the remote works. It's quirky."

I pull my hand free and follow him like a starved puppy. He proceeds to walk me through the tangled mass of buttons and directions on his plasma's universal remote, and I try not to notice how good he smells. I mean, *good*.

He places the remote in my hand, and I wonder if an airline pilot must look at so many buttons. "It's all yours. Don't let me hear you're throwing wild parties down here or anything." He laughs. "Never mind. Throw all the parties you want."

And what would I serve? Peanut butter crudités? "Thank you, Jake. I'm not sure how much time I'll have to use it, but, well, thanks for thinking of me."

He nods, and that dimple of his stares me down. *"Mi casa es tu casa."*

The words melt that frozen part of me—that inner gal who aches with loneliness—and I flee to my loft. Just what I need in my life, another restless Casanova-wannabe. *Lord, get me out of here!*

Fourteen

JUST HOW CAN I DESCRIBE that first cup of coffee in the morning? Oh, let me count the ways, baby. I hold the mug against my chest and breathe in the earthy scent of roasted beans mixed with a dab of half and half. Even the vague essence of fresh seawater, the kind that's drifting in on the breeze at the moment, can't overpower the euphoria of those first few sips of the day.

I sink deeper into a lounge chair on the back deck, the bliss over this moment heightened by the knowledge that Jake took off for parts far south of here first thing this morning. I saw him through my upstairs window, his black truck peeling down the street just as the sun crested the foothills to the east, and it hit me: I'm alone. Never mind that I'm usually in that predicament; this time, it truly is for the best. There's no excuse for nosey, gossipy neighbors, but secretly, I'm glad Iris warned me of Jake's lady-killer ways because last night my mind had begun to linger on my landlord past the point of comfort. It was time to pull up.

Anyway, life's just so ironic sometimes, you know. I lost my last boyfriend, my apartment, most of my stuff, and—ha, get this—I'm being sued! Yet I'm living in one of the poshest neighborhoods in the city. Who knew life could be so . . . so . . . so unexpected?

I down the last sip and stand, only to come face-to-face with Sarah, the neighborhood curiosity. Well, one of them anyway. She's standing behind the rotting lattice fence that separates our two decks.

"Good morning," I offer.

She flails a little and drops her watering can, which, if you ask me, is about three sizes too small to ever really be useful. You need much more water than that to get down to the roots. Her makeup's heavy and red and powdery. Not *let's find our seats because this circus is about to start* overdone, but severe just the same. Yet from behind the mask, the most gorgeous azure eyes stare back at me.

I reach over the dilapidated fence. "I'm Gaby, your new neighbor." Her eyes flit downward at my hand, like she's confused. Then, with a spark of recognition, she gives my hand a gingerly shake.

"Hi. Sarah."

She doesn't look crazy, although would I know crazy if I saw it? (Aside from Iris, I mean.) Maybe she's visually impaired. That would explain the overindulgence of Maybelline this morning.

Yet she's so quiet. And since I've seen her through her upstairs window, gabbing on the phone late into the night, I'm quite sure she's not mute. Oh! I'd rather apply acrylics with over-the-counter nail glue than stand here in silence.

I smile in the vacuum that is our conversation. "Wish I could stay out here all day." I give the sea a pity glance. "Duty calls though."

My gaze lingers on the sea. When I look back at Sarah, she has already crossed her deck and opened her back door. I wave, and she smiles demurely before disappearing inside.

That was awkward. I grab my coffee cup and drain it dry while turning to face the flowing channel below. I've got a hankering for chocolate, but Bri's been too busy to whip me up a batch of her decadent brownies, and that's just about ninety-seven kinds of wrong.

Best friends are supposed to drop everything when their friend's in a funk, are they not?

Something in the water catches my peripheral view, and I strain to make it out. Nope, it's gone again. Wait. There. A sea lion rubs its plump body against the narrow dock. How cute is this?

Since moving here I've seen crabs scaling the rocks below the deck like climbers on Half Dome. I've also heard about occasional bat ray sightings and harmless sharks. But this is the first sea lion to swim into my world.

I tiptoe down the ramp to the dock. "Hi, baby," I whisper. My whiskered friend stares at me through somber eyes, her drenched body smacking against the side of the dock with each rhythmic lap of seawater. She bobs there, watching me, and I'm not certain, but I think she may have just smirked.

"You lonely?" I'm not sure why I ask her this. Surely there are enough fish in the sea to keep her busy. Then again, she makes no attempt to bolt.

You would think that after all the years of playing childish games in an open-air shack at the side of a country road that I would have become one with the outdoors somehow—that I'd be spending my grown-up years coaxing stray kittens to drink milk or rescuing bunnies from construction sites. Reality is, I like pretty things that come in gold boxes: diamonds, Godiva chocolates, glittery shoes. And Marc Jacobs pumps, though I can't afford a pair at the moment, just wouldn't look right hoofing it on a mountain hike somewhere.

"You think you're going to change all that, don't you, now? Don't give me that soulful look, sweet thing. You and I have nothing in common."

Her fur shimmers in the early morning light, slick yet mottled like burnt oatmeal. She brushes an ear flap against the dock, undeterred, and her puppy dog eyes bait me. I laugh. Is it possible to be smitten by a sea lion?

Sweet Thing—I've just named her that—dives below the surface, disappearing completely. I sigh. Easy come, easy— Oops, she surfaces again, those gemstone eyes charming me once more, and I sprawl on the dock and watch her for who knows how long. After a while, the sounds of my neighbors waking and readying themselves for work and school pulls me from my musings. I realize the time and reluctantly pull myself up, careful to smooth the layers of my cotton skirt.

I glance back and sigh as Sweet Thing frolics in her watery home. "You've made my morning, little friend. Go catch yourself a squid or something." Slowly I climb up the plank toward the deck, but not before catching sight of Shonda, observing me from a sling-back beach chair perched atop her yacht, a trail of cigarette smoke dissipating above her head.

I hurry into my shop and stop short. "Wow, you're here early today."

Livi's bent over a spreadsheet, hair sprouting from a ponytail in every direction. My all-weather friend pulls her gaze up, revealing sagging rings beneath her eyes. "Hey, Gaby."

I approach her. "Are you sick?"

"No, I'm not sick."

"You look like you haven't slept."

"You could say that."

I plop down next to her. "Why . . . why haven't you slept? Is something wrong?"

She lets out a loud, exaggerated sigh. "I'm a light sleeper, Gaby. Is that okay with you?"

Who is this imposter, and what has she done with my peace-loving friend? I stand. "I'm going next door to get you a latte."

Livi opens her mouth to protest.

"Buh-buh-buh." I hold a finger to my lips. "I'll be right back."

When I return with her caramel-laced coffee, the one I bought with a pocketful of quarters, Livi's on the phone.

"Yes, Mrs. Ross. No more monthly orders. I'll give her the message. Thank you." She tosses the receiver into the cradle, then looks up at me. "Gaby, you're broke."

The coffee burns my hand, and I realize that I forgot to ask for a sleeve. I'm all for saving the environment and all—green is the new pink, you know—but requiring customers to ask for a sleeve that they'll most surely need to protect their skin from swelteringly hot drinks just so they can assuage any guilt over impacting our landfills . . . well, that's just not right.

"Did you hear what I said?" A vein pulsates at her temple. "Your business is bleeding faster than a hemophiliac."

I wince.

Livi reaches up and smoothes her ponytail, only to watch a bedraggled strand flop onto the bridge of her nose. She shrugs both shoulders. "I don't know what else I can do. It's simple accounting. Your expenses are higher than your income, and you just can't operate like this forever. I'm sorry."

I set the coffee down in front of her. "I can do this."

Livi looks away. I'm witnessing a new side to her. She's usually so accepting, so . . . so uncritical and easygoing. I know this because I've driven with her. Just try cutting her off in the fast lane. You can't, I tell you, because she'll let you in. Going twenty miles per hour slower than the speed limit? No problem. Just come on over!

"What aren't you saying, Livi?"

She huffs, her eyes downcast. "Where were you yesterday, Gaby? I cancelled my showing when you didn't come back to the shop."

"No. Oh, Livi. I told you to just close up if I didn't make it back."

"You can't afford that," she snaps.

I roll my hands into tight fists, jagged fingernails digging into my palms. Deep breath in. Start fresh. "Livi. I appreciate all that you've been doing for me, but I don't want you to give up your life for me. I never asked that of you, and I just don't expect it."

She pulls her hair out of its scrunchy and shakes it loose. "Sorry, Gaby. Sorry. I'm just exhausted. I've been here since three a.m."

"Why? Why would you come in so early?"

She shrugs. "Couldn't get any sleep at home."

I narrow my eyes. "It's Jet, isn't it? Your roommate's been smoking pot again, and dragging home all kinds of miscreants. Am I right?"

"Listen, she's a troubled girl, and she's hit a low point. I just figured if I let her be for a while, she'd . . ."

"She'd what? Livi, don't cover for her. She locked you out, didn't she?"

Her saucer-shaped eyes meet mine for the first time all morning. Just as quickly, she breaks eye contact, and scoops up her things. "You know what? I've got to go. I have a million things to do today."

I put a hand on her arm. "Wait, Livi. Don't run off. I think you need to confront Jet. Tell her she needs help, that she can't survive like this. I know confrontation isn't your thing, but do this for yourself. You'll feel better for it, I promise. Don't let other people run your life."

She stares at my hand, then slowly lifts her gaze to meet mine. She rights her shoulders. "Gaby," she says, "you're the one who needs help. You can't survive like this."

I release her arm and she's out the door.

Fifteen

I'D BE LYING IF I said Max's presence in my life wasn't the thing I'm clinging to at the moment. Figuratively speaking, anyway. I'm out on the dock, and I've just learned (accidentally, of course) that narrow heels and decaying wooded surfaces just don't mix well. As I hug a piling while attempting to pull my pump free, I'm thinking about the downhill spiral that has pulled me into its spin lately. It started a month ago and hasn't slowed a bit. *Au contraire*—it's actually revved up.

But my thoughts have turned to Max the past few days, his familiar face illuminated in my mind. Seeing him in a new and *muy macho* light, those delicious chocolaty eyes of his have sparked thoughts of a long-term romance complete with the conventional trappings of picket fences and 2.6 kids. Yes, these musings have kept my heart afloat.

Speaking of afloat, a gray kayak slices its way through the channel waters. Iris's daughter, Kit, paddles with fierce power, her dark eyes focused on the point at the front of her boat. Until she sees me, that is. I watch her coast in beside the dock as I twist and grind my shoe deeper into a jam.

She lays her paddle across her lap. "Take the shoe off."

I jerk a look downward, unlatch my shoe, and slide my foot out. Never mind the rosy glow to my cheeks.

Kit shakes her head of soot-black hair and dips her paddle back into the water.

"Wait," I call out. "Are you feeling better today?"

She grimaces at me as if I've just handed her a detention slip. "I'm all right."

"Good, because you seemed pretty ill the other day. That can be rough on a school day. Hope you took some zinc for that."

"Had some stuff goin' on. I'm over it."

The obnoxious roar of a dinghy screeching down the waterway muffles her words. I squint in its direction, still prying my heel from the deck. On approach, the kid in the driver's seat cuts the engine and floats on past. He gives a *whazzup?* nod to Kit, and she disses him with another grimace.

Ah, the mystery of young love. What did that old guy in *It's a Wonderful Life* say? Right, something about it being wasted on the young. I don't even want to think about being thirty-three, which I almost am, and how much time I've wasted.

Kit looks at me. "He's such a dork."

My heel pops out of its trap, and I nearly topple backward.

She laughs a snarky kind of laugh now. "Bet you don't even own a pair of flip-flops," she accuses.

I control my eyebrow. "I'd surprise you, then. I used to have a ton of them. My friend Bri and I love to walk the beach, and they're good for that, you know." I don't add that we usually have a basket of fresh-baked brownies with us, our wallowing food of choice, and that, truthfully, we don't actually walk. We lounge.

Kit doesn't leave. "So what happened? You give all your flip-flops away to the homeless or something down at the river camp?"

I straighten. "I lost them in a fire not too long ago. Actually, I lost most of my possessions."

"That sucks."

My eyebrow does its darting upward thing, and I do nothing to stop it. What's this girl doing out here all alone and so early? I take in her sallow skin, her stringy hair. Does she expect me to believe she's got the call of the wild in her blood? Or that this is her daily exercise routine? Please. I'd guess drugs or a guy.

"So where are you headed so early?"

"Goin' nowhere."

That's what I thought. I force a smile. "Is that very far away?"

Her lips stay flat as a line, but she bounces her chin in thought. She shrugs and stares into the air. "Gotta do my thing. That's all."

With both feet now naked, I make a move to step back to the deck above. "Well, thanks for your advice about the shoe, Kit. I guess I'd better mosey off to work." One step back, though, and a pin of pain sears me. I yelp.

Kit crows. "Everybody knows you can get splinters from an old dock like that."

So you'd think that after a confrontation like Livi and I had yesterday, she'd not be "darkening my door" anytime soon. Yet as I rush into the shop carrying tepid coffee, a cheap, non-flaky croissant, and bushels of lavender and willow, I nearly pass out from fright when I find her slumped over the laptop on my counter. My truncated shriek does little to disturb her. "Livi! You're here."

She drags her eyes upward. "Yes."

I set the flowers onto the floor and lay the rest of my things on the counter one by one. "I thought you were mad."

She frowns. "I'm just worried about you, Gaby. And I shouldn't have overreacted like I did. I'm really not sure what got into me. I just

feel like you really don't understand just how bad things are for you."
She scratches a spot on her cheek over and over again.

That's ridiculous. I've seen what's in my refrigerator. I've seen the
trash can after a day of tossing out rotting foliage, and I've held the
legal documents accusing me of creating ugly arrangements. I hook
eyes with her but stay quiet. She obviously has more to say.

"Anyhoo, I've revised your blog design, giving it more punch. I
keep finding your doodles, and using them to inspire me, although I
have lightened the color scheme on the actual design." She turns the
screen around. "Do you like it?"

I gasp. "If you ever think about giving up on real estate, you could
make a bundle in Web design, my friend."

She smiles shyly. "You ready to start posting yet?"

The phone rings, and I reach for it. "Almost. I promise to work
on it tonight." I press the receiver to my ear. "Florally Yours. This is
Gaby. How may I help you today?"

"Mornin', Beautiful."

Max. "Hi."

"Was thinkin' about you today."

I press my thumb and forefinger to my lips. "Really?"

"Gibson and I are taking off for a few days. It's spring break for
him. Time for some male-bonding activities." He laughs.

"Oh."

"But before we go, I'd really like to see you, Gaby."

Yes, that's my heart fluttering. "I may be able to comply." My girlish
smile makes Livi frown and shake her head.

He chuckles. "Well, good. Lunch today, then? Thought we could
maybe grab a hamburger or something."

I shrug inwardly. So, it's not filet mignon? It's lunch and—I remind
myself—it's free. With really, really cute Max. "I'd love it, but I might
need to eat here . . ." I peek at Livi and she waves me on. "Never mind
about that. Sure, I'd love to."

The morning flies by and—hallelujah—I sell three arrangements and take an order for a small retirement party to be held at the Tower Club. Ka-ching! Ka-ching! By the time Max strolls in to take me to lunch, Livi's mood has lightened and she's been able to take several calls from clients of her own.

Max winks at me, takes my hand, and we stroll downtown for a burger. Is it just me or do we look just perfect together? We pass another store window, and I make no attempt to hide my fascination with us in the reflection. Our chemistry has symmetry!

We're seated outside, and the minute Max's order comes, I swipe one of his fries. "So what's this big trip you and Gib are going on?" I ask him.

"Bora Bora."

I giggle. "You're too funny. No, really, where are you headed?"

"I wouldn't make that up. Gib's got the chance to surf some big waves down there, so I thought why not go with him? Should be fun."

That's for sure. I swallow a bite. "So you've been planning this a long time, then?"

"Nah. It just came up a couple of days ago. It's actually a surf tour, and a couple of friends had to drop out at the last minute. Gibby asked if we could take their places, and since the deposit was already paid I figured, why not?"

No wonder he hadn't mentioned this before. Not like he should have at this point in our relationship. I can call it that, right?

"I would've said something before, but I wasn't really sure if it would happen. Had to call in some favors to get our passports in a hurry." Max tosses me a wink.

"I take it you two don't travel much, what with your business and Gib's schoolwork."

115

"Nope, not much at all." He stares at his plate, and either he's really loving the pattern, or he's lost in thought. I'm hoping for the latter. "Actually," he says, "I've got a few trips in mind for later this year."

Now, see, this is where a girl could come to all sorts of conclusions. Is he testing the waters with me? Thinking of taking me to meet the parents? Hinting, maybe, at a fall wedding followed by an exotic hop to a private island? Deep breath in. Start fresh. "Later this year, huh? Something fun, I hope."

"Maybe." He's doing that staring thing again, only this time his fork has apparently snagged his attention. "I actually have an ulterior motive today. I wanted to ask you a question."

Do tell. "Sure. Ask me anything."

"Would you feed our dog?"

"Excuse me?"

"This trip is on such short notice, and my neighbor Casey usually stops in to take care of Rover." I watch to see him crack a smile. He doesn't. "Problem is, she's already going away for break. I've been wracking my head trying to figure out who could help us out at this late date, so would you mind?"

I hesitate. I've never owned a dog, nor ever taken care of one, but that doesn't make me a dog-hater. I always wanted one, but Mama and I just never had room and none of my landlords were open to the idea . . . So there you go.

"She's old and tired. She'll love you."

How exactly do I take that? "Of course I'll feed your pup for you, Max. You don't even need to ask. I'm happy to. Rover, huh?"

A smile of relief fills his face, and he hands me a key. "You'll need this."

What is it lately with men and keys to their homes? I'm one step away from being asked to dust and vacuum while I'm there. I can feel it.

I take the key, and Max takes hold of my hand. In one swift move, he leans across the table and plants a soft kiss on my lips, the moment sending a warm shiver through me. "Thanks."

"You're welcome," I whisper back.

I just agreed to feed his dog, and I have to wonder, what would an agreement to clean house get me?

Sixteen

ONE KISS AND NEW BOYFRIEND awkwardness is *over*. Praise the Lord and pass the wedding bands! Okay, maybe it's too early for that, but really, I've known Max for years. Shouldn't that account for something?

I'm back at the shop. Livi darted out of here the minute I returned, and I haven't heard from her since. The quiet has gotten me thinking, and my earlier elation over The Kiss has now settled into a question. Had Max planned on kissing me all along? Or was his amorous move simply a reaction to his relief that Rover won't be starving while he's gone?

Hmm.

The bell on my front door rings as it opens.

"Hi, Gaby."

"Doug! Oh, my lawyer extraordinaire. Come in, come in!"

"Thought I'd stop by and pick up a bouquet for Bri, and while I'm at it, talk to you about the suit."

I lean against the counter and drop my head into my hand. "Must we?"

He smiles regretfully. "I'm afraid so."

I slap my hands on the counter. "Okay, tell me everything. Don't leave out a thing. I'm ready!"

His forehead shifts with his thoughts. "First, Gaby, we're going to have to file that demurrer I told you about."

"The what?"

"Basically, I'll be asking the court to throw out this case."

"Well, hallelujah to that!"

"If that is overruled—and it very well may be—then we will need to file our answer to the complaint within about fifteen days. This means we'll have to peel apart the bride's lawyer's legalese and assert our defenses."

Clear as silt. "I can defend myself. She's strange and awful, and I'm nice."

Doug stares at me with piercing lawyer eyes, and I see him in a new and frightening light. I almost want to scream "I'm guilty, guilty, guilty!" and pay the price if it means I can escape that steely gaze of his.

He clears his throat. "We'll assert that the bride's specifications were met. She knew which flowers she wanted and that what she ordered is what was delivered."

"Bing, bing, bing, and then it's over. Right?"

"Not so fast. Her lawyer will say that you should have known that these particular flowers would not work with her décor."

"I did tell her that! Red anthuriums, white pompons, and blue lilacs—those were all her idea."

"Well, he'll say that you, as the expert, should have talked the bride out of ordering them. He'll lay the responsibility on you."

I wrinkle my nose. "Florist malpractice?"

Doug's mouth twitches. "Something like that."

"Well, I just hope my insurance comes through for me."

Doug's forehead shifts this time, and he's as quiet as a clam.

"What? No way. They're not covering me?"

"I'm sorry, Gaby. I tried, but they won't consider it."

I find the stool behind my counter and lower myself into it. "So what's the damage?"

Doug gives me a closed-mouth sigh before eyeing me. "For starters, for the privilege of being sued, you get to pay the court's filing fee of several hundred dollars. And one more thing, Gaby. . . ."

The ding on the door breaks my absorption. A woman with shaggy white hair leans in. "Phew. I found you. This place is tiny." Her eyes flit around before landing on me. "I'm here to pick up the arrangement for our retirement luncheon, and I've been assured that you always bill my boss for these things. I don't have any money with me."

Join the club.

Doug slaps shut his portfolio, plucks a simple bouquet of spring daisies from a bucket, and lays two bills on the counter. "I'll call with more news later," he says on the way out.

I nod at him as he goes, then turn to reassure my remaining customer that, yes, I will bill her, even though her boss usually interprets due and payable upon receipt as whenever he feels like it. Without a hint of sullenness, I give her the red-carpet treatment, all the while hoping that something good will come out of this latest mess I've gotten myself into. *About that, God. What's up with all the messes lately?*

"Good news."

"Yippee, I need some of that right now," I say into the phone. *"¿Que pasa?"*

"Well, Gaby, I've, um, received my first listing."

"That's not just good news—that's so great, Livi! Congratulations!"

She's quiet.

I probe. "Aren't you thrilled?"

"I am . . . thrilled."

"Well then whoop it up, girlfriend!" Somebody around here needs to have something to celebrate.

"I'm so sorry, Gaby, but I won't be able to help you in the shop anymore. See, I've been offered a great job under one of the busiest brokers in town. She's. . . . she's promised to mentor me, and I just hate to pass it up. . . ."

Oh. I swallow my sigh. "You've already done so much for me, Livi. Of course you can't pass this up. Please don't think about it another second, okay? I'm excited for you. I am. Truly." Sick for me, excited for you.

We hang up. The shop surrounds me with silence. Reluctantly, I check my new blog, the one I've yet to personalize. Nada—nothing. Not one comment waiting for me. I glance around the room, then back to the laptop. With a sigh, I type in the address of Iris's romance blog.

Lovely Readers,

Today I'd like to offer some sage advice to my single readers:

Five Ways to Rope a Husband.
1. *Prepare for one. If you have a single bed, buy a double.*
2. *Take a financial-planning course at your local college. A man interested in money is a good catch, indeed.*
3. *Join a gym. Plant yourself on a stair-climbing machine that faces the entry doors and watch for The One to walk through.*
4. *Golf. Play with them, flirt with them, but by no means ever win the game.*
5. *Regularly visit a sports bar. Impress them with your knowledge, but hold back lest they think you're above them.*

And I wasted my time this way, why?

After closing up shop, I find myself standing on Max's porch, half-way down a lane near the State Beach, teetering with anticipation. My future could be just beyond that door, and I want to savor this moment. My mind flickers cruelly. What if Max's sweet old dog resembles a pit bull at recess?

Without warning, the door swings open. "You're here. Great." Max kisses me on the cheek, and suddenly I don't care if the creature I've come to meet is a big old bear. Some super-sized swooning is going on here. Max stops. "You've never been here before."

I loop my hand into the crook of his arm. "Why don't you give me the grand tour."

"Okay." We step over a pile of sleeping bags and backpacks large enough to scale, and I'm wondering if this just might be a sign of things to come, maybe this is what life with a couple of bachelors looks like. Then we turn the corner. I blink. Have we stepped into the pages of *Architectural Digest* or what? I've always loved a man with good taste. Who knew Max had an eye for mixing taupes, blacks, ivories, and golds into one sophisticated living room? Where's the surf motif, the sandy slip-ons, the surfboards laid up against one side of the room? Apparently Max doesn't subscribe to the notion that the preferred house cleaning method for men is to periodically hose the whole place down. It's spotless in here, and forgive me if I've missed it, but I don't see a drain anywhere in the place.

We end up in Max's black-and-white-granite-topped kitchen, and I feel the call to don an apron and whip up a Thanksgiving meal. "Rover hangs out in here most of the time, but Gib's walking her right now. We'll be leaving as soon as he comes in."

"So how old is your pup?"

Max's eyes don't meet mine. "Actually, she was Rosemary's dog."

I sense the crushing weight of caring for his beloved wife's pet. I pat his shoulder. "I understand."

He catches my eyes with a look of gratitude and what I can only describe as longing. Is it getting hot in here or what?

The boys take off to surf the world, while I'm still in the house. Before long, it's just me and docile, floppy Rover, listening to the dependable tick of Gib's *Surf's Up* clock. I think about this. In the last few days, two men have offered me keys to their homes, and more importantly, access to their plasma widescreens. My pandering to their sense of chivalry has, apparently, worked flawlessly.

Rover darts off, then growls. I wander back into the kitchen, hoping she hasn't just discovered a rodent. She still growls as I lean against the stark stainless-steel island, my eyes running over Max's mail strewn about the countertop: brochures for campgrounds, science camps, fishing excursions, and a father-son hike in the wilds. Not a romantic trip for two in the bunch.

I straighten up and Rover spies me. She snarls and then lunges like a lion onto its prey, but—thank you, Lord—she has no teeth. I shriek and coax out my calm voice, the one I use when I'm talking to myself. The same one that tries to convince my head that my life consists of more than comedy material.

Instead of being soothed by my reassuring platitudes, Rover, previously so floppy and docile, springs to life in her most ferocious form yet. She head butts me with her furry softness and growls like she means it. In a moment of daring, I pull out my cell phone, slide it open, and snap a picture of Max's old girl in all her unforgiving glory, her pink tongue unconstrained by blackening gums.

She stops. She bends her neck to the right. She licks my phone. Yuck.

I wave my phone at her. "Evidence, my friend. I'm glad we understand each other." I almost say that, if I marry Max, it's off to doggy boarding school for her. She must be a mind reader because I'd swear she just narrowed her eyes at me. With a whine of Scooby-Doo proportions, she lowers herself onto her haunches and begins to slurp away at an intriguing spot on the back of her paw.

All this has got me wondering if, somehow, a sign has appeared on my forehead: *Kicking while down encouraged!*

I take my disheveled self home and swerve to avoid Sarah walking in the middle of the street toward the beach, her face down. Just as I pass, she lifts her head. My wave falls on a vacuous gaze, her expression empty as if we'd never met.

That's me, memorable as early contestants from the first installment of *American Idol.*

Also taking up space in the street are Iris and Shonda, standing nose to nose in quiet conversation. I drive past, hoping they each had a breath mint. Not until I reach my front door do the heavens open and I receive a bit of a bright spot in a rather dreary day. Other than lunch with Max, that is. . . . Although, on second thought, maybe his invitation was just a ruse for his doggie-feeding request. I push away the thought.

Barbie Runnergirl jogs up to my gate. "I hear you're a florist."

"You heard that right. That's me. How can I help you?"

"I've seen you around."

Considering I'm not pencil-thin like Barbie Runnergirl nor my workout manic friend, Livi, I'm not sure how to take this. "Thanks," I say, giving her the, you know, benefit of my doubts. "I'm Gaby. It's very nice to meet you."

"You too. I'm Meredith." She continues. "I was wondering if you would want to do the flowers for my wedding." She startles me with her out-of-the-air question.

Wedding! "Congratulations, and yes! I'd be happy to do the flowers for you." Because, frankly, I've got nothing else planned, no matter when it is. "Have you set the date?"

"Not exactly. Probably two months from now. On the beach."

Sigh. Bri and Doug were married on the beach—and could there be a more happy couple than those touchy-kissy two? "The possibilities are endless for you." I reach into my cranberry-and-salmon striped bag. "Let me get you my card."

"Not necessary. I know where to find you. Gotta run. See you."

With that, Barbie Runnergirl—I mean, Meredith—and her staccato vocabulary dash off. I step inside the empty house and shut the door.

Seventeen

THIS IS MY FAVORITE PART. They've spent the night brainstorming themselves out of one whammy of a predicament. They sang; they danced. They watched the sun come up. He walks her home, in the rain, and he knows. She's the One.

I hit rewind and watch the entire scene from *Singin' in the Rain* again. That's love for you, a man willing to risk flu, or a head cold at least, to dance in a storm. Mama never got this flick. "Dancing in the rain? That's how you get sick!"

I gather up my half-empty bowl of popcorn, soggy and cold, to take with me back upstairs. I've got my principles. The man loaned me his TV, not his garbage can. Before leaving, I glance around. The doily on the headrest of Jake's man chair hangs precariously, and so I straighten it, smoothing the lacey fabric down with the fingers of my free hand. I just can't get over how different Jake's furnishings are from Max's. If my grandmother had ever owned a home of her own (instead of living with Mama and me when I was little) and if she were still living today, somehow this is how I imagine her home would look. Comfortable couch, an upholstered hassock, knickknacks, plain wooden dining set. Yes, she would have liked it here. Although

I doubt Grandmother would have allowed the dust to gather in such extreme quantities.

I pick up a picture of a pretty teenager grinning from a silver frame sitting on the dust-coated shelf. She looks familiar. Then again, sunny blondes grow wild here in beachside California, like poppies. I probably see her look-alike twice a day. Iris mentioned that Jake had years ago lived here with his young daughter. I assume this is her and wonder where she is now. Yet is it my place to ask? I run my index finger along the frame's upper edge, removing a film of dust before setting the photo down, and head back upstairs.

Morning dawns, and I wander out to the deck, coffee mug in hand. A splash draws my attention to the dock below, and for about half a second I wonder if Tom Hanks and Darryl Hannah might surface. Mermaids, anyone?

After sinking myself into brainless hours of movie-wallowing the night before, sans Bri's brownies—sniff—I managed to stay awake and blog for a while, visiting rather voyeuristically in other sites. My own site sits empty and not a little forlorn, but I also like to think it resembles an artist's canvas just waiting for brilliance to strike.

Another splash pulls me away from my thoughts, and I peer over the handrail to find my friendly neighborhood sea lion.

"Hello, Sweet Thing," I say. "You're lookin' fine today. Catch any good fish lately?"

Call me crazy, but I think I just saw a grin spreading across the narrow line of her mouth. She nuzzles the dock, and I'm drawn to walk down the ramp for an up-close view. As I do, she dives beneath the surface of the water.

"You ditching me too?" I chide. "Well, then. You just go on and join that club." I giggle as a tail pokes up through the water, then disappears. "Just keep on going." I call after the creature. "Don't mind me."

I glance around, and notice that just about every other dock has a boat tied to it. Except Jake's. Sure there's a beat-up red kayak tethered to one end but how seaworthy could it be? Why bother to live on a dock and not have a boat? Is that like bothering to run a shop with no customers?

"Hey."

I'm startled by a boat coming up from the right. It's Kit's.

"Hey yourself, Kit. How's it going?" *And why aren't you getting ready for school?*

"Nice shoes."

I glance down at my pink pouffy slippers—another Bri hand-me-down—and raise my chin and wink at her. "Gracias, chica."

She grunts, yet I notice a smile trying to surface. "You speak Spanish?"

"A little. My mother does, and she taught me some, but it's really more like Spanglish."

"Like the movie."

Let's see, Adam Sandler married to a crazy woman yet resisting the charms of his gorgeous Spanish-speaking maid. "Kind of," I say with a giggle, the second one this morning. The sensation feels good against my throat.

"You should kayak sometime. You're always so uptight."

Oh, really. "And kayaking would change that? The looking-uptight thing?"

She shrugs both shoulders. "Maybe. Kayaking's just sick, that's all."

Sick? Not sure what to say here. I reach back in my mind and remember Gib and Nathan talking outside on Bri's porch one day. Oh yes, *sick* is the new *good.* I give her a shrug back. "Maybe I will."

She snickers. "Sure."

"Maybe you'll teach me sometime."

She narrows her dark-ringed eyes at me, but a sparkle of sunshine lights up her uneven part and I notice a golden tinge to her roots. From behind that Goth facade, I'm seeing an angel peeking out.

"Because I've never been in one of those things."

"That's obvious."

I fight to keep my eyebrow from rocketing skyward. I watch her. "So I guess it's a date." She withers at my words. Okay, so maybe that was the wrong phrase. "So will you teach me sometime, Kit?"

She shrugs. "I guess."

I watch her row away. Get to school, dear one.

Two hours later, I'm prepping my shop for a full-blown invasion and praying one will come. I've dusted off a blue-painted bench, one often used to display floral arrangements, and I've relocated it under the outside awning, hoping it'll draw customers with its whimsical welcome. I've also wiped down windowsills, spritzed several new bouquets that I created out on the back deck at home, and filled stainless buckets with fresh, room temp water and lots of freshly-cut flowers.

I admire the results, which happen to remind me of my mama's touch. It'll have to do.

And it does. For an hour, I answer calls and help customers as they browse through my flip-book of floral images. Peruvian lilies, protea, tuberoses, all make the list. I even manage to collect a small sum of cash, but by lunchtime business drops off decidedly and I turn to my laptop and log on.

My blank blog stares back at me. I play air piano in front of the keyboard. I keep telling myself that any second, these babies are gonna fly! I start: *This is Gaby's blog.* No, scratch that. Start over. *Hello, I'm Gaby. Always the florist, never the bride—ha ha!* I shake my head. Too chummy. Okay, start again.

Welcome to my garden! I'm glad you're here. YOU are the star at Florally Yours. Think of your floral arrangement as art, something that will draw you into its creative embrace and brighten your life. We at Florally Yours aim to help you create your own masterpiece in which you, yes, YOU are the star. Again, welcome.

I stand back and scrutinize my first attempt at blogging. So it's not Shakespeare? All's well that ends well, and why not? I gave it a shot, and it's not half bad.

But is it half good? I answer the phone.

"Gaby-girl, what's up?"

My best friend's voice goes down like a chocolate smoothie. "I'm hanging in there, Bri-Bri. You know I am. How's life with a full house?"

"We're surviving. Just on a quick break here. Ned flooded the boat's engine this morning, so we drifted in the sea for a while until the Coast Guard came and got us."

"But you're okay?" *And was the guard yummy?*

"Yeah, sure. Only now some of the passengers want a make-up cruise tomorrow, so I won't be having a day off as planned." Big sigh. "Well, it was sorta a day off. I had to reschedule Aunt Dot's doctor's appointment that I had on the calendar for tomorrow. Yep, I've got her strapped in ready to go now."

A warbly voice hollers something unintelligible in the background.

Bri's back on the line. "Aunt Dot says hi. Oh, and she says to tell you that she strapped her own self in. Sheesh."

We say our good-byes, and I try not to let the lack of my best friend's presence get to me. Never even had a chance to mention that I hold the key to Max's classy digs, nor that Rover and I had an understanding. I glance at my blog, and would you look at that? A comment already. Who knew?

Glad to see your life turning around, Gaby. I hope you're enjoying the TV.

I lean forward. *What?*

I forgot to mention that I left a tray of my famous basil lasagna in the freezer for you. Bon appetit!—Jake.

Oh. My. I click on Jake's highlighted name, and locate his profile. I follow that to his contact address.

Dear Jake, Thanks for the comment on my blog. You are the first! I was wondering, though, how you found me so quickly (my curiosity is purely for marketing purposes). Cordially, Gaby.

I hit *Send* and fritter away the moments, watching the door, watching the clock, watching the laptop screen. A message appears. *Hello Gaby, Surprised you, eh?*

I look away and grumble. No. I was just curious. Didn't he read that? The screen draws me back.

I Googled you, then subscribed to your blog when I first noticed it show up in the blogosphere. Took some time for you to post, though, but I'm glad to see you finally write in. Have fun with it, all right?—Jake.

Yes, fun—some might call it that. The queasiness in my belly reminds me of the day Jake's voice boomed into my shower, and I have the urge to draw the blinds, lock the door, and crawl beneath my futon.

The door jangles and I straighten up. "May I help you?"

A round woman steps inside, then sneezes. "Gotta bill for you here."

Another member of that club. It's from my favorite wholesaler, and I'm about thirty days late. I thank her for it, you know, because it's the polite thing to do, and get back to my reading. She continues to stand there, sniffling away. I look up from my reading. "Can I help you with something else?"

She shifts her eyes to my display of mixed gerbera daisies, cut and vase-ready, then back to me. She clears her congested throat. "I was told not to leave without a check."

Oh.

She leaves, finally, along with all but $1.73 of my bank balance. Evening settles in, bringing with it dark shadows and a breezy chill. It almost looks like rain. I drain the till, turn out the lights, and hope for enough gas to make it to Max's and then home to my empty loft.

Eighteen

I SAVOR ANOTHER BITE OF basil and noodles, the herb treating my taste buds to a faint aroma of mint, and cozy myself into Jake's man chair with the latest issue of *Reef Report*. In it Iris waxes on about weekly date nights and the importance of making a man feel respected in the home. I stick my forefinger down my throat and pretend to gag—only it loses something when there's no one in the room to cheer me on.

Bri wasn't home when I called, something about driving Nathan and a load of friends to LA for an IMAX movie showing. Aunt Dot gave me an earful though. Let's see. Doctors around here are apparently inept, ignorant, and unattractive, unlike those rogue fellas out on the mission field, where she'd prefer to be. No wonder Bri escaped to LA.

I wander out on the deck, where the wind has turned warm and tropical. The moon glows from its prominent place above cool water-filled channels, full and bright like a spotlight for the big show, and I have to wonder if I'm the one on stage. Maybe my problems are all just figments of some screenwriter's overactive, dark imagination. Think *Adaptation*. An engine whirs in the distance, and a sudden slap against the dock grabs my attention. I find Sweet Thing lounging there.

"Nice night, isn't it, girl?"

She barks softly, followed by a high-pitched moan.

"I hope you're okay down there." I step down the ramp.

Her head bobs atop the water, eyes shining. Having a sea lion for a playmate hadn't occurred to me when I rented this place. Then again, stranger things have happened. Like being sued over supposedly ugly flowers. Yes, sea lions as pets must be this area's best-kept secret.

The echo of a lawn mower on steroids grinds into the air as that familiar dinghy whips around the corner, throwing a fan of sea spray onto the dock. Sweet Thing barks and dives below the water. My eyebrow travels north, but unfortunately the reckless teenage captain won't be able to see my ire.

Then he unexpectedly coasts to a stop in front of my dock. "Hey," he calls out.

"Hey, yourself."

"Cool night, huh."

I so wanted to wring his neck a minute ago, you know, for breaking my reverie. But he's really quite the charmer—if you can get past the long hair that hasn't seen a comb since I've lived here. "Yes it is. Do you live around here?"

"Yeah. I'm Willy."

As in free me?

He jerks his head in the direction of the corner. "I live around there. Hey, you're friends with Kit, huh."

Friends? Hmm. "We've talked a couple of times, and she's going to teach me to kayak sometime."

He nods. "That's cool. Her mom's weird. She probably needs a chick like you in her life."

His out-there comment causes me to burst out with laughter.

"I'm just saying. You need a life jacket? We've got a bunch of 'em in our garage."

Life jackets? "I don't recall you ever wearing one."

He shrugs. "I'm a strong swimmer. I don't need one. But chicks should always wear a life jacket."

Oh brother. "Is that a rule?"

"No offense. It's pretty tame around here, but if you get out into the mouth"—he points toward the harbor mouth where I often see yachts and cruises heading out to sea— "it gets hairy sometimes. Gotta watch out for that."

"Thanks for the advice, then. I wouldn't want to flip out of that thing, I guess, and not have some sort of float to help me out." Nor get any of that seawater in my hair.

He checks out my hand. "Guess you're not married."

"You're observant."

"I've heard that."

I laugh again. Oh, I so want to wring this child's neck.

"Well, gotta go. Have some fun on Jake's deck. He's a good guy, in case you're wondering."

My stomach tumbles a bit but I ignore it. "Why would I wonder about that?"

"Cuz, well, you know. Things've been said, but I think he's cool. So have fun out here and, uh, yeah."

Uh, yeah? I wave as he goes, trying not to laugh too loud, yet grateful that I still can. As I swivel back toward the ramp, my eyes catch on Sarah, standing at her window. I lift a hand but lower it when I realize she's not facing my way. She's on the phone, staring into the night.

Back inside, I spy Jake's man chair and indulge myself, plopping into its plump arms before I head upstairs to my rather empty loft. There's something conventional yet comforting about an old stuffed chair sitting in the middle of a living room, like a waiting granddad, ready to offer rest and comfort to a weary soul. And I'm weary. Weary

enough to drift off, for just a minute, until I can gather the strength
to head on upstairs.

I've no idea how much time has passed. Footsteps waken me, and
I'm curled, fetal-like, when one eye pops open. I smell a man.

"Sorry to wake you."

I gasp. "Jake?" I try to stand, but the room spins and I crash back
into the embrace of his recliner.

He squats and watches me at eye level. Man, he's beautiful. Truly
beautiful—like a hardy rugged rancher with some of *People's* Sexiest
Man Alive mixed in. I groan.

"You're perspiring, Gaby. Don't move."

Move? I couldn't even if you told me that a judge stood before me
offering to tear up that evil bride's flimsy lawsuit if I'd only stand up
and walk. Heat and ice compete to take over my body temperature.
My stomach hurts, my mind spins, my temples pound. I hear a groan
and realize it's coming from deep within me.

"You'll be okay, Gaby. Just sit back." Jake's voice soothes as he lays the
cool washcloth across my forehead. "How long have you been ill?"

"I'm not. I haven't been. Oh, oh, just now."

He notices the empty glass I'd left on his coffee table. Great. Last
time I'm invited to hang out in front of his big screen. Hope I didn't
leave a ring.

"Drinking?"

"Just water."

"What did you have for dinner?"

"Um, oh." Bright light showers down from the ceiling, like weights
over my eyes. Jake slides the dimmer to low. "That better?"

I nod. "I only had some lasagna."

Jake presses a hand against his face, and did I mention how meaty
they are? The man could rope cattle with one and stop a bull with the
other. Concern furrows his brow, and I watch as he rises. He yanks

open the fridge door, takes the glass serving dish from the rack, and dumps the rest of the lasagna into the garbage.

He grumbles under his breath, and it sounds like he's swearing. A hollow thud lands beside me, and I peek out from under heavy lids. Jake's hovering over me again. "Brought you a bucket. It's right here, when you need it." He takes my hand and guides it to the bucket's rim. His flesh feels more like a hot pad wrapped around my fingers.

"I'm sorry I troubled you."

He lets out a brief, low grunt. "I just came back for my cell phone. Tried to work without it, but I've got suppliers screaming at me from all over the country. Figured it'd be better to just drive on back here and get the darn thing. And you didn't trouble me. You're a very sick young woman."

I giggle, and it hurts my head. I moan.

"What did I say?"

I sigh. "Just hit me funny. That's all."

He continues to watch me. "You think you're going to lose your dinner?" He lifts the cloth and touches my forehead with the back of his hand, like a concerned parent. Vaguely I remember the young girl in the photograph on his bookshelf. Must be his daughter.

"I . . . I'm just weak, I think. Just so tired." Even I can tell that my voice has turned thin and wispy, unlike my waistline.

In an instant, two steady arms slide beneath me and I'm securely in the air. "No, no," I protest. "I can walk. Let me walk." I pull away from the place where my head had landed between his shoulder and neck. The movement causes the room to spin, and with one strong hand Jake pushes me back into him.

They say that some people have selective memory. Well, let me just say that I'm all for that, my friend. Frankly, there are just some things in life not worth remembering, and can you think of anything more worthy to top that list than this moment? Maybe that's why when I awake in my loft, cuddled and warm beneath an unrecognizable white-eyelet blanket, the blinds uncharacteristically drawn to just above the windowsill, the sun peeping through the sliver of glass, I've no recollection of how I got there.

I sit up, clammy and damp, and then I remember. Jake. I throw back the blanket and stand, only to quickly lower myself back into the sofa bed, which by the way, I can't recall opening up last night. The counter is lined like a pharmacy, with various potions and tablets. A jug of water, and a glass with lip prints—mine?—sits beside it. I hold my face in both hands and breathe deep.

Slowly I walk to the front window and peer to the street below. Jake's black truck is gone, and I almost wonder if I dreamed the whole scene. Iris and her pooch stand on the sidewalk talking with Shonda, and if I had the strength in me, I'd run downstairs and unleash the poor animal. The way my neighbor's arms flail as she talks and points toward Jake's house, and my window, I'm afraid she's going to injure the little guy.

My cell rings, but it's not in its usual place beside my bed. I spot it on the counter with my meds, and reality dawns that I was definitely not alone last night.

"Hello."

"Gaby, Doug Stone here."

Um, I know. Even in my less-than-healthy state Doug's lapse into lawyer-voice cracks me up. Only it hurts to laugh.

He continues. "Are you all right, Gaby?"

I blow a weary sigh. "I'm recovering, but oh, I had a bad night. I think I may have eaten something funny." I sneeze. Then again.

"I'm sorry to hear that. Listen, I'm out here in front of your shop. I was hoping to drop off a document for you to sign—the plaintiff's lawyer is breathing down my neck—but I guess you won't be opening today?"

My eyes whip toward the clock. Oh no. Midmorning and Livi's not there anymore. "Oh . . . oh. S-sorry, Doug. Can I pick it up at your office tomorrow?"

"Of course. I'll leave it with Darla. I'll also need you to drop off a check for the filing fee. Just write it out directly to the Court Clerk since I'm waiving all of my fees for you."

I hesitate.

"Will that work out for you, Gaby?"

"Sure. Absolutely." I grab a pencil. "Just tell me the amount." He does, and I nearly stumble backward. My account's several hundred dollars short—no surprise there—and I make a mental note to visit the bank and take out a cash advance against my Visa card. A wall of queasiness threatens to take me down again, only this time I doubt it has anything to do with food poisoning.

Nineteen

"AH-CHOO!" I HOLD THE PHONE in the air while I sneeze. Jake had called to check up on me. "God bless you."

"Thanks." I sniffle and press a tissue to my eyes and nose. "Again, I'm so sorry you had to find me like that, Jake. I promise to Lysol your man chair later."

"My what?"

"Oh. I mean your recliner."

He chuckles. "Forget it. I have to hire a housekeeper soon anyway."

"I'll say."

He sputters. "You tell it like it is, don't you?"

I smile through runny eyes. "Sometimes I do, but that was uncalled for. I apologize."

"Nah. You're right. The place is a dump."

He's being kind, and I really don't want to have to agree with him, but I do. While Max's home screams highly polished and cared for, despite the presence of a surfing teenager and weathered old dog, Jake's cluttered palace has been obviously neglected. I guess the neighborhood Don Juan has yet to date a woman with a career in janitorial service.

"So, again, gracias." *I may not be able to pay next month's rent, but loving money is at the root of all evil. Am I right?*

"No problem. You're light as a feather. I could carry two of you." *Charmer.*

"While I carried you up the stairs, you were murmuring about chocolate in Spanish, I think." He laughs in my ear.

"Well, if I'm going to get caught murmuring in a sickly fog, chocolate would definitely make it into my list of top ten topics."

He laughs heartily and that sense of his steady arms beneath me comes back, causing me to shudder. In those hazy moments of illness, I somehow remember thinking that Jake was hot. *Oh. My. Tell me I didn't murmur anything about that. It was the fever talking, I tell you, the fever!*

I shake it off. My head's still fuzzy, my nose congested. I flashback on the gal who sneezed and sniffled her way through my store the other day, the one who wouldn't leave without her boss's money. *You left me broke and sick, lady.* At least I now realize that Jake hadn't been trying to poison me. Like I ever really believed that.

I attempt to wrap this up. "Well, I need to go feed my boyfriend's dog." *Maybe boyfriend is a bit presumptuous, but hey, he trusts me with his dog. For some men, that's the epitome of serious.*

"Can't he do it himself?"

I sigh. "Not from thousands of miles away. He and his son are surfing the big waves outside of Bora Bora as we speak. Or they will be soon. Anyway, he asked me to take care of Rover while they're gone and I just couldn't say no. Not that I ever would." *And not that this is any of your business.*

"All right, then. Carry on."

We click off, and I let it sink in that I went all day without working. My store must have looked forlorn amidst the bustling Main Street businesses. Then again, it often sits empty for hours at a time. I know that will change. I know it will. It has to.

Within the hour I've bundled myself up to feed old Rover. Thank you, Jesus, that I left her a ton of food last night. Outside, I almost make it to my car, but don't. Iris stops me.

"Hello, Gaby."

"Ah-choo. Sorry, Iris. Hi."

"Jake sure tore out of here in a hurry this morning."

We stare at each other. *Is that a question?*

"Trouble in paradise already?" she probes.

She's decided what she's going to believe, so who am I to halt her fantasy? "Something like that, but we'll work it out."

Her expression falls. "Do . . . Have . . . Is . . . ?" She can't seem to spit it, whatever it is, out.

I open my car door, and call out to her before slowly climbing inside. "I'm off to Max's, Iris. See you."

Her eyes bug out farther than I've ever seen them go, and I drive off, hearing that ghastly old song "Torn Between Two Lovers" in my head. As I replay those ridiculous lyrics, I giggle all the way down the block.

An hour later I return to my loft, feverish and weak. Rover had looked happy to see me, but the way she slurped and slopped the outside of my coat with that sandpaper tongue of hers, I wonder if somehow she mistook me for a pork chop. It may be a balmy sixty-eight degrees outside, but try telling that to my body. Minutes after arriving home and stripping away my toasty coat, the one I borrowed from Bri, I had to dive between the covers to warm back up again.

Lethargically, I thumb through the mail I'd carried upstairs with me. After feeding Rover, I drove over to the shop and stopped only long enough to grab the mail and head on home. Sigh, I needn't have bothered. You know, I really need to start opening the mail over the garbage can, because that's where most of it ends up anyway. I flip through the pile, vaguely remembering the days of personal letters. Even a postcard would do. My fingers stop at an envelope with the familiar return address of my landlord of the Main Street shop, and I rip it open.

NOTICE OF TERMINATION OF LEASE

I blink and read it again. I've been given just two weeks to come up with the month's rent, plus the late fee assessed at precisely 12:01 A.M. just one day after the date due. Whatever happened to grace periods? If God can be all about grace, why can't landlords and credit card companies? I throw back the covers again, get up, and spill out the contents of my peanut jar. Desperate times call for . . . well, you know. I separate the coins and come to the conclusion that there's probably only enough here for a mucho grande latte with an extra shot of mocha cream. So all is not lost.

This is serious, Gabrielle. I drop my head back and stare into the rafters. "I know, Mama." I consider calling Doug, but doesn't the man have enough of my problems to worry about? Just what he needs: a nonpaying customer with another problem.

Max. He's a commercial landlord. I'm sure he'd be able to offer me some perspective. Deep breath in. Start fresh. Yes, that's what I will do. I'll just ask Max for some advice "for a friend."

Jake's doorbell squeals. I peek out to see Barbie Runnergirl jogging in place on the front stoop. I drag myself downstairs, satisfied that despite my landlord's threat, I may still have options.

"Hiya, Gaby." She moves at a rhythmic pace, no sign of breaking a sweat, and did I mention how wrong that is?

I sniffle. "Hello, Bar . . . I mean, Meredith. What can I do for you?"

She breaks eye contact and steps up the jogging pace. "Just wanted to tell you I won't be needing you to do flowers for my wedding anymore."

"Oh."

Silence lands between us. "So thanks anyway," she says. "Gotta run." She laughs at the pun, and I manage a weak smile.

Well. Whatever Iris said to her apparently worked well enough for her to rethink hiring me. I'm too sick to fight it, but I wish I knew what that woman's problem was, why she seems to have it out for me—even from my first day in the 'hood. *Hey*, I want to scream, *I'm a nice lady!*

Then again, nice ladies don't give up. Do they? I want to quit. As the words form a sentence in my brain, my stomach lurches. I'll blame it on the flu, but honestly, it's my mama's influence that just socked me in the tummy.

"Flores girls don't quit, Mijita," she'd always say.

Not after Amy McIntyre trumped me in the Miss Second Grade pageant.

Nor when Bobbie Gain knocked ink all over my prized art show sketch.

Nor when Alec Smythe dumped me before the senior prom!

Mama always told me it just wasn't in the Flores blood to quit, conveniently forgetting to mention the source of the rest of my DNA. Whatever that was. Deep breath in. Start fresh. I look to the kitchen counter and run my eyes over the pharmaceuticals lining it, opting for a fizzy vitamin. It goes down like bubbly fruit, and I imagine my cells bursting with new strength and energy.

Unfortunately, mind over matter doesn't really work. I still feel like a battered beach ball that's been spit up on a rocky shore. An image of a circus seal pops to mind, and I peek out the window. Sweet Thing's down there, floating alongside the dock, the water receding evenly around her like a stone thrown into a pond.

I slide open my window and call out to her in a loud whisper. "Hey, Sweet Thing. How you doing, girl?"

Her head swivels back and forth like a submarine's lens.

"Up here."

Her shiny eyes find me. Tell me sea lions can't speak human! I laugh. "I'm too sick to come on down there, Sweet Thing, but I'm happy to see you."

She cocks her chin like a teenage boy saying "What up?"

I settle my arms onto the windowsill and shrug. "Not much, *y tu?*" If she can understand English, why not my grandmother's native tongue?

I guess I just got too personal, because Sweet Thing dives beneath the watery surface and I can't find her anywhere. Like most of my boyfriends. I giggle at the awful thought, even though it's really too true to be funny.

Then again, there's always Max. Surf dad and local business owner extraordinaire, Max. I breathe in the sound of his name and realize that I miss him. I really miss my new chocolate-eyed beau. There's something so attractive about a man who's got it all together, who doesn't need my money (okay, so I'm currently broke), my cleaning skills (his home is spotless), nor my eggs (he already has a terrific kid in Gib—any children Max and I may have together one day will only add symmetry to their little family of two.)

Speaking of Max, I shove my landlord's warning into my purse, wishing I never had to see it again. The errant thought that I just might lose my business, tiny as it is, slices through me, and I feel the need to vomit. Or is that just the vitamin threatening to come back up?

Instead of giving in, I lower myself into my unmade sofa couch, sink my head into the pillow, and try to figure out what in the world to do next.

Twenty

Two days have passed since that awkward moment when I awoke to find that I'd been tucked into bed with no recollection of said tucking. Despite my lingering illness, I made a feeble attempt to go to the shop yesterday. I had hopes of receiving minute quantities of *dinero* to pay for more supplies and provide me with enough for a meal made from my own hands—as opposed to my landlord Jake's, as meaty and kitchen-worthy as they may be—but I couldn't get past brushing my teeth.

Sunday has arrived now, and I'm laid out on this lounge chair like fudge melted into an unwaxed tray. No intention here of moving anytime soon. *Don't be lazy,* I hear my mama say. I shake off the words I heard so often while growing up and glance toward the water flowing just beyond the deck. Wind chimes ring on the breeze, and the current makes me think of a flowing mocha sea.

I can barely hear the cruiser boat rolling its way through my backyard as naturally as a seagull soaring above the beach. On approach, though, a familiar voice perks me up. It's Bri, her carefree tone carrying boldly through a speaker mounted on the side and filling the quiet around me.

"The inhabitants of this fine castle on the water are often found frolicking playfully on their decks. Oh look!" she hollers. "There's one now." A dozen or so visor-covered eyes gawk at me, and Bri laughs and points in my direction, like I'm one of those monkeys swinging raucously at the Santa Barbara Zoo and they've paid admission to observe me in my natural habitat.

I lean against the handrail and cough to clear my throat. "Hey, Bri-Bri," I call out, only my voice squeaks, and Bri wrinkles her forehead, straining to hear me.

She forges on. "I see she's playing with us! Everyone, let's all wave to the playful beach girl!"

The visor-heads wave at me. Bri smiles for her part as a tour boat host but watches me with best friend eyes. I point toward my throat and hang my mouth open until recognition lights her eyes, and she turns off her mic.

"You sick?" she mouths.

I nod vigorously.

The visor-heads turn in unison. They look at me, then at Bri, then back at me, and finally at her, like synchronized swimmers gone whacky. Bri's driver, Ned, however, seems oblivious to the fact that his boss has stopped speaking and just keeps on steering his way down the channel. I shrug at Bri, not even sure if she still sees me, and then give them all a proper send-off wave.

Sigh. Bri and I have become like two ships passing—only mine's actually stuck in port as hers sails on by. It's not like her to work on Sunday, though. Bri's a stickler for weekend family time, usually reserving the day of rest for church and chocolate-noshing at the beach that's just a shell's throw from her home.

Obviously, she needs the work. As do I.

I remind myself that I'm still recovering and decide that working will have to wait until Monday. My cell tells me it's Rover's feeding time, so I head out to my car with an idea.

Half an hour later, standing on Max's front porch to the sound of Rover's whine, I wrestle with the lock. "I'm coming, I'm coming." I halt. What if my scratchy voice throws her off and she doesn't recognize me? What if she charges me with those sopping gums of hers, and soaks my favorite—and only clean—shapely sweats?

After she's fed and watered, and after she's managed to only slightly desecrate my favorite cotton-Lycra blend pants, I plead and coax the old girl into my Volvo and head back to my neighborhood. Back on Harborwest Court, I take the reins of her leash and hold on tight as Rover bounds out of the car. I'm ready for a struggle, but after she lands on the sidewalk below, she just turns to me as if to ask, *What now?*

"We're going for a walk in my new neighborhood, Rover old girl." The gravel in my voice is loosening.

She stares at me for a beat and a half before reluctantly turning forward, obviously resigned to exercise with me. We stroll along, enjoying the sizzling sun and friendly faces along the path toward the beach until she gets in the groove and takes the lead. She sniffs the base of a tree, I nod and smile to my neighbors, she does her necessary dog duty, and I politely look away. It's all very civil. And normal.

A wisp of smoke curls its way into my nostrils, and I swivel around to find its source. "Hello, Shonda."

"Gaby." Dark glasses hide her eyes. Her mouth stretches thin and tight.

I cough, and Shonda flinches.

"Oh, don't worry." I push my voice to its fullest, current potential. "I'm past the contagious stage." One look at that tobacco stick in her hand and I'm thinking she has worse things to worry about.

Her eyes, although shielded behind spectacularly large eyewear, don't leave my face when she asks, "That your dog?"

I reach down and give Max's patient pooch a friendly neck rub. "She's my boyfriend's. Isn't she sweet?"

"Your boyfriend's?" Shonda's mouth hangs open, like she doesn't believe it.

I straighten. "Well, we've only been dating a couple of weeks, but we've known each other for years." I flick my wrist when I say that, and then feel like a dork. "Anyway, he's good friends with my best friend and her husband. Well, actually, his son is good friends with my best friend's son, so . . ."

I've lost her. Shonda's glancing behind me now, as if searching for a quick exit. I slow my mind down, genuinely sorry for that second cup of coffee this morning. That and the swig of cold and flu medicine I took with all its alcohol and caffeine-laden richness. It may not cure what ails you, but at least you'll feel like a million bucks during the healing process (until it wears off that is, and you're back sniffling and wheezing through the hours).

"So you've got a boyfriend. That's news."

I give a congested little giggle. "I doubt that anything I do would be considered news."

"Wanna bet?"

I pause. Fake laughter escapes me then, the kind that hides a rumbling missile ready to blast off at any second. "You're very funny, Shonda." I say this slowly, because what I'd really rather do is to tell her that gossip's not nice and suggest that there are better ways for her to spend her time. Instead, I make nice with a compliment and hope she gets the hint that rumors aren't a road that I travel on.

Only she just shrugs. "Not trying to be. I've got nothing to be funny about these days. Life's a beach, and then you die. Nothing funny about that." She glances away.

The whole "beach and then you die" statement isn't part of my theology, and a pang of compassion grips me for her. Shonda's got it going on: the designer sandals, perfectly tailored loungewear, expensive accessories, nails, makeup, hair—all of it "done." How bad could it possibly be for someone like that to have lost all hope for the future?

Then again, life hasn't exactly been a box of chocolates for me either. All I'm saying is that I know what it's like to grow up without a dad around and no other children to play with while Mama worked 24/7. I've been strung along by too many beastly men, lost most of my belongings in a preventable apartment fire, and because of a ditzy, greedy bride, I just may lose my business forever and be driven to bankruptcy. I pause, swallowing all those harsh realities. Maybe Shonda's got something there. Is this it? Do I struggle along through life only to eventually die worse off?

Rover wiggles the leash, breaking my concentration. "Shonda," I say, my voice suddenly just a gravelly whisper. "Rover and I are heading to the beach. Would you like to join us?"

She doesn't answer right away, but by the way her brows shift up and to the side behind those glasses, I know she heard me. "No, not me. I've never really been very fond of all that sand. It's really quite dirty."

Oh.

"Moving here was my husband's idea; I just live with it."

Maybe a new subject would help. "Could I ask you a question?"

"Yeah, sure."

I hesitate. "Why is Iris so obsessed with all things Jake? Every time we meet she seems to have something new to tell me."

"You don't know?"

I turn up my palms and shrug. Rover whinnies against the tug on her leash.

"Those two have old issues. Things that don't die away easily, you know? You moving into his house stirred up those memories in her mind." Shonda holds her cigarette in the air. "I have noticed, though, that since you moved in, maybe even a little before that, Jake's partying ways seem to have died down. Before that, the man liked to show off his . . . fun-loving side."

"I shouldn't have asked. He's just my landlord, but Iris seems to think I've got the inside on all he does."

"Best not to involve yourself. You've got a boyfriend, so rumors about you should quit now." She takes a long drag. "Unless of course Iris has reason to wonder about you and Jake."

"No. None at all." Rumors? What rumors?

"Good for you. By the way, that's too bad about the lawsuit. Our sins always seem to find us out, don't they?" She nods, her mouth pressed back into that flat line, then slips past me.

I croak a stunned good-bye and turn my eyes toward the west.

We forge on, Rover and I, and she drags me down one of the lanes that lead to the sand. With the sun overhead, the water shimmers invitingly, and if I'd thought to wear a swimsuit under my slouchy pants, I'd be stripping them off and diving in. A salty mixture of air teases my skin, and say it ain't so but I'm positively longing for some of Bri's brownies. Frighteningly so.

A dark shape in a building wave catches my eye, and I shield my face from the sun, straining to make it out. Sweet Thing? I turn to Rover. "I'll just be a minute." Like she understands.

She whines.

I hide a smile. "Sorry, girl. No dogs on the beach. Says so right there." I point to the sign.

She whimpers again just as a couple of schnauzers trot past dragging a boy and his iPod. With moxie, Rover stands, picks up the leash with her mouth, and nudges me with it.

Oh. My. "All right. Let's go see Sweet Thing."

I stand at the water's edge, just a couple of body lengths away from a girl showing more skin than bikini as she glides along on a skim board, and search for my sea lion friend. Rover, who's shown a surprising amount of energy for an old dog, whinnies and squeals by my side, splashing mud on my flip-flops (and messing up my homemade pedicure, I might add). I shush her and she spins. Okay, it was one turn, but still I'm impressed.

"You win." I unhook her leash. "Don't do anything crazy."

As if those words invite the worst, she becomes like a horse from the chute and flies into the water scattering the party of sandpipers hunting for lunch. She tromps along, undeterred by rising foam and deepening waters. I run forward, but my spongy flip-flops stick in the wet sand.

"Come here, girl. C'mon back!"

Suddenly Rover's gone deaf.

"Rover! Come!" I'm stretching my vocal cords as far as they'll reach.

Skim-board girl laughs. "You really call her Rover?"

Sweet Thing's telescoping neck pushes through the water again. Apparently she's as fascinated by Rover's dog-paddling technique as I am. Rover holds her own, unlike me in the public pool while growing up. I have no regrets though. How else would I have come into such close contact with all those burly lifeguards?

A devil wave hits, and I gasp. "Rover!" My breathing tightens. I kick off my flip-flops and tromp into the water up to my knees. "Dear God, dear God." That's all I can get out, but something tells me God hears that prayer anyway. "Rover!"

She surfaces, but her little paws quickly lose steam. I try to reach for her but a slosh of deep water carries her beyond my grasp. I charge against the tide, knowing that if I'm not careful, two of us will need saving. "God, please."

Sweet Thing's head pops up through the water's surface. Her shiny, round eyes focus on Rover and I'm not sure if I should rejoice or pass out.

Twenty-One

SEA LIONS CAN BE AGGRESSIVE, I've heard, but *do they eat dogs?* I suck in a breath and push myself into waist-high water, trying to keep my eyes aimed on Rover's struggling form. Sweet Thing disappears, then resurfaces and begins to circle Rover.

"The seal's going to get her!" Skim-board girl's shrill voice cuts me with fear.

Sweet Thing circles several times, then inches closer to Rover from behind. The sea lion nudges Max's dog with its nose. "Rover!" Sweet Thing does it again. Then again. I blink rapidly, trying to wrest the salty water from my eyes. Within seconds Sweet Thing has nudged Rover right into my arms—and then she's gone.

I wrap my arms around Rover's stinky wet body and crush her to me, keeping myself as steady as possible against recurring wave slaps. She whimpers and nuzzles her nose into my armpit. "It's okay, girl. You're all right."

I drag us both onto the sand and collapse into its hard-packed surface, never letting Rover go.

A passerby named Janice gives us a ride back to my neighborhood in her banana-yellow Thing. If I weren't so overcome with the shakes, I may actually have enjoyed the drive in the open-air beach buggy. Unfortunately, as we enter my block with all eyes on us, waves of fatigue careen over me, creating the longing for a hot bath and cozy bed, maybe even a spoonful of brownie batter—if Bri were around.

One look at who's standing at my door, though, and I realize my quest for rest is kaput.

Max's eyes widen as he steps quickly down the path toward the street. He flings open the gate. "What happened?

Rover still clings to me. "What are you doing back already?"

Max reaches into the buggy and takes Rover from my arms.

What did he just mutter? I open the door and climb out. No bother. I'll get my door. Janice leans forward into the steering wheel. "That's a lucky pup you got there. Might want to run her by the vet's, just to be sure."

"Thanks so much for the ride."

"Hey, no prob. What a show it was!" She shakes her head before rattling off in her retromobile.

A mixture of anger and confusion shows on Max's face. "We had to leave Bora Bora early because of a monsoon. When we got home, Rover was gone. I couldn't understand it." He glances down at the sopping mop in his arms. She licks his chin. "I never thought I'd find her like this."

"We just went for a walk, and sh-she got away from me. I kept calling after her but she wouldn't come back." My voice, already shaky, begins to sound scratchy too. "That's when Sweet Thing showed up and saved her."

"Saved her?"

"Rover kept getting carried off by waves. I . . . I tried to reach her." The tears are welling now. "But I couldn't. A sea lion nudged her back to shore."

"Gaby, no." He hugs Rover close, making me feel suddenly alone and afraid. He rocks his dog like a baby, his eyes shut against her damp head. "She could've been killed," he whispers.

Me too. I stand there shivering in the pale sun, thankful I'm not wearing anything sheer or white. Not like he'd notice.

Max passes me slowly, still cradling Rover. I reach out to give her a pet, but he keeps walking toward his truck.

"I'm sorry," I say to his back.

The back of his head just nods.

"I'm coming already." My cell trills on and on until I'm awake enough to find it among my things. Even in the haze of sleep, it occurs to me that if I'd had it in my pocket at the beach when I had leaped into the ocean, access to a cell phone would be yet another necessity that I'd have to do without. Like good food. "Hello."

"Gaby, you are there. Why didn't you tell me you were so sick?"

I groan. "I'm fine, Bri." And grumpy.

"Well, you don't sound fine. Have you been to the doctor?"

"No, Mom, I have not. I'm sure another day's rest is all I need. It'll have to be."

"Are you mad about something?"

"No."

Bri blows a huge sigh into the phone. "Yeah, you're mad. Okay, what's up? Boy troubles?"

Tears prick the rim of my eyes. If Bri weren't so busy all the time, she would know all my troubles and I wouldn't have to fill her in like she's some therapist and I've taken up residence on her couch. I know that controlling my temper is my new thing, but right now? Not so easy.

A glow from outside illuminates the dirt on my harborside window. Then again, does Bri really need my issues to solve right now? Making my problems go away shouldn't be on her to-do list. That's my job.

Bri's voice cuts in. "C'mon, Gaby. Spill it. Tell me how you're feeling."

Deep breath in. Start fresh. "You know, you're right, Bri-Bri. I'm just not feeling very well. I went for a walk . . ." I trail off, unready to divulge the latest disaster in this drama that is my life. "And anyway, I think it was just too soon to be out in the wind."

"Yeah, you should have waited another day," she says, agreeing with what I'm telling her. "Promise me you'll drink something hot. Do you have lemonade? You could zap it in the micro and have a hot toddy for your throat."

"I probably do." Lying, again. "Thanks, Bri-Bri. Maybe we can talk better tomorrow."

"Yeah, let's do. Wait a minute . . . I've got a newly booked cruise at nine, then another at one, and hmm, then I'll be picking up Nathan and taking him to be tortured at the dentist's office." She sighs. "I'll try and call you in between."

"Yeah, maybe."

We say our good-byes and click off our phones. I desperately need to deal with the Max and Rover fiasco. Maybe I should have told Bri about it. Now she'll probably hear all about it from him, then call me. Eventually.

An echoing bark calls my attention to my waterside window. Sweet Thing's out there, so I pull on a robe and dash down the stairs to meet her.

"Sweet Thing! You're my hero." I tie my sash tighter at the waist and squat down to take a closer look at my sea lion pal, who's swimming around in the channel just beyond my dock. Her lustrous black eyes stare back at me. The eyes of a friend. "That was some rescue you did out there today. Gracias, *mi amiga*." My voice cracks on the words, and I realize that the shock of the whole incident is wearing off and leaving me exhausted. Fragile. Confused.

Sweet Thing barks again, and I wish I had a fish to toss her. A lobster tail drowning in salted butter sounds pretty good to me too. I'm sitting cross-legged on Jake's rickety dock, and just how long has it been since I plopped myself down like this to play? Sweet Thing cocks her head in my direction.

"My mama used to let me play dolls in her old flower stand. She had to, really. What else was there for a young girl to do?" I shrug at her with my palms upward and laugh at Sweet Thing's earnest expression, like she's really trying to understand.

"Yes, I spent more time up here"—I tap my temple—"creating my own little worlds than doing just about anything else. Except for studying a lot. My mama believed in education! In the American way!" I pump my closed fist into the air. "She wanted me to only learn English, but you know what? When I was young and I was supposed to be asleep, she would talk with my grandmother. After she died, my mama would call her sister on the phone and I would listen very hard to all her Spanish words. That's how I figured out so much of what she was saying." I smile, remembering how I always knew way ahead of time what my mama had gotten me for Christmas and birthday presents. Like me, my mama talks too much.

I grin at Sweet Thing. "You have no idea what I'm talking about, do you?"

"You expect her to answer you?"

Kit glides close to where I sit on the dock. "Hello, Kit."

"Hey. What're you telling that lion?"

Sweet Thing disappears underwater.

"Just my life story."

"Must be pretty boring if you have to tell it to a sea lion."

If she thinks she's going to rile me, well, she's not. "Yes, I guess it is."

Kit watches me, her face a rendering of inky black on white porcelain. To have skin like that and not frame it in the organic color of her youth seems nearly criminal. Or maybe just sad.

"Why you wearin' a robe? Sun's not even down yet."

I shrug a shoulder. "I just felt like taking an early shower. Besides, it's my backyard. Why not dress as I like?"

"Because duh . . . everyone around here can see you."

My hand holds the flaps of my robe closed. "Well, what-ev!"

Kit cracks a smile—a little one, mind you, but at least she's showing teeth in a non-menacing way. And she's beautiful. "You're a funny chick," she tells me, and I flashback to Willy and his earlier assessment of my potential relationship with Kit.

"Hey, well, gracias, chica."

Kit huffs, but there's still a hint of smile on her lips. "Heard you speaking Spanish to that lion. That's sick."

"*Sí!*"

She rolls her eyes. "All right, already. Gotta go now, but I'll come back next Saturday or somethin'. You gonna be here?"

I bat my eyes. "Maybe."

"Ch-yeah. You'll be here. Wear something to get wet in, because we're gonna take out that old kayak of Jake's."

"So you think it's seaworthy?"

"Only one way to find out."

I watch her paddle away into the evening and almost wish I could hitch a ride into the sunset, so to speak. And though I have successfully avoided openly acknowledging him for hours, Max has been on my mind. His stunned voice. The hurt expression. The steady but quick exit. Just thinking about this crazy day and our last encounter sends an ache through my chest.

I lean against the lower railing, just below deck, and drop my head back. "Are you there, Lord?" I ask into the atmosphere. "It's me, Gaby." Okay, so maybe He's heard that line somewhere before. It couldn't hurt asking again though, could it?

As the dusky sun begins its fade into the night, casting a reddish glow all around, I wonder if an answer will come.

Twenty-Two

THE SIGN FROM GOD I'D been waiting for out on the deck never did show. No bolt from the sky nor snow along this stretch of the Southern California coast. Not even fire burning on water. Really, it was a rather dull night.

That dullness continued its little romp through my home, when I realized I was waiting for a possum-playing phone to ring. I know; waiting by the phone is so '80s. True, those were my elementary years, but who could forget Mama hovering near the phone that hung on the kitchen wall? I remember skipping up to it and yanking on the coiled cord, watching it spring back with a slap against the receiver. (When Mama wasn't looking, of course.) Anyway, in those days, long after we'd watched the ball of sun set behind the trees and closed up the flower stand for the night, Mama would scold me into taking a bath, and that's when I would hear her pacing. Her ballet slippers would slide against the linoleum, scraping to a stop every once in a while, and I'd hear her unhook the receiver, pause as if waiting for a dial tone, and then plunk it back down again.

Funny how memories pop into my head at moments like this, when I too am hovering near a silent phone. Only it's a cell phone, and since

I've got voice mail, there's no need to check to see if it's working. It is and no one has called.

My blog, on the other hand, has seen plenty of traffic, and so I indulge myself with lazy reading time, pausing only to wax poetic (mentally, that is) about the benefits of rich chocolate. I read on:

Congrats on your new blog! Rock on, Florally Yours!!!!

What can I do to keep the leaves on my African violets from turning brownish black?

Hey! You gonna post a picture of yer-self in here? I need to see who I'm talking to.

Just checking in, Gaby, to see how you're feeling these days. I forgot to mention that I whipped up some chicken enchiladas for you before I left the other day, after seeing that you'd gotten back to your loft safely. I hope you're getting your rest and taking the meds I left. Anyway, they're in the freezer for you, wrapped up tight. Enjoy them (and sorry about the lasagna incident).

I wag my head at Jake's comment, making a mental note to tell him that my illness most probably came from my exposure to the sneezing and wheezing accounts receivable gal from a vendor's office. Then again, I could let him think he nearly poisoned me. . . . I squint and continue reading my blog comments, especially enjoying this one:

Who's that guy who just wrote in? Your papa? Hahahahaha . . .

Seriously. Jake's taken a real fatherly interest in me, something I've never really known firsthand, nor cared to. Then again, maybe that's his shtick, as Bri would say. Maybe he wines and dines his women with a homemade meal and manufactured concern, circling them like prey until they're too weak to resist his culinary charms (and manly hands, I might add).

Let's not go there. I click on over to Iris's site, expecting what? A good laugh maybe? Some solid romantic advice? We'll see.

Lovely Readers,

Today I find myself simply compelled to write about judgment. In my humble opinion, you can never find reconciliation if you adopt a judgmental attitude toward another person. Instead, try understanding as a way to improve your relationships, and your relationship skills in general.

I straighten. Doesn't that just beat it? That woman is like the cat calling the dog furry. One peek at the comments section, though, and I'm just floored by the response.

Thank you, thank you, Miss Iris! I followed your advice the other day, you know when you told me to start thinking of my boyfriend's love language instead of just my own? Well anyway, it worked. (I think he's going to propose.) Bye, and thanks!

My father and I have not spoken in years. YEARS! As a last-ditch effort I gave the old geezer a call and dropped a few lovey-dovey words on him—just like you said to do in one of your posts. It worked like a charm! You should open your own office—I'd pay ya.

And finally, this little nugget:

If you weren't married, Beautiful, well then I'd marry you myself!
                                    Signed,
                                    Not too ripe for the pickin'

I'm holding my head in my hands. Things are just never as they seem, are they? Iris casting her romantic notions like weeds among the rye grass while I sit here waiting by the cell phone hoping for Max to call.

Maybe you should call him and drop a few lovey-dovey words on him.

Iris's unwanted advice drops into my head, sparking a flash of anger. Not to mention the frustration that's already been building, the kind I've vowed to bury yet have been unable to curb completely. Angry thoughts bottleneck in my mind, like two lanes of traffic vying for the one narrow lane left open. I know I should throw up a road construction sign, one to warn away the words that rile me to no end, the ones causing me to want to toss aside my plan to always take a deep breath! And start fresh!

I tried all that, and you know what? Those angry traffic words just refuse to yield to the orange cones I've carefully placed along the road. *Deep breath in.* It doesn't work. I saved that man's dog, for heaven's sake! Where's my apology, Max? My thank you? My box of truffles!

And the part about starting fresh? By calling Max? Well, that's just not an option.

I sign into my blogging account, ready to unleash myself into the Internet.

The past hour of working on the computer seemed more like wrestling an octopus. Awkward. Frustrating. Sometimes a downright test of wills. Thankfully, though (and may I just have an amen here?), I won. Yippee! I, Gaby Flores, have mastered the ability to upload a picture onto my blog. And I only had to chop off a few unwieldy tentacles to do it. Bu-dum-bum.

I glance back at the screen, marveling at the punctuation of color, attitude, and pizzazz characterized by the picture staring back at me.

It's a still shot of Tobey McGuire and Kirsten Dunst in the clinch as Spidey and Mary Jane. I've drawn around them an undulating frame of deep azure and peppy yellow. Sweet! So much prettier than a boring floral advice column, don't you think?

My fingers have been drumming on the countertop for I don't know how long. Computer enhancement of an existing picture has taken over the world, but I do miss the smell of graphite and the tingles I almost always get when seeing color exploding in nature. Makes me want to express it somehow on paper.

When my cell rings, I nearly miss it. I gasp. My cell's ringing!

"Hello!"

"Hi, Gaby. It's Livi. Got a sec?"

Sigh. I thought it was Max, even though I'm starting to wonder if I can handle a man who caresses the dog but leaves her rescuer without even a morsel of regard.

If you don't mind waiting while I pick up my heart, Livi, then sure, I've got time. "Hi, Livi. What's up?"

"Are you closing on Saturdays now? I was just wondering because, well, when I was showing a new client around town yesterday, or I guess she's a potential client, anyhow, I pointed out your shop to her but it was closed."

"Not to worry. I've just been sick." I cough for effect.

"Oh, so, is it serious?"

I don't know. Is a breaking heart fatal? "Just a bad cold. I'm sure I'll be up and running by tomorrow, though. You're the best for checking on me. Really, Livi."

"Because if you need me to help you out on Saturdays I think I can fit you in . . ." She drifts off. "Uh-huh. Yes. I think this would work okay. I just won't take any meal breaks next week, and come in and help you in the early afternoon."

"Livi? Don't take this the wrong way, but you've got your own life to lead, you know? Stop worrying about me and get moving on that career of yours."

"If you're sure."

I continue. "I'm working on a plan anyway. Thanks so much for trying to help me out, but I've got it all under control."

"Really. Are you sure?"

No, of course not. "Yes, yes, Livi, I am."

With one more lie under my belt, I log out of my blogging account, taking one more look at my newly uploaded picture of two movie lovers. I bat away the question of what such a picture has to do with flowers, and give myself an Outstanding for effort. Acquiring new tech skills has got to be worth something. Am I right? Computer off, I start my evening ritual of releasing my bed from its day job as a sofa, and turn out the lights.

Twenty-Three

ON MY WAY TO WORK this morning I stopped and had a little chat with Peter. Later today, I'll pay a visit to Paul. I ask you, with the proliferation of available cash advance opportunities, how can anyone be truly broke these days?

The shop looks the way I left it. Simple, clean, empty. I click open the door and step inside carrying an armload of the freshly cut flowers I picked up on the way. Unfortunately, I assess my paltry supplies and make a mental note to call in a rush order. And just like that, much of the cash in my purse has already grown wings.

One check of voice mail, though, and things may be looking up. Three messages await me.

Beep. "Gaby, Doug Stone here." Again, his lawyerly ways just make me laugh. Of course I know it's Doug Stone. "We have something to discuss, so give me a call when you get in."

Beep. "This message is for Gaby. This is Cassandra from Realty World and I really do need to get the rent check from you today. Did you get my client's notice? Call me back when you're in. If you're in."

Beep. "Gaby, it's Bri. Hey, have you checked your cell this morning? Tried to reach you but no go. Anyway, what's up with you and Max? Gib came by for Nathan this morning and told me about the quick trip back from Bora Bora. Bummer. Also said something about Rover and drowning. Uh, ya gotta fill me in, girlfriend. Call me."

So much for good news. My lawyer needs to talk to me—that can't be good. I jot down his new number. And if I remember correctly, that rent notice gave me two more weeks to come up with the moola, so Cassandra's going to have to wait until I can give her a solid answer. As far as Max? This has gone on long enough.

I pick up the phone and punch in his number.

"This is Max."

"Why is Gibson telling people that I nearly drowned your dog?"

"Who is this?"

I set my jaw. "If that's supposed to be funny, well, it's not."

"I didn't tell my son what to say to Bri."

"How did you know I meant Bri? Never mind. He got the idea from someone, Max, and I think it was you."

"Gaby, listen, I was shocked when I stopped by your house and found Rover in that condition. You see that, don't you?"

I'm silent.

He continues. "The vet said she was physically okay, but Gaby, she's too old for adventures. She shook the whole way home."

He's right. I can't even take care of a dog. What kind of mother would I be? "Never mind, Max. I've got to go. Customers, you know." Liar, liar.

"Can I ask you something, Gaby?"

"Sure."

"What happened to your fire?"

"Excuse me?"

"You're just not the same saucy thing I used to run into over at Bri's. The old you would have been cussing at me in Spanish by now."

"I never cuss, *Loco* Boy." And did he just call me saucy?

"See? Like that."

"What does this have to do with anything, Max?"

He pauses. "Nothing really, I guess. Just an observation I'm making. You've changed."

"Maybe you really never knew the real me."

"Could be."

"Bye, Max."

He hesitates and I almost think he has already clicked his phone off. Wait. He's still there. "I'll call you, Gaby."

I hang up first. He'll call me? Isn't that what guys always say when they mean exactly the opposite? I should know! I hold first prize for having been on the receiving end of that statement more times than Ugly Betty.

The bell dings on my shop door. My shoulders stiffen. I've had a process server, a lawyer and a bill-waving vendor pass through my door in recent days. Who's next? A charter member of PETA, ready to protest my inhumane treatment of one Rover Rispoli?

"Hello, dear."

"Agnes! Come in." She's gorgeous, regal, and tiny in her rich purple suit and lavender hat. Just the right amount of powder and rouge—not blush, she always tells me, it's *rouge*. I hold myself back. If I didn't curb my enthusiasm, I could smother the frail woman with it. "What can I do for you today?"

"Well, I decided to do a little shopping on Main Street today, dear." She speaks quietly and slowly. "It's been weeks since I've been able to find some kind person to drive me here. Is Livi working with you today?"

"No, Agnes. Actually, Livi's found a good position working for a real estate broker across town." I give a pathetic little sigh. "I miss all her help around here."

"And who do you have to talk to, dear?"

I laugh, trying not to think about my unwanted visitors of late. (Not including Doug, of course, but must he always come here on official business?) "Just talking to myself these days." I, of course, neglect to mention my chats with Sweet Thing out on the dock.

"I see. Do say hello to Livi for me, won't you? Oh my, aren't these the loveliest daisies today. They look so fresh."

"They are, Agnes. I picked them up just this morning from the grower and put them in my strongest freshening agent. They should last quite a while."

"Lovely, dear." She glances around. Her face wears a pensive expression. "My, it is quite sparse in here." Agnes searches my eyes. "Is everything all right, Gaby?"

Can I lie to her too? *Gah. No, I cannot.* I let my gaze drift to the bare front window. "They could be better." I shrug. "It's been a rough couple of months, but I'm certain things will turn around eventually."

"May I pray for you, dear?"

She always makes me smile. I attempt to placate her with one of my own, strained as it may be. "Sure," I say, "please do that."

"I meant now, Gaby."

Just why does that make me want to cry? If I didn't know how little I had actually eaten for breakfast, I'd swear I had just swallowed a scoop of sand. Such is the lump in my throat.

"Father in heaven," she begins, "we know that you have a plan for dear Gabrielle. We pray that you will make your blessings known to her, that she would walk in abundance and not lack, and that she would believe that you want the very best for her. Oh, Lord, you are good. Bless Gaby and help her to use her gifts to glorify you in every way. Amen."

The gates fly open on her amen, causing a few well-controlled tears to spill every which way. Agnes's prayer gives me the lift I need to face this day and all its ugliness. And hours later, long after she has moved on to spread her brand of cheer to other business owners on Main Street, I'm still feeling the love. An occasion like this calls for a celebration of the chocolate variety—am I right?

I click the lock on the shop's front door, closing early enough to give me time to stroll up the street to my favorite local chocolatier. My fingers jingle the coins in my pocket, the ones I pilfered from the peanut jar at home this morning. Other than the cash advance I plan to spread thinly among my outstanding bills, the coins are my only chocolate-buying resource at the moment.

Standing in front of Truffles by the Sea's spotless display case, I'm torn between the deliciously decadent truffle fillings of mocha and Bordeaux. Decisions, decisions.

"Have you made a selection?"

I frown at the woman behind the counter. "I'm having some trouble here."

She just smiles and nods. "No hurry. Let me know when you're ready."

I'm not sure if it's the heady blend of cocoa and sugar or something else, but an uneasy wave of nausea hits me. I lean one hand on the case, inwardly flinching at the fingerprints I'll be leaving there. There's also orange, raspberry, and amaretto fillings to choose from. Why am I so weak?

I rally long enough to catch the employee's attention.

"I'll have two, mocha and Bordeaux." I take the bag from her and rush out to the sidewalk and back down the street, stopping only long enough to stuff the first creamy truffle into my mouth. Eyes shut, I breathe in its fragrance with every bite. Then an aroma of a different kind mingles in the air beneath my nostrils.

"Stuff of the gods."

I open my eyes to find a bearded homeless guy staring at me. His eyes shift to my bag.

I cinch it at the top like it's filled with swill and dash back down the street toward my car. The momentary weakness I'd experienced back at the candy counter has lessened, but not my yearning for a second helping of pure bliss. I pop the other truffle into my mouth, and let it melt there. "Mm-mmm." That's what I'm talkin' about.

On the way home, my cell rings. "This is Gabrielle!" I say.

"Gaby?"

"Uh. Ye-ah?"

"It's Bri."

"Bri-Bri! How are you, girlfriend? Tell me everything!"

She's quiet. "Have you been chugging wine?"

I crack up. "Silly girl! Can't a girl be in a good mood? *¡Muy bien!*"

"O-key. You know that Coast Guard guy I told you about? The one who towed my boat last week?"

"The yummy one?"

Bri makes a strangled sound. "Ew. He was ancient. No, it's his son I wanted to talk to you about. He cleans boats."

I giggle.

"What?"

"Just thinking of a guy swabbing a deck. Sounds so very rugged."

"What is up with you? Seriously. Spill it right now."

"Nothing, darling, nothing. Just stopped by the truffle store for a little snack, and I'm feeling quite giddy now. There's power in chocolate, you know."

"Hey, I do know. Sounds like you had more than two though. Did you eat a whole box or something?"

"Nope. But all I've had to eat are two truffles, all the livelong day." My mouth forms a big *oops.*

"Gaby! That's all you ate today? No wonder you're acting crazy. I'm inviting you to dinner. You don't mind meatloaf, do you?"

"I don't know. Does it sweat while it's singing?" I laugh aloud at my reference to the oversized entertainer. "Hee, hee. No, seriously, chica, I'm good. Jake actually left me enchiladas." *Thank you, Jesus, for reminding me about those!*

"Shut up. Your landlord cooks for you? That guy's up to something. I can smell it! Has he tried anything funny?"

Phone still stuck to my ear, I let myself into the main house, and spy the freezer. "He carried me upstairs the other night."

"Excuse me? You let him touch you? What about Max? What did he have to say about that!"

I roll my eyes, something Bri does hourly. "I was sick, but what about you?" I accuse. "Weren't you getting ready to fix me up with some old fart's son? *¡Basta!*—enough already!"

Bri blows out a long breath. "I admit it. Max is a great guy, and you're my best friend. You're beautiful together, but I just don't see it. I never have or I would've suggested it a long time ago."

I pull the tray of enchiladas from the freezer and set them on the counter. "Really. Why not?"

"Max needs . . . Oh, I don't know. Just a gut feeling, I guess."

"Max needs something I don't have?"

"No, no. Aargh! Okay, when Gibby came over today, chattering on about Rover's near-death experience and how you and Max seemed to be on the outs, I thought, here's my chance, and I merely suggested to Wendell, the boat captain, that his son, Wendt, would be a good catch for a friend of mine."

"A good catch." Isn't that what Iris said about Max? I clear my still-recovering throat. "Wendell has a son named Wendt, huh? I bet they make quite a pair."

"Hey, don't judge a book by its cover! So baby naming wasn't his thing? He's a sweetie, and I think you'd like his son."

I unwrap the enchiladas, my stomach leaping at the sight of corn tortillas stuffed until bulging with shredded chicken and grated cheese. They lie there, smothered in frozen, spicy sauce and I'm overtaken by hunger. Enough to keep my mind off the fact that my best friend apparently doesn't think I could make Max happy, whatever the reason.

Twenty-Four

It's not easy to upset Bri, but I managed it. So what are best friends for anyway? But really, if anyone's going to do some apologizing, it's her. Trying to fix me up with the harbor guy's son just because of a little spat with Max? Are you kidding me?

After nuking myself a plateful of enchiladas last night, I flopped into bed and zonked the whole night through. Between the remnants of my cold, a stressful day at the shop, and a rapid sugar high that wore off after dinner, I slept nearly nine hours.

I close my eyes, but light from yonder window beats down on them anyway. I'm reliving yesterday in my mind, not ready to give up the dream of Max Rispoli, hunky prospective husband who's handy with a carburetor and financial statements. An admirable combination, if you ask me.

God, give me another chance with Max. I know I can make things work better between us this time. I promise.

With that prayer, I put away all thoughts of Max—and everything else in my life that's troublesome. Stepping across Jake's back-door slider, I'm slightly disgusted by the buildup of silt lining its metal frame. The air is still, and except for the distant buzz from cars flying along the 101 freeway, the channel stands quiet in the morning mist.

I made myself an extra-large coffee this morning, and I'm cradling it now while leaning against the handrail and breathing in the day's seaborne air, watching for signs of life. Willy's been by. He left a copy of the *Reef Report* down on the dock. I scan the channel and see evidence that most of my neighbors have yet to retrieve theirs.

I pad down the ramp in my pink slippers, openly inviting more of Kit's ridicule, and that's when I notice a pile of exquisite shells left haphazardly near the corner of Jake's dock. Must be a new promo for the *Reef Report*. They knock together in my palm like jewels and I wonder how they'd look strung on a shiny cord.

My name floats in on the mist and I turn. Shonda flashes me a peace sign from two doors down; guess this means supposed rumors have little bearing on her opinion of me. I send her a nod and head back to my loft to grab my keys. Before I can leave, though, there's a firm rap on the main door to the house.

Opening the door I see a squat woman, her face exotic and beautiful, like she's an artful blend of the myriad cultures we have in California. She's wearing a black skirt and a plain cotton tee fitted snuggly against her padded waistline, holds a tall mop like a pitchfork in one hand, and zeroes in on me with intense eyes. "You the lady of the house? Yes, yes. I think so."

"Mmm, I think you've got the wrong house. Which address were you looking for?"

She steps in. I step back.

"No," she says. "This is right house. I hear you are the lady."

Calm. Calm. I reach back and close the door to the main house—having forgotten to lock it last night before my mad race for sleep—and block it with my body. My hand rests on the knob. "I'm sorry, but I didn't call for a housekeeper. . . . Wait. Who called you?"

"Jake call me. He say I should talk to Gaby. That's you. He describe you."

I let go of the door. She narrows her eyes at me, and I'm getting the feeling she doesn't like me.

"Okay. I start with kitchen, then move to bathrooms, then the rest of the house. You got vacuum?"

My eyebrow does its customary dance, knowing that the dirt buster I have tucked away beneath my counter would choke and die on even half of Jake's living room rug. My thoughts scurry around my mind trying to recall where—or if—I've ever seen Jake's vacuum cleaner, because, frankly, this pretty maid is scary mean.

"Oh boy, oh boy." She's talking to herself while assessing the neglected first floor, and I have to say, that is a suitable alternative to her speaking to me.

"I found it." I push Jake's vacuum over to her. When I let go, it falls backward under the weight of its old age.

"Ay."

I check the time on my cell. It's late, and I'm hoping my grower has plenty of stock left by the time I get there. Do I just leave her here?

"Excuse me, but what is your name?"

She doesn't look up. "It's Jane."

I giggle, and this time she looks at me sharply. Oh. My. "Well, Jane, I have to leave for work. Did, uh, Jake give you specific instructions?" Like where the silver is located?

"He say you give me cash. I take it now. Before you go."

"Um."

She stops working and watches me.

"I guess I'll have to give Jake a call."

Jane gives me a perfunctory nod, and I step out onto the deck to call the landlord.

"Yo. Jake here."

"Hello, Jake. It's Gaby, and we've got a pickle here, I think."

"Would that be dill or sweet? I just can't work with that bread-and-butter variety."

"Your maid wants her money."

I hear him suck in his breath, and then groan. "Whoops!"

Whoops?

"Listen, Gaby, I planned on calling you, but with this restaurant opening in just a couple of nights and the owners going wild, well . . . Ah, I blew it, plain and simple. So would you do me a favor?"

I already am. "Sure, Jake," I say in my sweetest voice. "What do you need me to do?"

"Run upstairs to my bedroom, hon, and grab the cash from my T-shirt drawer. I'll wait on the line to make sure you find it okay. Would you do that for me?"

Hon? Oh. My. He wants me to paw through his underthings. I might just die on the spot. "I'm in a hurry to get to work, Jake, but all right." My voice shakes.

The phone's in my ear as I dash upstairs, and through the receiver I can hear the swish of water and clank of pans characteristic of a busy kitchen. Jake's calling out instructions, and I imagine the steam and the bustle, the sweet and the savory all blended into one heady aroma. It occurs to me then that I know very little about the man whose dresser drawers I'm about to rifle through in order to pay the help. Forgive me if I'm overthinking this, but isn't that just so wrong?

Upstairs, I peek around the corner and down the long hallway. "Jake?" He doesn't answer, but it sounds like he's explaining the best method of chopping onions to a sous chef or something. I venture through the narrow hallway with doors on both sides, unsure of which room is Jake's.

I glance into door number one on the right. It screams pink, and somehow I can't imagine my brawny landlord living there, or even setting foot in there, for that matter. But I want to. Once inside, my mind takes me back to 1984 and I'm a princess from Villa de

Barbie. I twirl once, creating a delicious strawberry and vanilla swirl out of the room's generously pink-and-white color scheme. My eyes alight on a picture of that same young girl who graces Jake's bookshelf downstairs.

Jake's back on the line. "How's it coming, Gaby?"

"Huh? Oh." I dash from the room. "Haven't quite made it there, Jake."

"It's all right. Listen, I've got to put you on hold for two shakes."

He does and I'm at the threshold of door number two. I twist the handle and give the door a little push before taking a step inside. I've never really thought of Jake as the crystal-and-iron sort of man. Not that I actually think of Jake all that much. But if I did (think of Jake, that is), then I'd see him surrounded by rough hewn logs, a leather footstool or two, maybe even the skin of a buffalo spread beneath his boots. Not this. Beveled glass, curved iron tables, sleek hammered copper . . . none of the furnishings in this room say *Jake*. At least not in my mind.

"You there, Gaby?"

His hearty voice reaches through the airwaves via my cell phone and pulls me forcefully from my thoughts. I look across the hall to what must be another bedroom. "Y-yes. I'm here, Jake. Is your room down the hall and to the left?"

"That's the one. Go on in there and you'll find an envelope with Jane's money in the dresser at the front end of the house."

"So her name is really Jane?" I ask as I reach the door to his domain.

"It might be. I don't care—just as long as she gets the place cleaned up. She came recommended, but I spoke with her on the phone and she's a doozy, let me tell ya."

"I'll say."

He bursts into laughter, and I cross the hall and step into his bedroom, surprised to find it unlike any other room in the house—at least the ones I've seen. Definitely has a man's touch. I giggle remembering the time Bri hired a designer to redo her kitschy beachside living room and she ended up turning it into a cigar lounge. Ha! That didn't last long.

This is different somehow, though. Warmer. More homey, even for a room with masculine touches all around—tan walls, maple wood furniture, and chocolate bedding mixed with basic blue striping—no expense spared here. And like my loft, this room lies lengthwise across the house, long and narrow. He has a harborside window in the back and a street-side sliding glass door that leads out to a small balcony. Probably the very same deck from where he threw his voice into my shower. Oh. My. Not wanting to go there at the moment.

"Now in my dresser, Gaby, you'll find a metal box with a latch in the second drawer down." I flit across the room and tentatively tug on his drawer, holding one eye shut so as not to shock myself. With what, I've no idea, but I'm just not all that interested in becoming shocked at the moment, you know? (Not any more than I already am, that is.)

Thankfully—yes, ¡Gracias a Dios!—there's not a tighty whitey in sight. Hallelujah! Instead, just your garden variety stacks of polo shirts in primary colors, pressed and folded neater than I thought a straight man could. I feel like I'm violating some kind of intimacy code by fingering my way through them, and a giggle escapes me.

"What's so funny?"

"Um, well."

"Well?"

I laugh aloud, my eyes caught on a white polo tucked into one the color of vomit green. "Tell me you don't layer your polos. That's fashion suicide, my friend!"

"Hey, don't make fun. That was the style, Gaby."

"Yes, and when was that—1985?"

He huffs. "Such a baby you were then, so how would you know?"

"I'm a fan of the oldies, you know—*Pretty in Pink, Some Kind of Wonderful, The Breakfast Club*. You know, the classics."

His laughter roars in my ear. "Honey, if you call those classics, we've got some talking to do." He laughs again, and this time a warm ripple rolls through my cheeks as I smile in response. "Besides, in the '80s I was in my prime, sweetheart. No time for teenybopper flicks back then, classic or not. Not a one."

So exactly how old are you, Jake? Shoving that personal question aside, I pull the box out from under a stack of shirts and plunk it onto the top of his dresser. "I'm opening the box now, Jake. Just so you know."

"I'm with you."

The words give me pause. I haven't had anyone "with me" in a long, long time. I open the box and an invisible swirl of his cologne fills the air around me. Is it possible to fall for someone's smell? Inside the box I find an envelope with more cash than I've had in my possession since . . . possibly ever. Unless you count borrowed money, and let's face it—that's virtually the same as never having it in the first place. Am I right?

I count out the amount Jake asks me to, then close up the box and slip it back into the drawer. All would have been just dandy in that moment of holding a stack of green, if I hadn't glanced out the window and seen Iris wavering on tiptoes, staring straight up at me.

I back up slowly, as if being caught with the daily till in my possession (a la Sammy), and hurry down to pay Jane.

Twenty-Five

Lovely Readers,

Image matters. Consider how your actions look to others. For example, married men should not be entering cars with single women, and vice versa. Nor should members of the opposite sex be seen in each other's intimate confines.

What may seem innocent to you has the potential to appear just the opposite to others . . .

GAH! I KNEW IRIS SAW me pawing through Jake's drawers! How did she get to her blog so fast—and why did I take the time to torture myself with her thinly veiled gossip? I quickly log off, grab my keys, and dash out the door.

When I arrive at Florally Yours, there's a note from Doug stuck to the window. I rip it down and make a mental note to answer his message from yesterday. The one I (conveniently) forgot about. I'm already late, late, late! And I'm wondering if I should have demanded a finder's fee from Jake.

Deep breath in. Start fresh. I'm here, and that's what matters. Am I right? Thankfully, over the next hour or so, I'm breathless from the rush. The premade arrangements I sprung for on the way to work—my wholesaler accepts Visa—sold out completely. Not a whole lot of profit, but there is some built in, and besides, the goodwill of actually having attractive stock goes a long way.

The door dings. I'm counting out change to a lingering customer, so I don't look up. When I do, tall and impossibly blond Summer Briens—the disgruntled bride—appears before me. She's wearing a chic Coach bag on her shoulder, its wide black strap linked by her thumb and a world-be-darned attitude.

"May I help you?" I ask, as if I've never seen this woman in my life because—let's just face facts, shall we?—I wish I never had.

She drops me a condescending smile. "I thought I'd come by and take a look around, if you don't mind."

Actually, I do. "From what I've been led to believe, there's nothing in here that you want."

Her lips spread like taffy across her face. "The place certainly has taken a downward spiral. That I can see. But"—she punctuates the word—"surely the store's well-established name and supplies on hand will serve me well when I take over."

I laugh, and her eyes stare at me in falsified wonder.

"Oh dear. Perhaps your lawyer hasn't told you yet. You have few assets, Gaby. Of course, you know that already, don't you."

My blood begins to boil, joined by the three cups of coffee I've already had today.

"Since your assets are rather piddly, Gaby, I'll be taking over your business. You can make this easy on yourself, dear, and just hand it over. It'll save you legal costs in the long run, now, won't it?"

"You need to go."

She cocks her chin slightly. "Of course I may be able to offer you a job, if that's what you are looking for." Summer slowly glances around my one-room shop, like a designer surveying a fixer-upper. I can almost hear the *tsk, tsk* rattling around in that head of hers. "There will have to be big changes around here first, though. Have you ever thought of making this space more welcoming? I wonder why you haven't put much effort into that. . . . Well, anyway, Gaby, as my case gets closer to being finalized, perhaps we can chat."

"You know what, Summer? You're crazier than that man who married you." Her eyes shrink and I continue, even as my mind tells me to stop. "Don't think it's gone unnoticed that you had to go all the way to LA to find a lawyer to take up such a frivolous suit. No one in this town would be stupid enough to sue for something so subjective."

She spits out a gasp. "Oh, really?"

Summer stands there indignant, and although I want to pull her hair as if we're two braided-head girls on the elementary playground, I'm also overwhelmed by the feeling that something's desperately wrong with her. Why would a woman who's in the enviable place of finding true love forever want to mar the memory of her wedding with a lawsuit like this?

A pang of missing the dream of Max hits my heart. I take a deep breath and start fresh.

"Go home, Summer."

Her face falters but is quickly replaced by a hard mask. "All that stock you used in my arrangements made my wedding smell like a funeral."

Something tells me that was appropriate. "You mean the blue stock you begged me to use?" We talked all this out before the wedding. I made her a sample bouquet and hoped she'd see how inappropriate it was—but guess what, she loved the colors and the flower types and placed an order for the entire hall to be filled with them. I sigh. "Go home to your new husband, Summer. There's nothing for you here."

"We'll see about that, won't we?"

She turns away and I watch her walk, her stride less confident than her words. I wait until the final click on the front door's latch before picking up the phone.

"Doug Stone here."

"Doug, it's Gaby."

"My elusive client."

I bite my tongue. "Just had a little visit from Summer."

He pauses, then groans. "That couldn't have been pleasant."

"No, but that would have been a nice change." I sigh. "Did you know she thinks she's taking Florally Yours from me?"

"That's what I've been hoping to speak to you about."

"So it's true!"

"Now hold on a minute. The other side has taken steps in that direction, but absolutely nothing has happened on this, Gaby. It can't. All they've done is filed what's called a petition for prejudgment writ of attachment."

"A huh?"

"It's a document asking the courts to put a levy on your assets—including business assets. We're going to contest this, but I wanted to strategize with you."

"I've been meaning to call you, but I was sick and . . ."

"Avoiding me."

"Maybe a little." My mind suddenly turns to mocha truffles, of all things, and I'm wondering if I brought enough change to make a quick stop at my favorite chocolatier.

"Gaby? Did you hear me?"

"Hmm? Yes, I admit it! I was avoiding you. Sorry, Douglas. Ten lashes for that."

"I asked if you could meet with me tomorrow. We can do it after work since I know you have to staff the shop during business hours."

I blink rapidly and glance at my daily planner, the one I hardly ever remember to fill out. I flip to tomorrow's date and see that, of course, it's blank. "I'm penciling you in right now, Doug. Okay?"

"Better make that pen. We can't afford to lose time on this."

We hang up and I stand in the silence, stunned by this latest development. Who knows how much time has passed when I hear the front door ding, announcing a customer's coming. I pull myself out of my funk and glance up. That's when Max's soulful eyes hook with mine. I'm not all that ready for another bout of bad news, so I just stand there lamely, staring at him, hoping that he'll start.

Apparently, he's waiting for the same thing.

"How's Rover?" I ask, keeping the conversation away from the elephant that's landed in my shop (not to mention the one I kicked out about a half hour ago).

"Not a scratch on her. The vet gave her a good once-over, and she's fine."

I swallow. "I'm glad."

"You okay?"

You mean other than feeling humiliated in just about every area of my life? In the past few days I've nearly drowned saving my boyfriend's dead wife's dog, a woman with more beauty assets than I have of any other kind has promised to take what little I've got left, and just this morning, Iris "caught" me rummaging through Jake's drawers. You ask if I'm okay? Well, I'll tell you. "Yes, I'm fine, Max. Just fine."

He takes another step toward me. "That's a relief. I came to apologize, Gaby, for the way I treated you. Wasn't right of me."

Dueling thoughts freeze me in place. This is where I accept his apology and forgive him for trampling my heart with his hasty retreat on Sunday. I'm supposed to forget all about how quickly he dismissed me, despite my attempts to explain. This is what I asked you for, God, right? It hits me then. What if Rover wasn't okay?

What then? I shudder. I might not have been able to forgive myself for that, either.

He waits for my response, and it melts my heart to see him and his humility standing there. If he wore a hat, he'd be holding it in his hands right now.

"Of course I accept your apology, Max." I look away, so relieved to have something better to think about.

His shoulders relax and he leans against the counter, crinkling those eyes at me. "I like what we've got going here, Gaby. I don't want it to slip away."

Neither do I. Yet I need something more. The old me would have taken that comment at face value and not expected more, but the me that's attempting to change, the one that's determined to get to the root of things, just has to ask, "What do we have going here, Max?"

"Two longtime friends having a good time together."

Oh. "Friends?"

He shakes his head side to side, never losing eye contact with me. His grin's infectious. "More than friends. You're a looker, Gaby. I've seen that for a long time, and you're independent. I like that about you."

"You do?"

He nods, takes my hand from the counter, and kisses it. "I'm very sorry about hurting your feelings the other day. Let me make it up to you, all right?"

I squeeze his hand back, my mind imagining all kinds of ways for him to do just that.

"Dinner?" he asks. "Tomorrow night? I'd make it tonight, but Gib's got me going to his open house at school."

I stiffen, not ready to tell him or anyone else about my need for legal counsel. "I can't make it tomorrow, but how about the next night?"

If Max wants to ask what I'm doing that makes me so unavailable tomorrow night, he doesn't. Unfortunately, the way he loosens his grip on my hand and shrugs out, "Sure," I can tell that his earlier affection for me has just lost a bit of steam.

Twenty-Six

GROCERY SHOPPING IN THE EVENING, when most nuclear families are sitting around a homemade meal playfully discussing the doings of the day, is the best time to meet men. That's the theory, anyway. Not that I'm looking anymore, but who am I to reject the honest-to-goodness testing of a long-held theory?

I squeeze an avocado, testing for its ripeness, and bump fingers with a man old enough to be my granddad. He smells of stale cooking grease and English Leather, and I've suddenly lost my appetite for guacamole.

Moving on, I'm in the yogurt aisle, trying to choose between Boston cream pie style or raspberry chocolate, when I throw out all caution and put them both in my basket. Add to that some precooked chicken, salad fixings, pasta and sauce for tomorrow's dinner, a few other goodies, and I head to checkout.

My basket's heavier than I'd planned, but thankfully, a bespectacled man in line ushers me to go ahead of him. With a nod of thanks, I do and begin placing my items on the conveyor belt, absentmindedly listening to the universal sound of items being rung up.

"Is that vodka pasta sauce any good?"

I swing a look behind me. The man who'd let me pass removes his glasses and puts them in the pocket of his distressed leather jacket, while watching me and waiting for a response.

"I like it." Oh, that was smooth.

"Maybe I'll try it sometime."

I nod, noting the flash of his unnaturally white teeth, but it's my turn at the register, so I punch my phone number into the machine—have to get my shopper's discount, you know—and watch my items tally. The total quickly moves up, climbing uncomfortably close to the dollar amount I have in my pocket. My neck and shoulders tense, and my mind's on alert. My face stays still, but my eyes move to the conveyor belt.

The total peaks and then moves beyond what I've got on hand. I draw in a breath. "Um, could you wait a minute?" The cashier, a string bean of an older man, keeps on trucking. "Sir? Um, wait."

He looks up, his comb-over unable to hide the sheen of sweat on his head.

"I'm a little short tonight," I say. "Could you . . . could I . . . remove some things?"

He lets out an exaggerated sigh and looks out at the snaking line of customers. "Yes, ma'am."

Leather man leans closer to my ear. "I could offer you a trade, if you'd like."

My eyes widen at him, and I pull back.

He winks, startling me. I push away the pasta and sauce with gusto. "Just put these back."

Again with the exaggerated sigh, the cashier makes a dramatic act of deleting the items from my total. Only I'm still eighty-two cents short.

Leather man jostles my elbow and offers me a dollar along with the creepiest smirk I think I've ever seen. I glare at the cashier. "And forget the yogurt." I push aside the Boston cream pie style container and hand him my cash. If I weren't so broke I'd have dashed out of there without my nickel change. After pocketing the coin and darting away with one large but only half-filled grocery bag, I think I hear a catcall.

Back at home sweet home, I yank the rest of Jake's enchiladas out of the freezer, serve a couple up on a plate, and nuke until they're hot. As the cheese begins to bubble and the spices in the sauce heat up, the ammonia-scent of the place disappears. Waiting, I admire the shine of Jake's kitchen counters. Who knew Formica could look so new?

Fortunately there were no more Jane sightings today. I'm not proud of how scared that bitty woman made me; I'm just glad she put the key back in the conch shell out front, apparently long gone before I drove up from my shopping disaster.

Thinking about shopping causes me to chew more slowly. I may need this to last awhile. I have to spread my bills out tonight and fig- ure out a plan to hold things together. And I will, right after I finish eating and step outside for some fresh air.

Sarah's light casts a glow onto Jake's deck. She's sitting now, sil- houetted against the window, more animated than I think I've ever seen her. I draw my gaze away from her, flip a light onto my path, and flop against the banister. By all rights, I should be living in a tent somewhere. Who am I to be surrounded by such luxury when I can barely afford my groceries? My mama, God bless her, always gave me a safe place to lay my head and three healthy meals a day. So she had trouble discerning the character of men in her life? At least she provided the basics.

I pad down the ramp to the dock below, perfectly content to let my money worries steep awhile longer, and focus instead on my own man. Max had me at hello tonight. Oh, I'd wanted to make him squirm, to make him think that any possibility of a relationship with me was over—or at least, decidedly damaged. He stood there so respectfully, though, daring me to stay angry while caressing me with those sincere eyes of his, and what could I do but fold like whipped cream?

Sarah's sliding door opens and shuts with a clank, pulling me out of my musings. My eyes catch on another pile of shells shimmering in the coming moon, and I scoop them up. Shells have always been an afterthought with me, something Bri and I would toss aside to make room for our waterside brownie-eating revelry. But maybe that's because chocolate at the beach has always been synonymous with wallowing for us. Okay, usually me. Our little cocoa-studded jaunts to the sea have always been our friendship's way of dealing with my catastrophe of the week. Hence, my blatant disregard for shells tossed up by the tides.

Goosebumps rise on my skin from the night's breeze, and I move quickly back up the ramp with my treasures. "Sarah?" I call out.

When she turns, the streak of tears on her cheeks glistens in the glow of light from my deck. She tucks her hair behind one ear. "Hi, Gaby."

She's a curiosity to me. "Everything all right?"

Sarah puts on a smile, but it doesn't reach her eyes. "Sure. Just fine."

I jingle the shells in my hand. "I found these on my dock." I hold them out for her to see. "Aren't they beautiful?"

She's considerate, but unimpressed. "I guess they are." She breathes in and her voice flutters, like someone who's just coming down from a good cry. "Have a nice night. I have to go."

"Wait. Are you sure you're okay? Want to talk about it? I could—"

"No." Her eyes flash me a startled look. "I just have some things to take care of on my own. You know how it is."

I nod and watch her slip back into her house, her shoulders round and bent as if carrying a weight beyond her strength. It amazes me how someone can so easily refuse help. Sarah obviously has deep issues, and wouldn't another shoulder help, even a little?

Then again, there's strength in independence. My mama may not live the life I envision for her, but she's doing what she knows and what she likes, and she's no pushover for it. That's for sure.

After tidying up, I yawn and head upstairs to my loft. Halfway up, the doorbell rings and I trot back down to answer it.

Andy and his eternally smiling self stands on the other side of the door. "How'z it, Gaby?"

"Hi, Andy. I'm doing okay."

He's standing with a tiki torch in each hand. "Heard about your dog rescue the other day. Man, that was whack!"

"What did you hear, exactly?"

"Oh yeah, everyone's talking about how you saved your boyfriend's dog from the jaws of a hungry sea lion. Some of the neighbors saw it and thought that was crazy, but not me." He stands straighter and taps one of the torches into the ground like a flagpole. "I am duly impressed. You've got it goin' on."

"You know, Andy, I was hoping to put this behind me, so I've decided not to talk about it. I'm wondering if you could help me out. If you hear any more about it, could you help me by just stopping the blather?"

Concern softens his features. "Ab-so-lutely! You can count on me. Mum's the word."

I smile, glad that's over.

He just stands there, staring at me with that positive smile of his. "Oh," he says. "I almost forgot. I came to give Jake back his torches. Now that he's back in the area, I figured he'd need 'em for parties."

Awkwardly, I take the torches from him, suddenly educated about the smell of burned bamboo.

"You just gotta join us sometime at one of Jake's parties. You'll have a blast, I promise you that."

I step backward, struggling with the torches. "Maybe," I say in my most noncommittal tone.

"Gaby?"

I peek around one of the poles. "Yes?"

"The man saved my life. Not like you did with that dog—and I know I'm not supposed to bring that up—but in every other way."

"What do you mean, saved your life?"

A thin layer of perspiration glistens along Andy's thinning hairline. "I'm an addict, Gaby. Wait. A recovering drug addict. Most of my family and friends abandoned me, but Jake didn't. I don't blame anyone for giving up on me, but I'm eternally thankful that he didn't let me die at the curb. That's where I spent a lot of my time—in the gutter."

I stare at Andy, now seeing him as someone other than a neighbor with questionable character. He's been broken and repaired, and who am I to judge him for the man he once was?

"Jake's just . . ." His voice cracks. "He's a great friend."

Some guys wear their emotions on their sleeves, or in this case, since I've never seen Andy in anything other than shorts and a tank, on his rotator cuff. And although I think a man and his emotions can be quite charming—think Zack Braff as Newbie in *Scrubs*—I'm not exactly sure how to react to them at this particular moment. I'm still reeling from his addiction confession.

So I say the only thing that comes. "I'm sure he thinks the same of you, Andy."

This, apparently, does the trick because the next thing I know I'm nearly bowled over by a sobbing Andy, the smell of old cigarettes mixed with spearmint, and two unwieldy tiki torches made of bamboo.

Twenty-Seven

"So she can't really take my business from me, can she?" I don't mention that the leasing agent has me on speed dial these days. *A few more days and there may not be any business worth getting.*

Doug's eyes dart back and forth across the page from beneath his newly acquired reading glasses. "Not if I can help it. You've given me plenty of ammunition here to fight this."

I nibble on another truffle, one of the two that I picked up on my way over here. Of course, I politely offered Doug one, and then when he said no, I waited a respectable amount of time for him to change his mind, but he still refused. I couldn't very well let them go to waste, now, could I?

Doug looks up and sets his pen down on his desk. Those glasses of his have slipped to the end of his nose, giving him that oh-so-distinguished look that Bri always coos about. "I'm satisfied with what you've told me, Gaby," he says. "And I believe the judge will throw this right out. Let's hope for that."

I head straight home, surprised to see Jake's house lit up when I arrive. These days, with angry housekeepers and tiki torches showing up at odd hours, coming home can be a bit disconcerting, to say the least. That thought, mixed with the fact that I've spent the entire evening being grilled by my lovable-yet-tigerish lawyer, has made this girl tired. I keep waiting for my dinner of truffles to kick in, but so far, not so much.

Inside the entry, Jake's French doors stand closed and his dated metal blinds shut tight. That's different. Voices carry through the thin glass, and I try (well, not too hard) not to hear a thing as I wander listlessly to my loft upstairs.

"You owe me this, Jake."

I stop. Iris?

Jake's booming voice cuts in. "Iris, I've heard this so many times that my déjà vu is getting déjà vu. I think you'd better go."

"Not until you tell me what you're planning. I've waited too long just to have you play games with me."

My hand rests on the banister, and I know that if those doors suddenly swing open and I'm caught, well, then that would be downright embarrassing. But this is Iris we're talking about—romance advisor, neighborhood know-it-all. . . . Suddenly my tired body has been revived by my curious spirit.

Jake's rising voice causes me to grip the rail harder. "Tell you what, if and when I decide to unload this place, you'll be the first to know."

He's selling?

"That's not good enough, Jake! After what you did to me? I believed you. I trusted you."

Okay, so maybe he's not actually selling his house, but the hiss in Iris's voice startles me, and I get the sinking feeling that I've stumbled upon a conversation that's just way too personal for even my curious ears. A flame turns up beneath their words.

"Are you ever going to let this go, woman? Go home to your husband. I've said my piece on this, and God help me, I don't ever want to discuss our past again."

"Then sell me this place. It should have been mine all along anyway! If I can't have you, at least . . ."

Their past? As in recent past? I hold my breath. And just when I had started to rethink my assessment of Jake. I quickly tiptoe upstairs, the heaviness of Iris's angst-filled voice fresh in my ears. She'd said, "If I can't have you . . ." What would make a married woman think she could have another man? Unless . . . unless Jake had led her to believe that to be true. My cell phone takes this awkward moment to trill, and I fumble with my bag for what seems like ages before finding it and sliding it open.

"Gaby!"

"Gaby?"

I open my mouth to answer my caller when I realize that Iris and Jake are standing at the foot of the stairs, gaping up at me. I toss them a weak smile and point at my phone. "Hello?" I say, maybe too brightly.

"Gaby, it's Max."

"Max! How are you?"

Iris glares at me, one bony fist jabbed into her waist, while Jake's expression comes across as a mixture of relief and interest. I turn away from them, Max's voice coming through. "You all right? You sound . . . funny."

"Just looking for my key. Hang on."

Jake charges up the stairs, his frame large enough to fill its width. I squeeze myself against the wall to let him pass, but he stops inches from me. "Let me take those." He grabs my work files from me and deftly finds the key to my apartment amongst my things. And need I say how grateful I am that he didn't whip out his own key to my apartment at this very moment?

I follow him up to the landing, around the corner, and up the final, brief flight of stairs. With a swift click of the lock, I'm no longer left to squirm in the narrow place beside him.

"Thanks, Jake." I manage to keep the mallet of judgment from my tone.

Max's soothing voice, though, takes a decidedly animated turn. "Jake? He there with you?"

"Hey, Max." I shut the door behind me, vaguely noticing my landlord glancing back at me before returning to Iris downstairs. Would it be terribly rude if I tacked up that towel again right now? "No, I was just getting home from . . . from a business meeting. Jake's back and he helped me with my things. No worries. I'm inside now and you have me all to yourself."

"Good. Just wondering where you'd like to have dinner tomorrow night."

I step out of my shoes and pad over to the back window. "Wherever you like. I'm easy." I shudder. "I didn't mean . . . I just meant that when it comes to food, I'm easy to please. It's whatever you like, Max, truly. I'm not picky." Okay, okay, he gets it.

"Let's do steak, then."

Oh. My. Not that place with the wood-paneled walls and vinyl seating that's seen too many steak-sauce spillings. As my mama's third husband used to say, surely you jest.

Max's voice cuts back in. "Say, just before six? Will that work for you?"

I make myself sound chipper. "Sure."

He pauses. "You okay, Gaby? That landlord of yours isn't giving you a hard time, I hope."

"No, not at all, but I do have a question for you, Max. It has to do with . . . a friend's rental situation."

"Livi's roommate giving her trouble again?"

"Jet's always trouble for Livi. I just wish she'd have the courage to move on, but that's not—"

Max cuts back in. "I've told her that myself, but she's hardheaded. Okay, tell me about your 'friend.' "

197

"Is it fair to serve a tenant with an eviction notice when they're only a few days late with the rent?"

"How much is a few?"

"Ten or so."

He lets out a blunt groan. "Gaby, Gaby. Let me ask you this: is it fair to keep the rightful owner of that property waiting for their money? They've probably got a lot invested in it. Shoot, from experience, I know they do."

"Okay, but what if that person has never been late before?"

"Doesn't matter. Bottom line is bottom line. If they can't hack the cost, they should move on so the property owner can find a replacement renter right away." He pauses. "We're not really talking about Livi here, are we?"

"Oh, pffst, no way. Livi's good; this is another friend."

"I'm glad to hear that."

"So would that make a difference?"

"Not really, Gaby. Failure to enforce the terms of a lease can be construed as a waiver of future defaults. And the courts! Man, the courts almost always favor the tenants over landowners. It's like a law or something. No offense, but I just don't believe in cutting renters any slack."

"Oh."

"So listen, Black Bull it is. I'll pick you up tomorrow around five-forty-five. All right with you?"

"Sure. See you then."

So he's not the teddy bear I've always pictured? Hawkishness is a noble quality, I say. Never underestimate the power of a good businessman—they make even better husbands. I try to convince myself of this while upending Grandma's coin jar, and counting out its contents.

A penny rolls onto the paper-wrapped painting I left sitting on the floor weeks ago. Who knows why I decide to finally tear away its paper, but I do, and it's one of those "ahh" moments when color and life and art intersect and catch my breath.

There's a tap on my door and I glance over to see Jake standing behind the glass, pretending not to stare through it. Reluctantly, I set the painting aside.

"Just came to apologize for that scene you came home to."

I turn away from him and plop on my couch. "Come on in." *You will anyway.*

He's carrying a foil-wrapped tray and I'm beginning to wonder if he owns stock in the Reynolds company. He lifts the plate in the air. "Brought you a snack. Beef sirloin tips over egg noodles."

Beef. Great. Yes, I want some more of that.

Jake turns toward my counter. "I'll just put it over here." He stops. *"The Boating Party."* His voice is almost inaudible as his eyes rest on the painting of a man rowing a small boat that carries a woman and child. He picks it up and turns to me. "Is this one of your favorites?"

I shrug, although I have to say that I am intrigued that this man has any concept of the painting at all. The explosion of doilies and knickknacks downstairs doesn't exactly lend itself to a backdrop of fine art from the Impressionist period. And don't even get me started about the museum of glass and iron on the second floor. "I've just always liked that picture."

He stares at it. "Really."

I step into my microscopic kitchen and glance at Mary Cassatt's famous painting, swallowing the memory of my first viewing of it. "Yes, I studied art in college some. Almost majored in it, actually."

His eyes travel from the painting to me. "So you're an artist?"

His question startles me, somehow, and I flinch. "No, just a florist. But I like to look at it." Although I used to fiddle with different media. . . . "This painting has always been an ideal for me,

I guess. There's something so warm and serene about it. Why am I telling you this?"

He smiles down at me from his incredible height, and I'm aware of our closeness. My skin prickles, and I cross my arms to rub away the goose bumps. I'm enveloped by that familiar scent of his, wavering between a strange, lingering comfort and an infusion of distrust. He helped me when I fell ill, and Andy credits Jake for saving his life, but what about his past with Iris that I just became privy to? Not to mention Shonda's warning to steer clear of Jake and his partying ways?

"Maybe you're overwhelmed."

I try to center myself in this moment and focus on the painting. "I guess you're right, Jake. There's so much trust in the woman's eyes and the eyes of her child. The way they watch the father as he rows them safely across the water just moves me, you know?"

Jake's voice thickens, and I wonder if his argument with Iris, the one I haven't mentioned yet, has taken its toll on him. And is that any concern of mine?

"How do you know the man's the child's father?" he asks. "Maybe he's just a hired servant."

"A servant wouldn't care so much! I can just tell by the way he watches them with intensity while working the paddles that this man must be her husband and that baby's father."

I hear Jake's breathing for a beat. He sets the painting down, backs away, and checks his watch. "It's late, so I'll let you get back to your night. You'll want to refrigerate that meat if you're not hungry."

I nod, and silence hangs between us.

"Lately I've been motivated to clean up the place, maybe do some renovations, but the loft looks great, Gaby. I appreciate how well you've cared for it."

I haven't exactly thought out what I'm about to say, but as is my way, I just dig right in and blurt it out. "And I appreciate you for saying that Jake, but I have to tell you something."

He stops backing up toward the door, expectation on his face.

"I'll be moving out soon."

Twenty-Eight

NOW, SEE, I DIDN'T EXPECT to see distress flash across Jake's face just now, after telling him I'd be moving soon. Nor did I expect to feel the wind utterly knocked out of my lungs when I said it. I haven't spent much time on the particulars, but it hit me tonight that I can no longer afford to live like this. Nor do I care to have to continuously fight off growing feelings for yet another Mr. Wrong.

Don't ask me where I'm headed, though.

"Where you headed?" he asks, finally.

I said not to ask. Deep breath in. Start fresh. "Oh, that's still up in the air, but I have some good ideas." Or at least, I will have some good ideas. When I think of some. "Anyway, I thought I'd better let you know now, while you're home and able to find a new renter." I glance away, unwilling to look Jake in the eyes because, frankly, that last statement felt like yet another blow.

He's quiet for a moment, and I don't really get that. He's my landlord, not my father—despite all the fatherly concern he's shown toward me. Although, word on the street is that he's like that with all the girls. That deep voice of his draws me to look at him, and I

202

see that his eyes have landed on my spilt coin jar. "Can I ask, Gaby, if the rent's too high?"

I laugh off his question, which of course is none of his business. "The rent's more than fair, Jake. I'm not complaining about that or anything."

He nods vigorously, his eyes still stuck on that stupid jar. "Didn't think you were, but I can bring it down to a number that's better for you. It would help me out a lot, actually, if you stayed."

I slide myself in front of the jar, blocking it from his view. Unfortunately, he's got me squarely in his viewfinder now, and there's a tension between us that I can't describe, but let me just say that the old song about magnet and steel has popped into my head. I mentally shake that thought away. "If you must know, I'm trying to be a good steward. It's a biblical concept that—"

He cuts me off. "I'm aware of it, and I can respect that. I too am trying to be a better steward of this place." His eyes linger on the silt embedded into the walls, the splotch I'd tried to scrub away but so far hadn't managed. Jake massages his lips together, as if he's thinking deeply, and I've just noticed that he's recently taken a razor to his usual stubble. "Knowing you're here to look after the place while I travel gives me a lot of . . . a lot of . . . peace of mind."

I cock my chin. "Really?"

He nods firmly. "Really."

"Because I can't pay a lot. Just between us, business has been a bit slow lately. Oh, I know it'll pick up. I'm doing plenty to . . ."

Jake takes my hand and shushes me. "I'm sure you're doing the best you can, Gaby. Just say you'll stick around and help me take care of this eyesore."

I pull away. "Wait a minute! You're looking for a new maid, aren't you? Uh-oh."

Jake roars with laughter, and I'm glad I hadn't hung my painting on the wall yet because he just might have knocked it over from the sheer volume of it. "Forget about that. Just stay here and make the place look lived in. Pay me whatever you can. Would you do that for me?"

I close one eye and look up at him. "Do I have to let Jane in?"

"Affirmative."

I give him a dramatic shrug. "Guess I can handle that all right. But she's pretty scary, you know."

He's still smiling. "I know. I like it cuz she keeps my renter in check."

I gasp and muster up the sternest glare I can, considering I've just been given a temporary reprieve on having to search for new digs, the one bit of light in a rather dismal day. I stand at the door as Jake leaves. "Thanks for dinner . . . I mean, the snack."

"Hey, don't mention it. I'm heading out again in a day or two, so I'll leave something for you in the freezer."

I groan. "Oh, Jake. That's not necessary."

"I know," he says and tromps on down the stairs.

With him gone, I devour the tender chunks of steak he left me, appreciating each bite more than the last. My shoulders drop and I sigh in a decidedly unladylike way. Truffles for dinner seemed like a good idea at the time, but Jake's culinary skills have played a number on my palate lately. With the last bite still left on my fork, I swirl it in sauce and remind myself to slow down. This is only a temporary situation. I wish I didn't know anything about Iris and Jake's past, but I do. And despite my growing, irrational attachment to him, sooner or later there'll be another mistress of this manor. And wouldn't she just love having me living above her all the livelong day?

Twenty-Nine

EARLY THE NEXT MORNING I'M out on the deck, sketchbook on my lap, bacon by my side. Jake must have taken off early because I didn't hear him, but when I looked out my front window, the street was quiet and his truck gone. Didn't stop him from leaving a covered plate of bacon and eggs just outside my door before he left, though, like I'm some cat. I munch another strip of the marbleized meat and wonder again how I should take Jake's incessant room-service calls.

Outside, dew coats the deck handrail like watery lace, and a blue heron streaks across the sky, her twiggy legs stretched long and lean behind her. Few of my neighbors are up and about this morning, and that's fine by me. I'm in a zone today, and like Garbo once said, "I vant to be alone."

Breakfast meat aside, it all started after Jake left my loft last night. Spurred on by the relief that I still have a place to live, even if only temporarily, my eyes opened to the possibilities. Sure my love life's on eggshells at the moment and my business is running on dental floss, but at least I know I won't have to sleep on the beach. So I found my pink girlie hammer and the box of nails I keep for emergencies (you never know when you might need to erect a wall or something), and hung up that picture of Cassatt's *The Boating Party.* Hung it right over my bed. Considering California's penchant for earthquakes, this may not have been the ideal place, but at least it's out of that brown-paper wrapping and up for me to enjoy while I can.

And that got me thinking and remembering. My poor mama had such a hard time keeping me busy while she worked at the flower stand when I was a tot. I always had my hands in her supplies, so she finally bought me my own sketchbook and graphite pencils, and told me that's what the professionals used, so I'd better get busy and make something worthy for her to hang—no crayons or markers for her mijita.

Oh, I know she was kidding about that.

Anyway, I made a mess of things at first, but eventually sketching became the one thing that slowed me down long enough to make Mama happy, and as for me, it became my comfort, my addiction. Like salty chips. Or mocha truffles. Ahem.

An engine purrs off in the distance, probably somewhere near the harbor mouth. I step over to the handrail and lean against it hoping for quiet and inspiration. Scanning the waters and dock below, I watch for signs of Sweet Thing, but the only surprise I find down there is yet another pile of seashells. I schlep my sketchbook aside and trot on down the ramp to scoop them up. When I do, they toss together like coins in my palm, valuable and sturdy, yet far more beautiful than money. Most of them have a hole or a chip, but that's expected, you know? They've been tumbling about in the raw sea, for goodness' sake. Yet one in the bunch is flawless, not a notch or scrape anywhere on it, and who could help but be awed by the Designer who thought this up? Oh, to have such a savvy architect for my dream home someday!

Sigh. The Chumash Indians lived in this area way back when, and they had it goin' on, that's for sure. Just think, if I could trade with shells like they once did, I'd be rich! Double sigh. One splash to the north, and a smooth, domed head pops up through the water, causing me to jerk backward.

"Hey, Sweet Thing." At the sound of my voice, my sea lion friend dunks herself underwater only to pop up again about two yards to the south. I lean one hand into my hip. "Oh, I know your type. Playing hard to get, aren't you?" I toss her a strip of bacon, without a thought to whether or not sea lions actually eat pig. But seriously, until she tried it, how would she know?

I don't see the sleek cruiser slicing through the water toward me until it's right beside me and the driver's glaring at me, bullhorn in hand. Thankfully, it stays at his side. "What are you doing?" the man screeches at me.

I sweep my gaze away from him, down the channel, and right back into his square jaw. "Are you talking to me?" And has anyone ever told you that you have a sexy chin?

"You can't throw food into the channel!"

"And why's that?"

"It's bad for the animals, of course. You're encouraging them to forage on the docks for food instead of learning to fend for themselves."

"Oh, of course."

He cuts the engine and floats beside Jake's dock. "You think this is some kind of joke?"

"Oh, shush. You'll wake up the neighbors."

The man runs a hand through his Dr. McDreamy hair, and I almost want to forgive his obnoxious entrance into my quiet morning. Almost. He stares at me open-mouthed and I laugh. "Okay, okay. I get it," I say. "Don't get yourself in such a snit."

The McDreamy look-alike shakes his head. "My perfect morning on the water—ruined."

I shrug. "Them's the breaks."

He rolls his eyes at me, but I see a sparkle. "You're real cute," he says, coming down hard on that last *t*.

I feign a curtsy. "Thank-ie."

"You do know you're not supposed to feed the animals, right? Tell me that information isn't exactly news to you."

"I won't and it was. But if it makes you feel better, I feel thoroughly scolded and it'll never happen again, Captain."

"You don't have to call me Captain," he tells me, those eyes alternating between hard and twinkling. "Sir would be just fine."

Kit pulls up in her kayak, her black hair unusually stringy, even for her. "Hey, Wendt. Caught any flies with that swatter of yours?" She doesn't smile but turns to me instead. "Hi, Gaby."

Wendt squints at me. "Your name is Gaby? You're not Bri's friend, are you?"

"Would it bother you if I was?"

He straightens and rubs his jaw. "Might."

I brighten. "Then I'm her."

"That so? Huh. She said you were lookin' for a man. Maybe you should be saving some of that bacon for your man's table rather than dumping it into the ocean."

Kit glares at him. "Get out o' here with that mouth. She's not lookin' for anybody—everybody knows Gaby's taken. She's got 'Jake's girl' written all over her."

I feel my eyes stretch to the size of that perfectly round shell I'm holding. "No, no, no," I blurt. "You both have it very wrong. I do have a boyfriend, and his name is Jake—I mean, Max! His name is Max."

Kit scowls at me, and Wendt just shakes his head and starts up the engine. "Not exactly my type, although I do like 'em fiery." He darts me a look. "Maybe when you figure out who is and who is not your boyfriend, I might just give you another try. Best to Bri."

Kit snorts and pushes a paddle full of water at him. "Loser!"

I just stand there on the dock and wonder what it is about me that brings out the very worst in men.

Thirty

Lovely Readers,

There are days when I feel as if everyone hates me, that I am of no use to anyone, and that I have no hope of a future because, lovely readers, I am not worthy of anything better.

Do you ever have feelings like these?

BRI'S VOICE TEARS ME AWAY from my thoughts on Iris's most recent post. "So what d'ya think of Wendt?"

I'm swabbing mascara along my lashes and I lean into the mirror, examining a glob of goo stuck on a lash. "You mean that brusque gentleman with the loud boat who insulted me during my early-morning quiet time? That guy?"

Bri sighs. "Tell me you didn't love his chin."

"I didn't love his chin."

"Liar!"

"Okay, Bri-Bri, he has a well-defined chin. Good for passing on to a son, but it would take more than that to make me interested in someone so . . . so . . . petulant!"

"Petulant? What is it with you and all those big words? Sheesh. It's like sparring with Alex Trebek."

"A little old for me."

"Yeah, but he's smart, and you always like the brainy ones."

"Can I help it if I have standards?"

"So you're going out with Max tonight." It's not a question Bri asks, just a statement she makes.

"Yes, I am. And I'm running late because he moved the time up by a half hour." I dip my brush into tinted powder, swirl and tap, painfully aware of the small quantity of expensive makeup left in the jar.

"So, going out with Max. That'll be fun?" Now she's asking me something.

I set my brush down and plop onto the sofa, which is actually Bri's. "Help me understand this, Bri. You and Doug have been friends with Max for years, and you've never said anything but the loveliest things about him. We start to date, and suddenly you have issues with him?"

"I don't have issues with Max. I love him; he's a great guy! And, hey, I'm the one who invited him for chowder, aren't I? I've just thought about it, and if there's chemistry between you two, I'm not seeing it. All I'm sayin'."

"Well, that is just terribly scary. Thanks so much for that."

"What d'ya mean?"

"I mean that my heart pounds like a fiend when Max looks at me with those chocolaty eyes of his. When he walked away from me last week over the Rover incident, I thought I'd die, Bri, just die right on the spot."

"Gaby," she whispers.

"I love being with him, but if you don't see it, then maybe he doesn't feel the same way about me. Maybe what you're trying to tell me is that you just don't see Max's feelings for me."

She's quiet. "That's not what I'm saying at all. I'm so sorry. Maybe I'm just too busy flippin' out about all the stuff going on at home to really see how good things are with Max. I just want you happy, Gabrielle. You know that, right?"

I sigh. "Yes, I do. So let me, okay? Just let me be happy with Max." *I am happy, right?*

"Done. Call me after your dinner and spill it, every blood-red detail. You are still going to that meat place, right?"

I roll my eyes. "I'll be ordering the prime rib, if it makes you feel better, Bri."

"It does! Order the best cut in the house. Believe me, from what Doug tells me, Max charges super-duper high rents, so he can afford it."

We hang up, and I hurry to finish getting ready for my date with Max, trying not to flinch whenever I relive Bri's comment about the high rents my boyfriend apparently charges.

"You haven't told me about your trip yet, Max." We're seated around a rugged wagon wheel topped by glass, part of the old west "charm" of this particular dining establishment. Never mind the Made in China tag tacked onto its side.

He leans forward, like he's got a secret to tell. "The meanest waves I've ever seen. Can't even swim out to them. Have to take a boat out to a motu, and then try to catch one. If you're lucky."

"What's a motu?"

"It's an islet—there's a whole string of 'em—like the biggest sandbar you've ever seen. Imagine standing on it, surrounded by water as clear as what's in your glass there."

I glance at my scratched, lemon-less water glass and shudder. There's a food scrap floating in it. "Sounds pretty."

"All except for the monsoon that drove us out." He wags his head. "Thankfully I demanded our money back and got it."

"Really? I would've thought there'd be something in your contract about them not being responsible for 'acts of God.' "

"You got that right, but I demanded my money back anyway. There's a loophole in just about every contract—Doug'll back me up on that—so I figured I'd go on the assumption that there was one in mine. Just held their feet to the fire awhile until they cut me a check."

"So I guess you'll be planning another trip with your windfall, then."

He sits back, crosses his arms, and smiles at me. "I've been wanting to talk to you about that very subject."

Oh, really?

Unfortunately, the waitress approaches our table—in heels and spurs, no less. "You folks ready to order?"

I look to Max. "I haven't had a chance to look over the menu yet."

Max takes my menu from me and hands both of them to the waitress. "We'll both have the surf-and-turf early bird special. We were seated by six." He turns to me. "Garlic mash or rice?"

Um, I'll have the prime rib au jus with rice pilaf and a Caesar salad. Who am I kidding? I couldn't even afford an early bird special on my own these days, so I'm not about to bite Max's providing hand at the moment. "Garlic mash, please." Potatoes stick to the ribs longer.

The waitress leaves and Max leans his well-formed arms onto the wheel, er, table in front of us. "No more beating around the bush. How would you like to join me on a cruise to Mexico this summer?"

I blink. Is that a trick question?

"Just heard about a great deal on a four-day, three-night cruise to Cabo in early June—before most schools are out."

"So would that be a problem with Gib? Taking him out of school and all?"

Max's eyes flash with amusement. I watch his mouth slowly form the words. "Gib can stay with Bri. This is for just the two of us."

"So . . ."

"So?"

Would it be too obvious if I asked the manager to turn down the a/c in here? I clear my throat, which until now, I didn't know was dry. "Max. I . . . I don't know what to say. I enjoy spending time with you."

He slides a hand over mine. "Same here."

Our hands really are the same size. It's kind of odd. I draw in a breath. "What I mean is, I . . . I just don't think I can go."

"I know it's hard to leave when you're the big kahuna." He laughs. "You know what I mean. Anyway, I thought that together we might talk Livi into pinch-hitting for you at the shop. You know she won't be able to turn us down."

"Th-that's not what I mean." A stray thought dashes through my head. "You know, Max, maybe if I could afford a room, I might consider it."

He drags his fingers along my arm. "This one's on me, Gaby. I've got our room covered."

¡Basta! "Max, I'm tempted by your offer, uh, more than you know, but I . . . just . . . don't . . . I can't . . . do . . . that. Not until there's a ring on this finger."

I hold out my left hand, just in case he doesn't get it, and make myself look him in the eyes. I expect compassion, understanding, maybe an embarrassed grin and a what-was-I thinking? apology. Instead, he presents me with silence, mixed with sarcasm and maybe even a flash of feigned hurt. His voice is low. "Time's passing you by, Gaby. It's the twenty-first century." His laugh sounds strained.

"So that's what you believe? Truly?"

"You bet. This attraction between us, in case you haven't noticed, Beautiful, just isn't going away."

Is that what you want? For it to just "go away"?

He continues. "Come away with me, Gaby. Let's find out what this—" he swings his pointer finger back and forth between us—"this thing we're doing is all about. Thanks to God we no longer have to live by outdated rules."

Now I laugh. "What is that supposed to mean?" He shrugs, and I continue. "Because last time I looked God was still on the side of modesty."

He throws up both hands. "Fine. Don't bring a thong bikini."

My face heats up, but not from attraction. I try to control my temper. "You know, Max, I can't believe you're making an issue of this. So what if I won't go away with you on the cruise to Mexico deal of the century. I set standards for myself a long time ago, and I stick to them. I'm not asking for you to agree with them." *Although that would be awfully nice of you.*

Smugness comes over him, and he nods continuously. "I understand. Oh, I get it now. You're a beautiful, successful gal, and I've always wondered why you never seem to have a steady boyfriend, Gaby. This makes perfect sense to me now."

"Say what you're thinking," I taunt. "You might as well."

"You're prudish, and not many guys I know are attracted to that type."

His words land like a slap. "You mean 'good girls'? Guys don't like 'good girls'? Is that what you're saying, Max?"

"Yeah, right." He refolds his arms at his chest. "My wife and I slept together before we were married, and don't you dare suggest that she wasn't good—she was holier than most church women I've ever met."

I sit back, utterly unable to compete with that. Who could? The waitress brings our salads, oblivious to our standoff. "Would either of you like fresh ground pepper?" she asks.

I snap out of it and answer her. "Yes, please."

Max just waves her off, never taking his eyes from me, which, by the way, have turned the color of dark chocolate. Have I ever mentioned that I prefer milk or mocha, maybe even a Bordeaux, but almost never dark?

I spear my salad, take a bite but taste nothing. Might as well be wilted celery, it's so tasteless in my mouth.

Max lets out a long, low grunt, unfolds his arms and mutters something about not wanting to waste a perfectly good dinner special.

Thirty-One

I'VE BEEN IN THAT PLACE before, where a guy *assumes* that at my age I'd think nothing about tumbling in the sheets with my latest boyfriend. Why wouldn't they, really, when safe sex is as close as the nearest vending machine? But I've never felt like *this*. Like by standing my ground I've not only lost a boyfriend, but also a dear old friend in the process.

Dinner last night grew more torturous by the minute, the infliction of each blow alternating between our waitress's incessant cheeriness and Max's cold stares. If it had been anyone else glaring at me over the surf-and-turf special, well, I would have called it a night and phoned for a cab. I wanted to work this out, though, so I stayed.

Worthless call on my part. Max drove me home in silence, and I gladly fled from his truck, slamming the door for good measure, of course. Of all the things to make such a big snit about, sex just isn't high on my list. I decided long ago to wait for Mr. So Right to gaze into my eyes and say "I do" before I'd give away that final, intimate piece of myself, and I've stuck to that belief. It's as close a part of me as my fingernails, ragged as they may be at the moment.

Honestly, though, I thought I would have conquered the "two becoming one" moment long before this. Mercy! If I had known God would take so long to lead Mr. So Right to my bedroom door, would I have made such a commitment?

And that's really what this is all about, isn't it? Commitment, or lack thereof. I said much the same thing to Max last night at dinner. "You say you've always wondered why I never seem to have a steady boyfriend, Max? Well, I've wondered the same thing about you. Why doesn't Max Rispoli, handsome local businessman and eligible bachelor, ever seem to have a steady gal of his own? Could it be the C word, Maximilian?"

Okay, now that was snotty. And the more I think about it, the more ashamed I become. I've no idea what it must feel like to marry for life, only to lose that person long before old age shows up with its terry cloth bathrobe and saggy ankles. Maybe Max's heart has been too broken by the experience to even dare to love again.

Yet why do I keep getting the sinking feeling in my belly that if Max were to meet Ms. So Right, he'd take the dare—even if it meant abiding by her wishes when it came to sex?

A customer breezes into the shop, and I continue with my prep and puttering. Earlier today, I took out my very last cash advance. I know it's the last one because I've made a commitment to myself—oh, that word again—to stop living on credit. That and the small fact that I've maxed out my Visa. So when Cassandra comes marching in here today with her overpainted lips and equally offensive highly teased hair, I'll have a check ready for her. It buys me a month, and a lot can happen in thirty days. Am I right?

My other customer completes her window shopping and makes a hasty retreat to the donut shop next door. The door to my shop clicks open, again, and I paste on a smile.

The guy who strolls in reminds me of someone. Don't you hate that? Someone looks so familiar, like you may have even held a conversation with them at one time or another, but nope, you just can't remember them. Short curly hair, a teardrop-shaped goatee, a Member's Only jacket from another era. Nope, he rings a bell, but I'm still not recognizing the sound.

"How may I help you today?"

"You don't remember me, do you, Gaby?"

Okay, so how embarrassing is this? The man knows my name and I think, yes, I definitely think I recognize him, but yet I don't. Strange. "Please," I say, "remind me of your name."

"It's Eric."

"Eric, uh, Eric . . ."

"Briens."

"Summer's husband?" The husband of the chick who's suing me? Well. What a difference a couple of months make. Last time I saw him he was standing at the front of the church in military dress, his hair shorn, his right leg shaking like he'd just stuck it into a bucket of ice-cold champagne. I didn't stay for the entire event, but while I was there, I noticed how often the photographer's assistant had to mop up this groom's perspiring face.

"How ya doing?" he asks me.

"Oh, just peachy, Eric. How's the wife? How's married life?" I hear Bri's sarcasm in my tone, and I wish she were here with me now, helping me keep my temper in check. Or at least feeding the inner chocoholic in me with some of her homemade brownies—anything to make this day easier.

He stands there with his hands in his pockets, surveying the room. Deep breath in. Start fresh. "Eric," I say, stepping out from behind the counter, "please leave my shop. It's not yours. It will never be yours. I've already told Summer that. If you want something, you'll need to get ahold of your lawyer and ask him at the rate of three hundred bucks an hour."

All color drains from his face. "Summer threatened that, huh?" He hangs his head and shakes it before drawing his chin up and looking straight at me. "I didn't reenlist in the navy, and I think she's gone off the deep end. She thought she married a career military man, and now she's stuck with me." He smiles and shrugs, drawing an ounce of pity from me. "She's suing every Tom, Dick, and Harry involved in our wedding. Nice touch, don't you think?"

I shut my eyes. This world is filled with nasty people who strike out at others when they don't get their way. It's as if all of humanity is stuck in middle school. I open my eyes and see a guy whose own small world has just experienced a quake, and I wonder if he'll survive the jolt.

"So," I ask, "is this a new side to Summer, then?"

He smiles knowingly. "Touché. All right, I admit that she and I had some good times together, but beyond the physical, what did I really know about her?"

Maybe I should replace my florist sign with Marriage Counselor. "Well, then, Eric. Maybe it's time you find out."

Long after Summer's husband, Eric, showed up with his tale of woe, I found myself dwelling on my own beliefs surrounding marriage. Ask anyone who knows me, and they'd tell you that I've had more close calls with the altar than the *Runaway Bride*. How many of those men did I really know, though? Maybe I'm not guilty of experiencing passion without substance, like Eric and Summer, but I have been ready to settle down with men who seemed ideal at the time. The demise of those relationships has usually landed on their shoulders, but I'm beginning to think I owe these men my thanks.

My cell rings, and it's Bri.

"Hi."

"Hey," she says back. "You didn't call."

"Sorry."

"I talked with Max. Um, I baked you some brownies. Wanna come over after work?"

So this is it. Max is breaking up with me through Bri. "He tell you everything?"

"Pffst! Not exactly. What happened, girlfriend?"

"He wanted sex. I didn't. End of story."

"I'll kill him."

"That's against the law."

"I'm married to a good lawyer. He'll get me sprung, or else."

I giggle, but the emotion fades away. "Oh, Bri-Bri. I thought this was it!"

"You're not crying."

"I'm too busy to cry."

"Gaby, can I be honest here? I know you, and you're never too busy for tears. Maybe deep down you get it that Max, great guy that he is, isn't exactly your type."

"I hate it when you say that."

"Truth in love, baby! Seriously, I think Max has issues that go far deeper than either of us knows. Do you really want to have to deal with his issues?"

"You mean, when I have enough issues of my own?"

"I didn't say that. Forget this. Just get your bum over here and eat brownies with me. I'd come over there but Aunt Dot's wacky when she's without her meds. Well, she's wacky with them too, but anyway, she's due for more in an hour. So come. I've already consumed enough batter to support cocoa bean farmers in several Third World countries for the next week, but I'm always willing to do more for a good cause."

Most days, the yes would come flying out of my mouth with no thought given to it. I'd just say yes and head on over to my best friend's beach pad ready for some serious chocolate feasting. But this supposed ending to the dream of Max and me has drained the energy and life right out of me and, simply put, I can't go.

"Sorry, Bri-Bri. Too much to do tonight. Save some for me, will you?"

She doesn't say anything right away, and then, "You don't even have time for one nibble?"

"Sorry . . . but thanks for the thought."

"Gaby? Um, I'm freaking about you right now. You don't even sound normal. I think I could get away for a little while if . . ."

I shake my head, my eyes taking in the empty shop. "Really, I'm good. Take care of that lovable family of yours and call me on the weekend, okay?"

She gives an exasperated sigh before signing off. "'Kay."

I begin the closing down process of my shop, aware for the first time ever that even best friends can't solve everything.

Thirty-Two

KIT DIVIDES THE WATERS IN her single kayak, gliding up to the edge of Jake's dock.

"You ready?" she calls.

It's early, but I've dragged myself out onto this chilly dock in hopes of silencing my confused and cluttered heart. If I hadn't promised Kit I'd be here waiting at this wee morning hour, then I'd be upstairs, burrowed beneath my borrowed blanket. Moving here was supposed to cheer me up, to help me forget about my employee's thievery and the loss of my home—and in some ways it has. In other ways though, like say, in relationships, I'm flailing like a churned-up crustacean.

"I guess so."

She tosses me a dirty orange life vest. "Put that on so you don't die."

I slip it over my head, silently praying that it's spider free. As I do, Kit ties up her boat and hops onto the dock in a pair of flip-flops with big chunks of rubber missing. "Getting in can be a mess. It's easier on sand. I'll hold on to the end while you climb in."

"How do I do that?"

She scowls. "Bend your knees."

I step closer to the side of the dock, shivers overtaking me in the nippy morning air. Or maybe it's the closeness of really deep water (containing real sea creatures) that's got me shaking so hard. One step off the dock and I could be face-to-face with Sweet Thing. I snort at the thought.

"What's so funny?"

"Oh, nothing."

"So, get in already."

I squat and lower one leg into the kayak, quickly realizing I've no idea what I'm doing, and I pull it back out. I turn around, and try with the other leg. Just as unnerving. I stand, straighten up and stare down into my boat's empty seat.

"Staring at it won't put you in it. Basic physics."

Deep breath in. Start fresh.

I lower my rear to the dock, put one foot in the boat, steady myself, and then put in the other. With both arms bent behind me, I scooch myself up off the dock and plop myself with an unwieldy *phwat* into Jake's kayak. From what I can tell, I only garnered one splinter in my rump.

Kit stands, her voice its usual sarcastic self. She hands me my paddle. "Wasn't pretty, but you're in there. Hang on. I'll be around in a minute."

For a girl whose main goal in life appears to be avoiding her mother, Kit treats me well. So she's sarcastic and lacks a dazzling smile? Some might even say that those characteristics alone qualify her to be called a teenager.

Deftly, she climbs into her own boat and grabs her paddle.

"Aren't you going to teach me to use this thing?"

She rolls her eyes. "It ain't hard. Just paddle." Kit shoves herself away from the dock and points herself toward the harbor mouth as if the boat's just another appendage.

I, on the other hand, try to use my paddle to shove away from the dock, but it slips beneath the old wooden surface instead, sending me nowhere.

"Try it again." Kit's voice sounds bored.

This time my shove sends me to the center of the channel. I dip my paddle in on the right, but not far enough and all I get is water on my lap.

"Try sticking the paddle in deeper."

I do, and my boat thrusts forward.

"Yeah, that's right. Now the other side."

Again, I dip the paddle into the water and give it a good, smooth pull backward, the motion having the opposite effect on my kayak. I keep it going, one side, then the other, then back again. There's a rhythm that I sense, my boat gliding forward, balanced and straight as I find my cadence with each pull, left then right.

She glides up beside me. "Follow me."

Wordlessly I do, my senses alert to the awesomeness of the rippling expanse of water we're heading into. We pass a blue heron, standing sentry-like at the edge of a dock, and I'm close enough to see the breeze flow through its feathers. In the distance, waves pound against the jetties that separate us from the open sea, churning up both trepidation and a surprising sensation of joy. I've never done anything so adventurous, yet frightening, all at the same time.

We make it to the center of the main channel when Kit lays her paddle on her lap and assesses me. "You're loving every minute of this, aren't you?"

I relax and let myself watch her despite my fear that any sudden movement may send me into the deep. When I watch Kit out here, she's not a lost teenager but a vibrant teacher, hopeful that her student is learning something new and worthwhile, even if I do look like a dork with this orange buoy around my neck. "*Sí*—I do love this. I never thought I'd be kayaking. . . ."

"Yeah, well you're a natural. Adults are usually so wimpy! I'm proud of you." She's looking pretty proud of herself too. "I think you could make it to the other side of the mouth."

I freeze. "I . . . I don't know."

Her shoulders slump and that familiar flat expression sullies her face again.

I paste on a grin. "Why not?"

She turns her boat toward the open ocean and I follow, trying hard not to wear away the inside of my cheek as I chew it nervously. Left pull, right pull, left pull, right pull. Despite surface ripples on the water, I'm finding this easier and more relaxing than I thought. Except when I see a sailboat the size of a small island navigating the turn with us.

I suck in air and puff it back out.

"Stay calm. You're not really gonna die today, Gaby," Kit says as she slows up next to me. "Not that I know anyway."

"Thanks for the calming words."

"Don't mention it."

After the yacht passes, the water's clear and it's just the two of us, bobbing along like toy ships in one enormous bathtub. "So what do your parents think about you being out here so often?"

Kit blows a raspberry.

"They do know you're out here, right?"

Her jaw clenches, her eyes shift toward me, then she shrugs. "My mom doesn't care. She'd never try it herself, but she couldn't care less that I'm out. And my dad doesn't know."

"How come?"

"How come what?"

I sigh. "Why doesn't your dad know? Or is he just a late sleeper?"

Kit looks at me like I've got seaweed on my head. "My parents are divorced. Didn't you know that?"

Divorced? So this is why I've never seen him around. . . . I take a breath. "No, Kit. Sorry, but I didn't know that about your parents.

Did this happen recently?" Like, say, in the past few weeks, because Iris told me she lived in the fourplex *with her husband and daughter.*

"Ch-yeah."

"Oh. It did?"

Again, she looks at me like I've lost it. "Oh, snap. That meant 'no.' My parents have been legally separated for a long time. They just decided to make it final."

"I'm sorry."

"Ch-yeah. Whatever." Kit spins her kayak around. "Let's go back."

A cascade of guilty relief drenches me. Maybe Iris wasn't married when she and Jake, apparently, had a fling. A small consolation, but one just the same. Makes me wonder about her recent blog post, though. Were the dire words in that post an attempt to reach out to others? Or is that how Iris herself really feels?

Kit digs her paddles into the water and strokes side to side. I surprise myself by how quickly I can turn and dart after her; unfortunately, I'm so intent on keeping up with her that I get no forewarning of Willy coming up from behind.

Until the wave of seawater hits me like an icy shower.

Kit screams. "Willy, you are such a loser!"

I gasp, trying to force warm air into my lungs. Otherwise I'd be screaming too.

Willy cranks his engine down and cackles. "Hey, ladies. What's shakin'? You shoulda seen the looks on your faces. S-weet!"

He's too busy cackling and holding his side to see the shovel-sized launch of water that Kit sends flying into his boat.

"Hey!"

"Don't mess with me, Willy!"

He wipes water from his face with his hand, barely hiding a grin. Me thinks the boy's in love. "You know you love it," he says, quietly. When he talks to her, the corners of his mouth flash upward.

Kit glares at him.

I'm cold and feeling the letdown of Kit's troubles on my shoulders. "Sorry to end the party, guys, but I need to get to work. How will I ever thank you, Willy, for saving me shower time today?"

Red creeps into his cheeks. "Sorry about that."

Sure you are. "Hey, it's part of the adventure, I guess. You're going to have to do more to convince Kit that you're sorry, though." The shy glances between them, despite Kit's anger of a moment ago, make me laugh again.

Kit shifts her attention to me. "C'mon. I'll get you back."

What am I, a horse?

I'm glad when I finally glide up to the dock. Not only are my yoga pants soaked (all I had to wear), but I've got a blister the size of a pebble growing on my right thumb. Every time water trickles onto it, I shiver.

A booming voice jerks my attention away from tying up the boat and almost sends me into the drink. "So I guess I'll be canceling that call I have into the cops." Jake is standing on the deck, leaning over the handrail and watching me, making me oh so aware of my wet bum.

I straighten. "Hi. You're still here. And why'd you call the cops?"

"Thought someone stole my boat."

Slowly, I lift Kit's lumpy lifejacket off my shoulders, trying not to catch my hair in its straps. "And why would you think that?"

"Just hadn't thought of you as the water sports type. So when I saw it was gone, I figured some kid had run off with it."

I squint up at him and see a twitch in his grin. And that dimple staring back at me. "You're such a liar."

He feigns a gasp. "You shock me, Gaby. I never would have thought I'd hear such words come out of that pretty mouth."

Kit's lips stay straight and flat, but I see her eyes dance, even though she keeps them focused on the task before us. And you know what? Maybe she's right. I am attracted to the man, but as I've learned, it takes more than that basic instinct to make for a great relationship. Guess Max realizes that now too.

Anyway, I sense Jake's presence just as strongly as the gust of wind encircling me as I climb the ramp. I close my eyes briefly against the breeze, remembering his heated conversation with Iris and also reminding myself of my own tender heart. The one that regularly falls for the wrong man.

Jake meets me at the top of the ramp. "Guess you owe me now."

I'm speechless. I don't know whether he's being serious here, although I suspect that he is not, or if there's a touch of truth to what he says. "I'll send you some flowers."

Something that looks much like pity passes in his eyes. "I was thinking more along the lines of dinner."

I laugh tightly. "You want me to make you dinner?"

"Actually, I'd like you to join me in hosting a dinner party I've been thinking of having here. I'll do the cooking, of course."

My stomach sinks. I knew there had to be a catch when he asked me to stick around despite my inability to pay the rent. Did he hook Iris this way too? Or was it the other way around?

I brush my gaze across his face, avoiding a connection. Stall, Gaby, stall. "I'll have to get back to you. Okay, Jake?" I turn and dash up to the loft.

Thirty-Three

I SKETCH FOR HALF AN hour and then drive to work—all the while praying that new customers would find my little shop today and be compelled to drop large amounts of discretionary income into my till. Not only would an influx of dollars help me wipe out my mounting debt and keep Florally Yours afloat, but it would provide me with a quick way of moving out of Jake's loft.

My mind wanders to the images that appeared on the page as I sketched this morning. No matter how I tried to shade less and highlight more, and even though I tried to think "happy" thoughts while drawing, the resulting product may have been the darkest thing I've ever done. So much for the healing power of art.

My heels click across the cement floor of the shop, and I dump my things onto the counter. There's a chill inside, but turning up the heat costs money and I've got to cut somewhere, you know? Besides, if it gets cold enough I could always use the shop itself for floral refrigeration.

My eyes take inventory of my floral supplies. Let me just ask—how can I be a successful florist and run out of wire and bear grass? My oasis foam supply has dwindled too, not to mention the rather uninspired choices of color within my stock of fresh flowers. I sigh. My head's just not in this game anymore. Thankfully, the phone interrupts my musings from the dark side.

"Gaby? Rudy here."

Air catches in my throat. Rudy has never called the shop before. "Is it Mama?"

"Yes, but I didn't say so."

I wind the phone's coiled cord around and around my forefinger. "What's wrong with her?"

"She not good, but she be mad as a tick for me saying so. Your mama miss coming to the stand today. She never miss coming to the stand. Don't tell her I call you."

Just how am I supposed to avoid that? "Is it . . . something serious?"

"She say she's tired, so maybe that's all. I don't know. I just thought I should tell you."

Deep breath in. Start fresh. I tamp down my fears. "Okay. What's happening to her stock, Rudy?" I know this would be important to Mama.

"I'm here, and I'm trying to sell, but your mama has her ways." That's the truth. Mama could sell her designs to a grower with acres of flowers in full bloom right on his own land.

A mere cold has never stopped her from her work, though, and the tightening of panic rises in my throat. "I'll call her, Rudy."

"Ah, Mija, no. She'll cut off Rudy's neck."

The old saying of his deflates my rising panic and I almost laugh. "You'll grow another one, I'm sure."

"Tell her you made me call, yes?"

I promise him, and dial up Mama, picturing her finely penciled eyebrow morphing into a pointed arrow with each ring of her apartment phone.

"*¿Bueno?*"

"Mama, it's me."

"Aww-ah! That Rudy! I cut off his neck next time I see his face."

"Oh, you will not."

"Did he say I'm sick? I'm just tired, Gabrielle. Everybody gets tired sometimes. I don't know why he makes such a big noise about it!"

My finger slips out from under the phone's coiled cord, and I rub the white indentations it made. My mind jumps backward then, to the last time I saw Mama, her hand trembling and twitching. That sinking feeling comes back. "I'd like to come visit you, Mama. Maybe bring you some soup or something."

"No, I'm going to sleep. You stay and work hard. You have a business to run, and you should not forget that."

"Yes, well, maybe I care more about you than my business, Mama."

"That's crazy talking. No. You stay there. You might be missing something if you go. Whatever you do, don't leave when you should be staying."

A stray thought crowds its way into my head. Other than the obvious reason of making enough money to live, why do I stay here? I remember wondering the same thing about my mama around the time I was ten. I whined about having to swelter the day away during the hottest month of the year. It was July and I wanted to be swimming with my friend Gigi at the Y, but Mama wanted me with her, so I made her pay with my sour attitude and constant grumbling.

In a flash, I see her onyx hair sprayed still, the blush of her cheeks, the inky black of those perfect eyebrows. Her eyes sparkled in that bitter sun, and I remember wondering why she watched the road so much that day. As the day wore on, though, my whining grew louder, and Mama's eyes dimmed considerably. Finally, she gave old Rudy (I thought he was old even then) permission to take me to the Y to meet up with Gigi's family.

I shake away the memory. "Mama, I'll stay if you promise to call me if you're not feeling better in a day. Do you promise?"

"I will feel better. Trust me."

"That's not what I asked. Please say you'll call me with an update on how you're feeling, or I will close my shop right now and come right over there with chicken soup and tortillas."

"Aww-ah! Okay, I'll call you. Is that what you want, Gabrielle?"

It's better than nothing. "Thank you, Mama. I'll talk with you tomorrow—or else."

Because I'd promised to stay put, I keep the shop open, but only until the stroke of five. After closing up, I walk down the street to Truffles by the Sea, splurge on a couple of raspberry- and rum-flavored truffles, and drive home.

Daylight savings time has begun, and thank goodness for that. To be able to come home and know there's enough sun to last for hours makes working all day all the more satisfying. Shonda doesn't look up as I drive past her vine-covered home, and Meredith jogs toward the beach, her running bra soaked in sweat, her eyes fixed straight ahead. I'm relieved to see Jake's truck gone, and so, after changing into some clingy, soft sweats and a hoodie, I escape to the back deck.

I lean against the rail and breathe in the salty air, which in my opinion is better than a prescription sinus drug any day. With eyes lolling shut, I think about Mama and convince myself there's nothing to be worried about. I would have driven over to see her, but what would that accomplish other than incurring her acute disapproval?

Seagulls twitter overhead, and when my eyes flop back open, I spy yet another hill of seashells on the edge of my dock. Carefully, I crane my neck, searching other docks in the area for a similar gift. I see none. So with curiosity in each step, I pad on down the ramp just in time to see Sweet Thing pop up through the waters just a yard or so away.

I stick a fist in my side. "Have you been bringing me these gifts?"

She stares at me with eyes like glassy marbles, and I wonder about the possibility of my bacon-loving sea lion friend collecting treasures from the sea and depositing them in the same spot each day on my dock. Kind of like dogs bringing their owners a bone, don't you think?

I fold myself onto the dock and scoop up the shells, exploring their intricate designs. They clink together in my hand, and I settle down as Sweet Thing begins to swim in smooth, oblong circles in front of me. As she does, my shoulders relax and giggles rise up unprovoked. The only thing missing is the bag of truffles I left upstairs.

For the next hour, as the sun shoots streaks of pinkish red into the sky, I allow my mind to meander aimlessly through a lifetime of thoughts. I realize that all this before me is temporal. I'm just a hitchhiker in this ritzy neighborhood, and it can't last forever. One of these days, I fear, my business will close, I'll have to accept a lifetime of singleness—there's no crime in that, after all—and the unspoken thoughts that have lain between my mother and me all these years will have their day in the sun.

A rustling to my left alerts me that someone has stepped out onto Sarah's deck. I glance up. "Sarah?"

We catch eyes with each other, but she turns abruptly, her face shaken.

I uncross my legs and stand. "I was going to ask you about these shells." I hold them up for her to see, but I find tears on her face. "Are you okay?"

She rocks back and forth on her heels, her mouth open, but says nothing. I dart up the ramp and over to the fence. "What is it? Let me help you."

She licks her lips and rubs them together, her eyelids drawn with worry, her eyes darting all around. "I don't know what to do. I . . . I tried to help him, but he says he's going to . . . oh no." She whispers those last words in anguish.

I reach out for her across the rickety fence, spilling shells everywhere. "Who's going to do what? You look so upset. What can I do to help?"

Her eyes widen as she stares at me head on, as if seeing me for the first time ever. In the light, I see how white she is—although she's usually wearing so much makeup, maybe this is her true color. Yet she looks stricken.

"Sarah?"

"Oh no, oh no." Her tears rush forth and all I can think to do is stand here and pat her shoulder. "I . . . feel . . . so . . . helpless!"

Gently, I pull at the tattered fence until one end pops out of its already decaying post making a way for me to step across the dividing line between Sarah's home and Jake's. I place an arm around her and guide her to sit in an Adirondack chair. I pull up close in the one next to hers. "If you could just tell me, maybe we could put our heads together and figure this out." *Jesus, help me help her.*

She hiccups quietly. "A man just told me he was about to commit suicide—and I couldn't do a thing to stop him."

Oh. My. I start to rise and then lower myself again. "Have you called 9-1-1?"

She sucks in a breath. "How could I do that? I don't even know him."

"Then how do you know he'd do that to himself? Maybe it was a prank."

She drops her head back. "You don't understand. He's been calling me for weeks. I thought I'd helped him, really helped him, but this time he was rambling and I could barely understand him. It was like he hadn't remembered a thing we'd talked about."

"Can I ask . . . who is he?"

Her head shakes back and forth like she has tremors. "M-my number's similar to a psychiatrist's number, and he called it by accident a few months ago."

"Months?"

"Uh-huh. Sometimes people call me by accident, and I just give them the right number. But Ainsley seemed to get better when we talked. He decided that he liked calling me and, I don't know, I liked him too and wanted to help him, so I just let him talk. I know it was a stupid thing to do, and now he's, he's in such trouble." Deep pink rims her hazel eyes. "He just called a few minutes ago, and I couldn't get him to stay on the line."

"No caller I.D.?"

"I don't believe in that. People should have their privacy."

"Did you press star-6-9?"

"What would that do?"

"It automatically dials back the last person who called you."

Sarah's eyes widen and she darts from the Adirondack chair. I follow her inside and watch her dial, her foot tapping uncontrollably.

Thirty-Four

I DIDN'T WAIT FOR SARAH to reach Ainsley by phone. Instead, I ran back inside Jake's house, taking the stairs to my loft a few at a time, promising myself with each step to buy a gym membership the very day that my ship decides to come in.

I'm nearly back outside when Jake lays a solid hand on my shoulder. "Ack!" I fall into him, my pulse beating furiously, the blend of exercise and fright sending my heart rate far beyond its target. "You've got to stop doing that, Jake! I didn't know you were home!"

"Where you going so fast?"

I grab his sleeve. "Come on."

Together we race outside, cross the now-invisible dividing line between his and Sarah's, and dash inside her home, knowing that we'll most likely find her upstairs next to the north-facing window, the one I often see her silhouetted against. In the midst of her living room, though, I halt.

Jake nearly bowls me over. "Whoa, careful. You're such a petite little thing; I could flatten you."

I shake my head. Is that the best he can do? I bat away his attempt at flirtation. "Look at this place. How do we get upstairs?"

Jake's eyes widen as he scans the room. I watch his face as he takes in the cases of porcelain dolls, the mountains of animals clothed in cashmere-softness, the life-sized Batman statue leaned up against a curio cabinet. Shock and awe takes on a whole new meaning in this place.

His eyes meet mine, and he takes my hand. Gingerly, we step over various piles of toys until we reach the stairs. Jake turns to me. "Why are we here again?"

I take the lead and drag him up the stairs. "Sarah thinks someone she knows is suicidal. She's upset. I thought I—we—could help."

His expression sobers, and he follows me without another word. When we reach Sarah, she's sobbing into the phone, and so I slip an arm around her shoulder. Jake takes the cell from my hand and flips it open, poised to call 9-1-1. We listen as Sarah begs Ainsley to tell her where he is, and then try to memorize the vague descriptions she manages to pry from him. The anguish in her voice does a number on my stomach, but it's my heart that takes the piercing when finally, after so many tension-filled minutes tick by, I hear her cry out, "But I love you, Ainsley. I thought you loved me back."

"There but for the grace of God go I." My pastor once told our congregation how Protestant Reformer John Bradford uttered those words from his prison window while watching another prisoner being led away to his death. Ironically, he later met that same end.

I'm thinking of this in the aftermath of learning how hard poor Sarah had fallen for a man who not only lied about his suicidal state, but about his love for her as well. What is it about some women—okay, women like Sarah and me—who regularly bestow our affections on those so terribly unworthy of them?

I toss another chip of wood from Jake's disintegrating deck into the channel, and the current carries it swiftly away. It's early morning, and the longer I live the more I appreciate this time of day. Night is for the bad stuff, it seems, and last evening had doozy-like qualities graffitied all over it. I toss another chip westward, but it hits the side of Jake's kayak before sliding downward into the water's silkiness.

I'm not sure what compels me to step into Jake's kayak, without a life jacket or towel, but in a blur, I do. Only one lesson behind me, and yet I head out and paddle like an expert, pulling my way through the water toward the main channel. A fisherman laden down with gear in a rubber boat chugs past, tipping his head in my direction. The world's a dour place sometimes, but out here on the water, I see contentment all around.

This thought drives me as I pull against the tide, left, right, left, right. The cadence in paddling lulls me into a sense of confidence, and with each pull I feel stronger and more ready to follow the current as far as my breath will take me.

I paddle slowly around the harbor mouth, watching early-morning sailors head out to sea while reliving the late hours with Sarah and the sobs that wracked her body as she burrowed her tearful face into my shoulder. As it turns out, "Ainsley" was a college student pulling a prank. If it weren't for the sudden appearance of his dorm monitor, who knows when Sarah would have learned the truth?

Jake surprised us both by quietly slipping out of the house and cooking up a late-night comfort meal of chocolate pudding and homemade whipped cream. A nice touch, I thought, especially for a man with a reputation for doling out his share of heartaches. And yet another reason why I can't get you out of my head, Jake McGowan.

A pelican jets along, inches from the water, startling me. I slow. "I'm hungry too, mister," I call out to the foraging bird. I lay the paddle across my lap and watch him glide effortlessly, his beak aiming at the waters just brimming with breakfast.

A sailboat cruises toward me, and although I'm aware of how tiny Jake's kayak must look in these waters, I'm not afraid. The captain skillfully turns his rig in plenty of time, sends me a friendly nod, and heads out to sea. My boat bounces in his wake, sending a newfound thrill through me. Who would've ever thought that Gaby-girl could be such an adventurer?

On that note, I grab my paddle and dig in, intent on making it out to the area that's been affectionately dubbed Mom's Beach. That's the beach Bri first dragged me to when her son, Nathan, was just a little guy. It's set in a cove surrounded by jetties, with no waves and plenty of ab-ripped lifeguards. And let me just say right now, she got no argument from me.

I sense the waters begin to agitate. As my boat makes its way through waters less protected from the open sea, splashes of cold water chill me. I can't actually see Mom's Beach yet, but I know it's not too far. Just around the bend, as Rudy used to say when he'd drive me long distances in his lumbering golf cart. Skiffs and powerboats motor past me, kicking momentum into the choppy waters and sending their wakes to pound up and over the side of my boat. A chick wearing a bikini-thong stands very Kate Winslet-ish at the bow of one particular yacht, sending an arc of water my way. Kind of early in the day, don't you think?

"Gah!" That last splash chilled me to my core, and for the first time since grabbing my paddle, I second-guess myself.

Yet it's too late to turn back. I'm halfway across the channel now and can see the opening between the jetties. Okay, I can barely see it, but it's there in view, so how can I not go for it? Easy, easy, easy! From where I'm getting this sudden burst of adventure, I do not know.

I rock on, crossing the channel's width, vaguely aware that my biceps have begun to tremble. I'm reminded of the last time I saw Mama, her hands visibly twitching as she handed change to a customer. Could her recent bout of fatigue have been related to something more serious? Heaviness fills my chest, and I sense myself reaching for every breath. With each dig of the paddle, I look up, expecting to be that much closer to Mom's Beach, but why does it feel like I'm drifting farther away?

I drop my head like that hungry pelican and dig in, playing a little game with myself. I won't focus on where I'm going for at least ten strokes, I decide, hoping that when I do finally look up and see the beach's welcoming sand, I'll feel relief wash over me at its closeness.

One, two, three, breathe, breathe, breathe. I slow, determined not to lift my head. *Four, five, six, breathe, breathe, breathe.* Almost there, I grip the paddle tighter, aware of the blisters that have formed on both thumbs and the sharp chills that accompany them. *Seven, breathe, eight, breathe, nine, big breath in.* I look up. Somehow, I've drifted sideways. The beach is no closer, and that sinking sense in my stomach has returned along with larger waves that toss up frigid wetness into my lap.

I sit bobbing and drifting and out of breath. The morning breeze sends shivers over my wet arms and couldn't I have thought of something a little less flimsy to wear? More boats join the parade out to sea, and I'm quickly becoming dwarfed by the onslaught. I twist around to figure out just how many boats are heading toward me, but the action causes my boat to wiggle uncomfortably in the choppy sea.

Deep breath in. Start fresh. With every bit of strength I still have, I pick up my paddle, turn the kayak toward the south jetty and dig in. *Right . . . left . . . right . . . argh . . . left.* I'm close enough to see the crabs scuttling between the rocky crevices when a rogue wave makes a sneak attack from the north. I gasp as my boat lurches forward, and in an impressive one-two punch, a tumult of seawater drenches me from behind.

I'm wet. I'm exhausted. And the salt water that stings my eyes makes it difficult to see. Between the call of seagulls all around, and the clang of shroud against mast, I start to think I'm hearing things. *Gaby . . . Gaby . . .* Again, the wake from a passing boat sloshes me toward the rocks. I reach my paddle out to stop myself from slamming against the man-made barrier, when I think I hear my name again. *Gaby!* I'm cold. I'm so tired. The blister on my right thumb has burst, the wound stinging with each wash of the salt-laden sea. In a flash I thank God Mama let me learn to swim at the Y. ¡Muchas gracias! I've got my paddle wedged between two rocks, hoping that I'm strong enough to keep my boat from bashing against the south jetty, when I feel the back end lift up ever so slightly.

I brace myself to slam against the rocks, but nothing happens.

"Gaby!"

I dare to swivel around, just enough to find Andy straddling a surfboard behind me. My mouth opens and shuts.

"Did you bring some line?"

I shake my head hard. Water splashes over both of us.

He points to a rubber seal. "Check inside the hatch. I've got ya."

I lay the paddle carefully on my lap, and twist around enough to peel open the hatch. Inside there's a coil of fraying rope, and I reach for it. But when I do, my only paddle slips off of my lap and into the deep waters.

Andy's mouth jerks. "Grab the paddle. Grab it!"

It's drifting away, sinking on one end as I stretch my arm toward it while hanging on with the other.

"Can ya get it?"

"I'm trying . . ." I stretch just that much more, when my balance snaps. I pull my arm in, wobble twice, but it's not enough to right myself, and my entire body flips solidly into the choppy, frigid waters below.

Thirty-Five

I WILL NEVER FORGIVE RUDY'S son Junior for making me sit through *Jaws* when I was twelve. The only thing I need to surface at the moment is some optimism. As my kayak continues to jostle and crest in the gathering waves while I hang on by a thin fabric strap, my mind flips through its internal Rolodex until it lands on the words I need. *"Do not be terrified! The Lord your God will be with you!"* That's what I'm talkin' about. I need those scriptural sentiments right now because something soft and slithery just wrapped itself around my calf before gliding away. *¿Eres tu?, Sweet Thing?*

"Grab the rope!" Andy calls out to me, and right now, he's my knight in shining neon shorts. He straddles his board while trapping my upside-down kayak against the rocks, and throws me a line to which I cling with abandon. With the strength of Samson and the speed of Apolo Anton Ohno, he heaves me onto his surfboard, while I simultaneously kiss my lingering dignity good-bye.

I hug the wax-pocked board, heaving air and spewing salt water through my teeth, as Andy dives into the surf and flips my kayak over with a thud. I glance around, but the only boats in view now are those that have long since passed through the harbor mouth and entered the open sea. And forgive my clichéd response, but we're up a creek without a paddle. Am I right?

"Andy? What are you going to do?"

"I'm gonna tow you."

Gah! I lay there watching him. Andy's got an amazingly boyish face, and he wears his hair closely clipped like Justin Timberlake. The sting of regret makes me ache as I realize how very, very kind he is. I clear my throat, which has begun to feel raspy. "I could climb up those rocks behind you and wait."

He doesn't look at me while hurriedly tightening the knot on the line that connects his surfboard to Jake's kayak, but the creases in his cheeks deepen against the strain. "I got this. Ya gotta trust me, Gaby. Besides, it'd be hard for you to hang on to this boat until I could get back to you. There." He slaps the kayak. "You're good to go. I'll help you aboard."

To say that my climbing from the surfboard and into Jake's kayak felt awkward would be to downplay the word's very meaning. I creep forward on my knees, trying to ignore the rawness of my skin, to the kayak that Andy continues to hold steady as he treads beneath it. Carefully—and clumsily, I might add—I bumble my way back into my boat and just lie there on my back.

Never has the unending sky enthralled me so.

I pull my gaze away from the expanse above just long enough to watch Andy adeptly heave himself onto his board, flop to his stomach, and begin paddling us out of the choppy waters. I lie back down and bob along behind him like a red-faced, overzealous injured skier strapped onto a gurney.

It's the mother of all lectures. Jake glares at me, his skin blotchy and red, though I can barely see it beneath all that stubble.

"Where's your sense? You could've been killed!"

I shrug, knowing he's right. But who made him my father?

He throws a beefy hand to his head and rakes it through his mess of wavy hair. "When I saw that boat gone, and all those ripples on the water, I thought . . ."

"*¿Qué?!* What did you think?"

Pain-filled eyes search mine before hardening into a stare. "I thought you were incredibly irresponsible."

"Oh, really?" I cinch my beach towel tighter around me. "Did you not tell me that I had access to your kayak? Or did you imply to take that right away after I confessed that I could no longer pay the rent? Because you never actually told me there was a catch."

He throws up both hands. "Fine, Gaby. Don't let people care about you. That's obviously what you want. I, for one, am glad that Andy happened to be as concerned as I was about your safety—or lack of. But, hey, that's the kind of guy I am. You go on and be Miss Independent, but be warned, you may not be as fortunate the next time."

I lick my lips, trying to send moisture into my parched mouth. "I've heard all about the kind of guy you are," I say quietly.

He looks away, a sarcastic smile, if you could call it that, parting his lips. He lets out a fat sigh. "You're so gullible."

"That's one thing that I most certainly am not."

"Is that right?"

"That's so right."

He huffs. "Let me ask you something. What did you think about Sarah when you moved in here?"

"Excuse me?" And just why am *I* being interrogated here?

"My bet is that Iris told you Sarah was a nutcase, and that you believed her."

I open my mouth and watch him in disbelief.

"I'd see you watching her from the deck, those intense eyebrows of yours shifting, and I'd wonder, Gaby. I'd wonder what was going on in that mind of yours. Your feelings seemed pretty obvious."

It takes strength to keep said eyebrow from darting northward after that statement. "Have you forgotten? I helped her last night. We both did."

"But you still thought she was crazy, didn't you? And how about Andy? What did Iris say about him?"

My eyes water. "Andy's my rescuer. I think he's one of the nicest men I've ever known. He went through a lot for me today, but even he didn't treat me the way you are right now."

"I'm just trying to point out, Gaby, how easy it is to mistake the truth for a lie. You've been shielding yourself from the people around you, and I just know Iris got to you. That's her MO, in case no one ever told you."

"You know what? Stop. Just stop. I think the problem you're having here is with Iris, not me. Maybe you need to examine whatever happened between the two of you—and from what I've heard, just about every other eligible woman in this city—before lashing out at me."

Okay, apparently, that did it. If ears truly could convey smoke, Jake's ears would be smoldering, and I'd be grabbing the canister of kitchen salt. Maybe I was a little too harsh. He doesn't say anything, and I can't stand the silence nor the incredible urge I have to grab both of his cheeks and kiss him square on the mouth.

Dear God, save me from myself.

Deep breath in. Start fresh. "I . . . I just meant that . . . I don't know what I meant, Jake. I'm sorry I took your kayak. I'm sorry I scared you and Andy. I . . . am . . . sorry!"

Jake stares out to the channel. "I just feel responsible for you somehow."

I walk toward the sliding door. "Well, don't. I'm not your daughter, Jake."

He flinches, and I slip into the house. I will not feel guilty for making a mistake. That man has no right to treat me as if I'm a stupid child. Especially when I long for him to think of me as a woman.

After a quick wash and toweling off, I smooth gel into my hair and fluff it up. I slip into my favorite cotton skirt, the one with large pink anthuriums splashed across it, a white tank, and sandals. There. No one would ever know that in the last twelve hours I've consoled a deceived neighbor, nearly drowned and had to be rescued, and had it out with my landlord. Although, can I really call him that when I'm not paying him anything for my room at the moment?

I'm late as usual, not to mention painfully raw, but I slip out of Jake's house quickly and quietly, and head for the shop. It's not as if I'll find a line of customers when I arrive. Minutes later, I pull into a spot just a few doors down and stride up the block, my flat heels making the sound of chickens scratching against the cement. I stick my key in the door, but it's already ajar. Has Sammy returned?

I peek inside. The overhead lights have been turned on, and an elderly woman hovers near my cooler. She doesn't look like a criminal. "Hello," I say, before actually stepping inside.

"Gaby?" Livi rushes toward me and pulls me in. "What . . . ? I can't believe you're here. You look . . . hmm . . . Gaby you look awful."

I jerk. "What do you mean, awful?" This is one of my favorite skirts!

She shakes her head and her forever ponytail swishes. "Are you okay? What are you doing here? Jake said you wouldn't be in, that . . ."

"Jake said!"

"Well, yeah. He called me and told me you got into some trouble in his kayak. He was really worried about you, Gaby."

My friend's face looks incredibly earnest. Her blue eyes search me up and down, presumably for signs of injury, and I've got the urge to poke her with my broken nails.

I spread my hands out in front of her. "Livi. I'm fine. I . . . I don't understand, though, why Jake called you."

"He didn't think you'd be able to open the shop today, so he called me. And you should know, Gaby, I'm always willing to drop what I'm doing to help you. I'm just so glad he was there to find you. That's so lucky!"

"Andy found me."

"Well, who do you think called Andy in the first place?"

I rub my forehead, aware of a coming headache. *Gaby-girl,* as Bri would say, *you've made such a mess of things.*

My lone customer steps toward us. "How much for the vase, dear?" Her voice sounds so tender and sweet that she could easily be Agnes's sister.

I open my mouth to give an answer, but Livi steps up and does so before I can. The elderly woman nods. "I'll take it. Do you wrap?"

Livi's on it. "We most certainly do! I will meet you at the counter." She turns to me then, and in a motherly tone says, "I'm sending you home to find yourself. Oops!" She laughs. "I mean, to pull yourself together. I will not take no for an answer, so go on."

She waves me away and turns toward the counter, intent on taking care of my first customer of the day—and closing the doors after my last. It seems that I've got no choice but to turn around and walk out the door.

Thirty-Six

I NEED BRI, AND IT'S just that simple. Okay, it's a little more complicated than that. I need Bri *and* a basket of her fresh-baked brownies, the only recipe my friend is truly qualified to whip up. *Sigh.* She's probably too busy carting Aunt Dot or Nathan around, or hosting a boat tour, to get involved in something so frivolous. But I *seriously* need her.

The only way I'm going to find her now, though, is if Ned takes a detour through the harbor mouth and into the open sea. Wouldn't her passengers, the ones hoping for a cruise along calm waters, just love that? I dig my toes into the sand and watch as a couple of surf dudes seesaw over a wave. Those guys have the life.

I've landed here after being unceremoniously sent away from my business. My own business! At midmorning, I'm ready for a nap, but I can't crawl back home, not after this morning's little adventure on the high seas. I cringe. I'm such an idiot, but must I admit it so readily? One thing I know: I won't be admitting that bit of self-deprecation to Jake anytime soon. The man's put a spell over me, I think. As I sit here on the beach just walking distance from my loft, in one of the most alluring places on earth, I can't erase the image of Jake's face twisted in emotion. Sort of a cross between anger and anguish, and although it pains me to admit this, he's beautiful when he's ticked.

But . . . our relationship, if you can call it that, has its limits. Except for his cooking, and the moments spent consoling Sarah together and my embarrassing morning rescue, this thing between us has to go away. *Thank you, Jesus.* I hug my knees and think instead about the relationship that had mattered to me most recently, and how we parted ways. Max hasn't called me in days, and guess what? I don't really care. Upsetting as that is to admit, I think my dreams about Max and his chocolaty-goodness eyes were just that: figments of my imagination.

One of the surf guys eases onto a nice wave. It looks like a steady one. He catches it, stands, rides for two seconds, and then *wham!,* he's underwater and his board flies over. I feel your pain, my friend. J. R. R. Tolkien once wrote, "Not all those that wander are lost." Not that I've ever actually finished anything by Tolkien. I just like that quote of his. And so I stand, dust the sand from my skirt and hands, and head off to who knows where in my decrepit yet trusty old Volvo.

At the first stoplight, though, I throw my arms around the cracked covering of my steering wheel, bury my head and briefly consider calling Bri. *Why me? Why me? Why . . . ?* When a horn blasts behind me, I snarl. How dare that driver interrupt my sniveling. I sit up and rotate my shoulders before depressing the gas pedal. I'm headed north on the 101 freeway, and if Bri were here with me right now, she'd have insisted on that anyway. With the aqua-infused ocean on my left, and sculptured foothills on my right, this drive is the very best direction for getting away from it all.

Too bad I only have enough gas to get away from some of it.

Sugarland's on the radio singing "Something More," a song about a woman who realizes there's got to be more to her life. And how apropos is this? I'm thirty-three; single, even though I've dated enough men to bring a football team back to LA; and living rent-free (because I'm broke and he's desperate) in seaside Romeo's third-floor loft. And have I mentioned that I only have three days left to pay the rent for my floral shop or I'll be evicted?

Lead singer Jennifer Nettles has just reached that point in the song when she decides to cut herself loose and follow her passion. The idea strikes a chord. Selling flowers? Is that my passion? Or is there something else?

The gas gauge needle drops lower, so I pull off the highway at the next exit, more depressed than ever. I haven't even left town yet. If this were a movie, my car would roll to a stop just outside a quaint church surrounded by oaks. There I'd find a kindly, aging pastor inside who'd offer me thoughtful, wise advice and then, with much joyful anticipation, send me out to turn my life around.

If only.

The holiest place around here is that historic cross planted atop the city's highest peak, the one I often think I can see from my third-story loft when I stand on my tiptoes and crane my neck. It was erected so that travelers could find the city's mission, and the coincidence isn't lost on me. I'm on a mission myself. So I make a quick turn up California Street, head toward city hall, and then climb the twisty hill that leads to Grant Park, where the cross rises beacon-like from the earth.

The climb, although it sucked more gas from my tank than a criminal siphoning from cars during an oil crisis, reveals a vista more expansive and clear than I've ever seen it. I can see all the way from Mandalay Shores on the left to points north of Ventura beach on my right, the ocean glimmering and shaking like unset, emerald Jell-O.

Despite the breeze, a flock of women mills about the rock wall that surrounds the cross, while others relax on beach towels and blankets on the grassy knoll. They look happy, like they're enjoying the world's best potluck with some of their closest friends. Instead of crashing their party, I step out of my car and over to the edge to take in the view. I'd rather be alone.

A woman breaks away from the group, climbs up the steps, and strolls toward me. Her face reminds me of my mother's—intense yet elegant. "Would you like to join us?"

I glance around. She must be talking to me because I'm the only one here.

She smiles. "I'm Amata. This is our quarterly support group for single mothers in the area—although not all the women are mothers. Just most of them. Anyway, a number of us treat them to a brunch of chocolate-feasting." She laughs, gently revealing several chins. "We brought some other foods too, but the chocolates have been the most popular."

"Nice to meet you, Amata. Thank you for the invitation, but I'm not a mother. I don't think I'd fit in. . . ." *And you really don't want my troubles and me joining you.*

"Oh, sure you would. Come join us so we can get to know you better. Do you have the time?"

Let me think. I nod. "Yes, I guess I do."

We walk together down the steps and to the lawn that's splayed out beneath the soaring cross, its thick, coarse surface mighty against the elements. Amata continues to talk. "It's hard enough to have young children in the house, let alone to do that on your own."

I nod, as if I understand, which I really don't, but I'm being nice.

Amata beams as she continues. "Many of these women don't have a father-figure for their child, so while they are here, some of the dads from church have taken their children over to the park off of Main for games and popsicles—they always love that."

Okay, now that's something I can understand. My father's been a mystery to me. Mama's always been evasive about him, and the few times I brought him up seemed to bring her intense pain. So early on, I learned to steer away from the subject of the man who helped bring me into this world.

But the questions remain.

A short woman with impeccably bobbed hair and a face full of freckles pops up from her spot on a fuzzy blanket and touches my elbow. "There's an extra seat next to me," she says. "I'm Jen."

Her earnest face draws me to sit cross-legged beside her. Far below us, the Pacific Surfliner, Amtrak's coastal train, rumbles and roars its way toward Santa Barbara.

Amata stands in the shade of the cross. "Ladies, thank you all for joining us this morning. It's been such a pleasure having you here. I hope you have enjoyed yourselves."

That last statement sounded more like a question, and the women laugh spontaneously.

"I'll say!"

"May I have a doggy bag?"

"Same time next month?"

"I'm not ready to leave."

Amata smiles and nods. "That's all right. You don't have to leave yet, not unless you'd like to, and of course, we're sending you all home with your own goodie bag of truffles, so no worries there."

Truffles!

She continues. "As is our tradition, we'd like to invite you to take communion with us before you go. It's purely up to you. If you'd like to join us, then please, get comfortable and we'll get started."

My face has just flushed as red as the inside of those cherry cordials. *Taking communion outside of church?*

Two women circulate, one with a tray of bread chunks, and the other with a bottle of grape juice. Jen leans toward me. "They use juice instead of wine, just in case wine bothers anyone." She giggles. "That wouldn't be me."

I bite my lip.

I watch as each woman takes a piece of bread and waits as her cup is filled with the juice. Everyday foods used in a sacred way. When all have been served, Amata stands and addresses us, and her genuine smile intrigues me. "The night before the Lord Jesus was betrayed, He took the bread." She holds up a ragged chunk of sourdough. "He blessed it and offered thanks and then said, 'This is my body, given for you.'"

Amata lays the bread in her palm and stares at it with a reverence that's anything but detached. A few seconds lapse before she looks up again, eyes shining. "Afterward, He took the cup and again offered thanks before sharing it with His disciples, and He told them, 'This is my life poured out for you, for the forgiveness of sins.'"

Except for a flap of wind that moves through, rustling various strands of hair, all around me is quiet as the women dip the bread into their cups.

Amata continues, "He asked His disciples, just as He is asking us, to do all of this in memory of Him."

Many of the women who only moments before had been chatting and laughing sit with eyes closed, as if savoring each morsel of the bread they are ingesting. I hesitate. Communion is important, but how many times have I sat in church and taken it with a remote spirit? My eyes rivet on the juice-soaked bread between my thumb and forefinger, my mind trying to wrap itself around the significance of the moment. I'm nestled into tall grass, taking communion with women I do not know, and somehow it doesn't feel weird, just tender and right. Eternal.

I continue to stare at the bread between my fingers, aware of soft prayers being said all around me. I close my eyes now and take the bread and juice, offering Him the only thing I can: myself. *Father, thank you for the bread that sustains me.*

A gentle hand rests on my shoulder, and despite the fear that had driven me north in the first place, a sense of calm blankets me for the first time in years. That and the surprise of elation.

I reach up to touch the hand on my shoulder but find nothing there other than my own flesh and bone. My eyes whip open, and the women near me continue to sit and pray quietly. Jen's eyes flutter open, and she smiles at me.

"Was that you?" I whisper.

"Was that me what?"

I glance around. "Did you touch my shoulder?"

She wags her head no and shrugs.

Huh.

Two knee joints crack as an older woman stands, a cue to the rest of us that the morning has ended. I watch as the women gather their purses and generous bags of chocolaty-goodness. They smile and laugh and hug, making me wonder what brought me here and why everything that has been so wrong suddenly feels so right.

Thirty-Seven

THE MINT-FILLED BONBON COOLS MY mouth as I lounge here, back on this familiar beach, and contemplate my next step. Something powerful happened to me in that impromptu communion service. Well, impromptu for me, anyway. It's not that I heard A Voice or watched a bush burn undamaged for hours, but there's a lingering sense of that guiding touch on my shoulder, and I can't let it go. The wave it sent over me was just too powerful to miss.

Only this wave is unlike the doubt that's been tossing me around lately.

With no fanfare, a familiar voice comes up from behind. "Penny for your thought."

I laugh and turn to find Bri walking barefoot in the sand. "I'll have you know that I have more than one thought in this head o' mine."

She plops down beside me. "Really? Then it has been a while since we've talked, hasn't it?"

I hug her. "What are you doing at my pity party?"

"Hey, you too? Maybe we oughta make it a big ol' wallowing bash."

"Tell me you brought them."

She snorts. "Of course. Only I didn't know I'd find you up here. Sheesh. Now I hafta share." Bri rifles around in her striped beach bag, the same one she's had for most of the time I've known her. "Here." She hands me a convoluted foil pouch.

"Wait. So you didn't know you'd be sharing and you brought all of these? What's going on, Bri-Bri?"

She huffs and looks out at the sea. "I don't know. Just been kind of depressed lately. Things aren't exactly as I thought they'd be at this point in my life."

"How so? Is it Aunt Dot?"

She slides me a sad smile. "Auntie's doing just fine."

"I thought she's been acting loopy. What about that?"

"Turns out we were right about it being the meds. She's such a healthy old soul that she rarely takes pills for anything. Not even an aspirin." Bri's shoulders rise and fall quickly. "She quit taking everything on her own, and now she's back to her usual self."

I cut in. "But leaving again."

Bri's a strong one, but she's wearing a glum expression. "Yeah. She is."

"Good thing you still have Nathan to mother, huh? Now he'll get you all to himself."

"I guess."

"There's more, isn't there? What else is bothering you?"

She makes swirls and scribbles in the sand. "It's been tougher than I thought it would be. Doug's new firm has taken up most of his time and money, and I don't know, I guess I just thought things would be easier at this point in our lives."

She talks as if she and Doug are at retirement age, instead of early thirties (her) and early forties (him). Bri drops back her head. "I'm thinking of renting out the spare bedroom."

"That bad?"

"Depends on who you ask. Doug's being optimistic, but I'm just nervous about the future."

This is not like her. Bri's usual devil-may-care-attitude has just taken a hit, and except for the blip in her judgment a few months ago when she allowed herself to believe that maybe Doug was straying, I'm not used to seeing her this way. Then again, it's amazing she's as stable as she is considering all the shuttling around she did as a child while her parents were flitting about and saving the world. Good thing Aunt Dot stuck around for her.

We sit in the breezy quiet. She seems lost in thought, and I'm beginning to sway beneath the activities of my own day, which pretty much covered the breadth of my life: physically, emotionally, and spiritually. And just how long can I keep my eyes open after all that?

Bri startles me by peeling back a strip of foil. "Here, let's get to it."

"Don't mind if I do. And here. You have to try one of these babies." I hold out the sack of truffles.

We continue to stare into the sea, but now we're doing it while savoring Bri's fudgy, irresistible brownies and a handful of holy truffles. It doesn't take long for us to become targets here on this beach, having already drawn the attention of seagulls and their ravenous appetites. One rather loud and portly bird put out the shrill call to his feathered buddies just a few seconds ago, and now they've encircled us as if we are prey.

Bri stomps her naked feet in the sand. "Scat!"

I giggle.

"What?"

"Isn't scat some kind of animal dung?"

Bri slaps my arm. "Ew! Who uses words like dung? Ga-ross!"

"Well, you're the one who said it!"

Bri scrunches up her face. "What is it you always say? *¡Basta!*"

I love it when she throws my own lame attempts at Spanish back at me. "Okay, okay, I hear you. Enough!"

"Not so fast. Why are you here? What about the shop?" She nabs my wrist until I look at her.

"Oh. My."

"What?"

My insides shake as I try to suppress my laughter. "You need a napkin."

She drags the back of her hand across her brownie-lined mouth, then licks her fingers one at a time, without apology. "Now. What's going on in your life? I hate that I don't know!"

Where exactly do I start? I slide a look sideways. "I nearly drowned this morning."

Bri's eyes grow wide.

"Okay, don't look at me that way, because it wasn't that bad. I decided to take out Jake's kayak early this morning when—"

"You on a kayak? Stop it."

"Are you going to let me tell you or are you not?"

She throws up both hands.

"Anyway, my neighbor Andy rescued me when I flipped out of the thing, but then Jake and I got into an argument about it. I don't understand him at all. Sometimes he treats me like a child. It's all very strange." And wonderful.

"So this is why you're here?"

I sigh. "Well, no. Oh, Bri-Bri, my business is out of money—I'm this close to being evicted." I press my fingers and thumb together. "Then of course there's the lawsuit, and I think my mama's ill but won't admit it, and my relationship with Max just sputtered, and I don't have enough money to pay my loft rent, but Jake asked me to stay anyway to keep an eye on his house. . . ."

"You're kidding."

"No, I'm not. There wasn't supposed to be a catch but, it's almost like he's watching me." Or something. I don't tell her how I'm beginning to feel about Jake's open displays of concern. "Anyway, I just can't afford to leave yet."

Bri straightens, and she becomes animated. "Stay with us. Aunt Dot's leaving in two days and you can move right in. The room's yours."

"Bri-Bri? You don't need another mouth to feed, and like I told you already, I can afford to pay very, very little."

"Forget it! You're my best friend—although I could slap you for not telling me all this sooner! You can make it up to me by moving in and letting me fuss over you."

I glance at her hopeful face and think, yes, that probably would make her happy. But what will it make me? And do I dare consider my happiness when I'm truly just a beggar these days? *I was a stranger and you invited me in.* Okay, so not exactly a stranger, but still. How can I deny Bri the opportunity to fulfill God's Word?

I flash my eyelashes at her. She loves that. "Bri-Bri, you're the best! You truly, truly are, but can you give me a few days to figure out what I'm going to do about Florally Yours first?"

"You really don't have the money for your rent?"

"Well, uh, no. But Livi's at the shop today, so who knows? Maybe her charms will bring in more than I ever could." Saying that gives me a strong déjà vu moment. "Her charm sells everything in this place." Rudy used to say that about mama, and was he ever right about that. I just don't know why she stays selling her wares from the side of a dirt road when she could've moved indoors long ago. That thought repeats inside my head. *Why does she continue to stay at the side of the road?*

"Gaby, did you hear me?"

I snap out of it. "Sorry, no."

Bri sighs a huffy sigh. "This isn't right. Ugh. There's just too much going on in your life right now for me not to have known about it. Too much, missy! So what are we gonna do about it?"

"For one, I'm going to stop being so gullible. Yes, I've said it before, and I've been trying, but look at me and Max. Everything was too perfect. He fixed up my car for free and invited me out for a few meals, and suddenly I'm trying to decide between traditional lilies or red roses for our wedding!"

"You're not that bad."

"Yes, I am. But that's okay, I'm finally figuring things out, and I just think maybe I need to get away from people in general, you know. It's obvious I can't pick a boyfriend. Or a landlord, for that matter; one burns down my apartment and the next one scolds me like a naughty child. Maybe it would be better if I found a nice desk job somewhere where the only person I'd have to communicate with would be an avatar named Valkarie."

Bri's eyes bore into mine. "Gabrielle. Just because you believe what you see in people doesn't mean you're gullible. It just means you need to dig deeper, and that takes time. So maybe you moved kinda fast with Max? Big deal. Better than not moving at all—which seems to be what you're suggesting." She plops another wad of brownie into her mouth. Not that this keeps her from continuing. "Believe me, Gaby," she mumbles. "Those people in your life who love you also sustain you. Don't shut out that kind of love."

Her words startle me in their familiarity.

Those people in your life who love you also sustain you.

Father, thank you for the bread that sustains me.

I let her words and those that I had prayed earlier in the day wash over me like the tide that's just washed upon the shore. Bri hands me another chunk of gooey brownie and I think, *Sustenance never tasted so good.*

Thirty-Eight

"SHE REQUESTED THAT YOU DO the flowers, Gaby."

My pastor's secretary is on the phone, after hours, rattling off details while I stand here, still taking in the news.

"She even set aside money for the arrangements. Now wasn't that thoughtful?"

I blow out a harsh breath. I just talked with her, didn't I? And when did she find time to plan her own funeral?

"Now it doesn't say here exactly what type of flowers she'd like, but I suppose you'll know what to do."

Of course I do. I glance out across the night sky and sigh. Agnes Trilly has died, and I have a job to do.

Pebbles and dirt rustle beneath the wheels of my car as I pull up in front of Mama's flower stand early the next morning. At first I see no sign of her and my heart drops. Maybe she's still sick. Maybe I should have driven straight to her duplex.

Then I see her. She's bent over a plastic tub and deadheading a bunch of spent alstroemeria blooms. Out with the old . . . I shut my door and step inside the tottering building, the air within its walls moist and weighty.

"Hi, Mama."

She turns around, holding her arms behind her back. "Mijita?"

"Are you feeling better?"

She scoffs and glances away. "That Rudy. It was just one day."

"Well, you look good to me, and I'm glad." Birds perched on the fragrant branches of neighboring orange trees fill the air around us with chirpy songs. Soothing sounds after a restless night. "Mama? I need to talk with you about something."

Her eyebrows shift up and down, and I sense that mine do the same maneuver. Weird. For some reason, my nerves flutter and I don't understand that. I'll never understand it. This is my mother, and I'm afraid to speak honestly to her.

Deep breath in. Start fresh. "Mama, I'm nearly broke. This is not easy for me to admit, but it's true. I've made a mess of things, and it's time to face it." My pride rises up to protest, but I give it a virtual slap and move on. "Anyway, I've tried to turn things around, but in my heart I realize that my efforts were not my best. Something's been missing."

"You should be there now. Preparing for your customers."

"Is that why you wait here day after day, Mama? Watching for customers to come by?" *Don't you want more from life?* I almost ask.

"Who is at your store?"

I sigh. I'm trying to reach out here, to face my mistakes, but maybe she just doesn't care to hear it. "Livi's there this morning, and thank God for her. She's such a great salesperson, she truly is. Thanks to her I'll be able to pay the rent tomorrow. But she has a career of her own, so I'm just not sure how much longer I'll last at this."

Mama touches her cheek with one hand. It trembles against her pillowy, honey skin, and when she sees that I notice, she drops it to her side. Inside, I too am trembling at the thought of what sort of illness is bringing this on—Parkinson's? MS? A stroke? Mentioning my fears, I've learned, will get me nowhere.

She's nonchalant. "What will you do?"

My eyebrows do that uncontrollable, shifty thing again. Do I tell her what I've been thinking? Won't she think me frivolous or lazy? Then again, the thought of something new dropped into my heart two days ago at that impromptu communion service at the cross, and I haven't been able to shake it away. I've turned it over in my mind, prayed about it, and even asked God to remove the desire, but nope, it's still emblazoned in my thoughts.

"I'd like to attend art school, Mama." You know, after I move in with Bri, sell the shop, and figure out how to pay for it all. "I've been doing some sketching, and it makes me feel peaceful."

Mama blinks rapidly and reaches one arm behind her, steadying herself against the scratched up counter.

I rush forward and wrap myself around her. "Mama, what's wrong? Let me take you to the doctor. Come on, let me help you."

She waves me away. "Gabrielle, stop." Her face cracks into a measured smile. "I'm not a baby, you know. You just made me surprised."

I swallow, not sure how to take that. Is she surprised because she doesn't believe I've got talent? Or that I can try something new after failing so miserably at running my own business? From age two, I figured I'd run a floral shop, just like Mama. Maybe she thinks I will change my mind and want to go back, and then it'll be too late. So I ask her, "Why does that surprise you?"

She rights her shoulders and stares into my eyes. "Your father was an artist. Constantly painting or making things with his hands." She waves her own hand into the air. "I wondered how long it would take for you to find your way."

Really? "And you didn't think this was something I should know?"

"Of course I did. I'm telling you now."

"I don't understand you, Mama."

"Even as a tiny one, *pequeña*, you went your own way. When I would say up, you would say down. I gave you the tools to draw when you were young and you were so good. I knew you had the artsy way in you, but then you said you wanted to do flowers. What could I say? It's a good living, so why not?" She looks toward the road. "I thought maybe someday you would see it as a means to your art."

Resentment rises in me. "Where is my father, Mama? You always clam up when I've asked. And please stop staring at that road!"

Mama turns back to me, and her eyes have turned red and glossy. Surprising, startling, not like her at all.

I'm having a light-bulb moment here and decide to go with it. "Mama?" I implore. "Are you, maybe, still watching for him?"

She holds eye contact with me. "Is that so wrong?"

I see her in a new way, my proud mama, usually so tough and level-headed. At this moment she's fragile, and precious, and so very human. She allows herself to fold into me. I'm stunned by her admission. Imagine her here, pining away for the one customer who's most unlikely to show. Not really sure what to say, I utter the simplest reply. "No, Mama. That's not so wrong." And I mean it, somehow.

After her brief bout of tears, she blows her nose on a paper towel from the counter and shrugs. "Your father doesn't know about you, Gabrielle. My father didn't like him, didn't think he was worthy—a lowly artist with stars in his eyes. Aww-ah! His father sold tractor parts but he didn't like it here in California, so he moved the whole family to Kansas or Oklahoma or somewhere else in the middle. I was never sure where they went. But Vlad liked it here, and I thought that someday he'd come back."

"As in Vladimir?"

She presses the wadded paper towel to her nose again, and honks like a wild goose. "He was prettier than his name, Mijita."

Now I'm the one who needs to sit down. "What about Vic, Mama? And Tom and Hal, for goodness' sake?"

She shrugs dramatically. "I loved them all. Well, all except that no-good Tom. But the others, I loved them. Or at least I liked them well enough."

I shake my head. "So you've waited here all this time."

She's finished with showing her emotions. I watch her turn and begin deadheading flowers that need it, and maybe some that don't. Both arms tremble as she works, but she ignores the obvious. The air's heavy with our silence, as I gather courage.

"Mama?"

"*Sí*, Gabrielle."

"My friend died yesterday."

"Bri?"

"No! An elderly friend who meant so much to me. Her name was Agnes, and she left behind a request that I handle the flower arrangements at her funeral. Will you help me today? I . . . I need you."

Mama doesn't skip a breath. "Of course. I will get my things."

"There's more."

Again with the eyebrow. "More?"

"I need you to take over running Florally Yours, not just to work for me like I've asked you to do in the past, but to actually manage the place. It needs your touch, Mama."

"And what would I do with this place?"

You mean this mold-stricken building that has more holes in it than a mesh bag? "Sell it. Or you could keep it and let Rudy and his wife and children run it. You can come back and check on it anytime you want or just ask Rudy how things are whenever he makes our deliveries."

She slows, and I think she may actually be considering my proposal. Her cadence isn't what it used to be, and as she straightens her back, her teeth bite down on her bottom lip, as if to redistribute the pain.

"I can't pay you much, but . . ."

She snorts.

"Bri has a room available. You could stay with her and her family."

"Me? With that beach girl? Aww-ah!"

"But she wouldn't even charge you."

Mama straightens fully and looks squarely at me. Instead of tears, her eyes sparkle as if reliving a joke. "What makes you think I can't pay?" Her chin juts forward.

I stutter. "Well, uh, I don't know. Selling flowers can be . . . I mean, it's been tough for me . . . I mean, how are you doing, Mama?"

Her face, often so stoic, opens with a wide grin and dancing eyes. "I can hold my own, Mijita. I have a mutual fund."

"So you convinced her?"

Bri just learned that my mama's going to be moving into her spare bedroom, and not me. That idea came quite suddenly while talking with her this afternoon, and I went for it, knowing that my best friend in the whole world wouldn't mind. So much for finding my way out of Jake's, though. I breathe a sigh of satisfaction. "Bri-Bri? I can't thank you enough for this. My mama's not well."

Bri cuts in. "But I thought you said she was her spunky self?"

Quickly, I move through my shop, wiping dirt and dust from shelves, after a long day of planning bountiful arrangements to honor Agnes's memory. "She's spunky all right. Outspoken, unyielding, proud as can be, but . . ."

"You've hinted about her health, but what makes you think it's really so serious?"

"Her hands tremble, and her arms too. She tried to hide it from me, but I noticed it a few weeks ago, then again today. I'm scared, Bri. Really panicked."

"Don't be. I'll spy on her and report back anything suspicious."

I smile. "She's going to be working with me, you know, so I'll have plenty of opportunity to assess what's going on with her."

"Yeah, but she'll be on her guard around you. With me, not so much."

I cluck my tongue and turn the Open sign to Closed. "You sure you're ready for my mama?"

Bri clucks back. "Yeah, baby, bring it on."

Thirty-Nine

JANE WAS HERE. I CAN tell by the gust of ammonia that hits my nostrils as I sail into the house. After arranging sweet peas all day for my dear Agnes, the chemical scent is even more offensive. Then again, at least it's cleaner, and Jane's gone for the day.

Tomorrow morning Mama will be back in the wee hours to help me finish all the arrangements. In addition to those that Agnes paid for posthumously, I've been flooded with phone calls for more from congregants. Thoughtful as always, Livi plans to come help us before she heads off to her own job later in the day.

Jake's avoided me the past couple of days, and, you know, I'm good with that. I really am. Agnes's sudden death has had me thinking about the fragility of life, and the importance of faith. Her life was the epitome of not just saying what she believed, but living it too. I need to do that as well. Even when I'd lost so much, I told myself that things would look up, but did I really believe it?

Anyway, it's too bad I'm not able to give Jake notice that I'll be moving out soon, but Mama needed the place more than I did, so I'm here to stay for a while.

Yet I know inside that I'm ready for some change in my life. Hopefully, talking Mama into managing my store will prove to be fortuitous and profitable. Then I'll be able to afford a place for both of us, a place where I can care for her should her health continue to decline.

I just hope we both last that long.

Upstairs in my loft, I step out of my sandals and pad around, trying not to notice the specks of dust and silt sticking to my bare feet. Maybe someday I'll be able to afford a Jane, only I'll be hiring someone who doesn't petrify me with one hard stroke of her eyes. I plop onto my couch and flip open my sketch pad, when a gasp escapes me at the image reflected on the page.

I'd forgotten all about the drawing of Sweet Thing that I'd done just days before, but the feeling that the sketch evokes brings a catch to my throat. My sea lion friend's watching me from the page with those soulful eyes of hers. She's set against a background of black and gray in variant shades, each layer darker than the next with a rising moon filtered by similar coal-like shades. Only minute quantities of white appear anywhere in the image.

I close the pad with a slap. Telling Mama and Bri about my dream of attending art school was the first step toward making it happen. I think Agnes would be pleased. Despite all the uncertainties facing me at the moment, I'm happy that this hope made it to the surface of my consciousness. Imagine . . . my father was an artist. So many questions, so much he could answer, yet chances are I'm on my own. At least I know that there's hope for my calling. It's in my blood, after all.

A tap on the door nearly sends me into the ceiling. I set my sketch pad aside, and tentatively step over to the door, knowing full well who stands behind it. Jake gives me a grim smile when I open the door.

"I've brought a peace offering." He's holding two mugs, curls of steam rising out of them. He holds one out to me. "Vanilla milk."

I take it from him and open the door wider. He follows me to the counter, where I set mine down without taking a sip.

"Gaby, I'm sorry for the way I barked at you the other day."

"Apology accepted."

Silence.

His eyes alight on the picture above my couch bed. "You decided to hang it. Good. I guess that means you'll be staying awhile."

I stare at him.

He laughs. "What? I had been wondering about your plans. Oh, and here." He reaches into the back pocket of his jeans and pulls out a slick, trifold brochure. "It's for the art center near the restaurant I've just opened in Pasadena. Thought you might be interested."

He remembered? I take the brochure and allow it to linger in my hands before I lay it on the counter. "Thanks. As for my plans, I just turned down an offer to stay with my friend Bri so my mother could move in there instead. It's just a temporary situation, though, because eventually we'll find a place we can share."

Jake's face turns sober. He reaches out to touch my shoulder, but I hold myself rigid. "I meant that as an apology. I've come to care about you and went nuts when I thought . . ."

"Thought what?"

"That maybe you were in danger."

"Thanks. And I'm sorry too for rankling you like that."

"You didn't rankle me." He brushes my arm again, this time bringing out goose bumps. I suck in a breath. "You okay?" he asks.

I grab up the mug, letting its heat warm me. Because I've been warned about Jake's way with women, I guard myself. He's been good to me in many ways, and I'm grateful, but I'd be foolish to fall into the relationship trap with him, especially now with my emotions in an extra-fragile state. I still need this loft to come home to, so why mess that up?

His expression seems earnest though, so I muster a smile. "I'm good."

"Good, good. Then I have a favor to ask of you."

The man doesn't waste any time. "Okay."

"It's Andy's fortieth birthday, and I'm planning to throw him the bash of all bashes. It's time this neighborhood buried the hatchet and had some fun, breaking bread together and all that. I thought since you and he just had an adventure together, that you might want to help me."

"With flowers?"

"Sure, but I'd like you to actually host it with me. It'll be bigger than the dinner party I first mentioned to you. I'll do the cooking, cuz that's my thing—but I'd enjoy your input and your help in putting it all together. What do you say?"

I'm on the spot. Andy saved me from my own stupidity, and how would it look if I refused to help him celebrate a milestone? Inwardly, I'm groaning, but outwardly I put on my best face. "I don't know how much help I can be—my mother's moving into town soon—but of course I'll help. I owe Andy that much."

Jake gives my shoulder a firm rub, then stops, his hand lingering on the fleshy part of my upper arm. "Great. We'll have fun together, you and I."

"Hmm." He smells too good for me to stay in here one minute longer.

Jake leans his head to one side and eyes me. "Don't you think?"

My cheeks flush from the scrutiny. "Fun, hmm, yes."

He lets out a heady sigh. "Gaby."

"Hmm?"

"Are we going to keep ignoring our feelings for each other?"

Ripples run through me, and one of my eyebrows pitches up, questioning him. He sets his mug down, sending the scent of vanilla into the air that's already infused with his own tropical cologne, and takes another step closer.

I step back.

He drops his head back and stares at the ceiling as if searching for words, then lowers his gaze to meet mine. "You're an incredible woman, Gaby. I want you to know that."

"Thanks," I squeak. From what I've been told, Jake doles out compliments like poker chips, and to my mind that just sends their value downward. Not that I'm not hopeful . . .

His eyes knit together. "You don't have to like me, Gaby, but I think you do anyway. Come on; despite what you've heard about me, I think you might even care about me. Don't you even a little?"

I tuck away my emotions and try not to acknowledge just how good Jake smells. It's the vanilla, I tell myself. Only when I pause and take in his whole face, just inches from mine, I melt. A voice within urges me to tell him everything I'm feeling. That I'm thankful for all he's done for me. That I can't remember much at all about other men I've cared about, yet I recall everything about him—even what he wore on his feet that first night we met (gray topsiders). That his worry, although cloaked in anger, touched me deeply.

But then the voice changes, and I hear Iris's, tortured and desperate. The pitch increases, crowding out the other voice, and I stiffen. Am I in danger of making the same mistake I've always made? Jake stands there, waiting for my answer, and I glance off to nowhere. With a forced shrug I turn back to him. "Of course I like you, Jake. You've been nothing but kind to me, so what's not to like?"

He winces. "That was cold." He pauses. "It's unbecoming."

His words sting. A lump forms at the base of my throat, and my voice comes out sounding thicker than I'd like, irritatingly so. "I thought maybe this arrangement of ours would work out, Jake. It seemed a bit unconventional, but I figured that maybe I could be a helper to you while you traveled. But my living here isn't going to work, is it?"

"Maybe not."

"I'll pack my things tomorrow."

He hesitates. "Where will you go?"

Do I admit that I have no idea? That Bri's spare bedroom would be awfully cramped with Mama and me sharing it? That although I've managed to stave off the imminent closing of my business—with help from Agnes—it just may be a temporary situation that'll need addressing in just a few weeks?

I slide a look at Cassatt's painting, the image of the happy family suddenly breaking my heart. When my eyes briefly find Jake again, his countenance has softened as well as my resolve. He turns my chin with a gentle touch, sending an unsurpassed thrill through me, and I want to pull away. I need to pull away. Yet I can't seem to do it.

That bold voice of his cuts through the silence. "Look at me, Gaby. Please."

I force my eyelids up, and find Jake's face just inches from my own, his eyes caressing me in a way I've never known. Imagine that. I've had a dozen boyfriends, yet this feeling is totally, completely, frighteningly unique. Nothing makes any sense. We're both breathing as if we've just run up the stairs, yet we haven't moved.

Jake changes that in an instant when he leans toward me and finds my lips, kissing them lightly. It's too much, and I gasp. I promised myself I wouldn't be misled again, but here I go. Not now, not ever. Before he finds my lips again, I turn and his mouth lands on my cheek. Abruptly, he pulls back.

"Sorry to have bothered you."

That lump at the base of my throat threatens to burst. I want to believe in him so badly right now, but that argument he had with Iris screams through my mind. What if this soaring passion I have for him gets shot out of the air by yet another rejection? Can I take another chance with someone like Jake, especially so soon after Max?

"Life hurts too much, Jake. I'm sorry. I can't do this."

He walks across the loft and flings open the door. Before he leaves, Jake turns to me. "You've chosen to believe what you want. Whatever you do, don't let it be said that I ever threw you out. If you want to stay, then stay. Or go. I really don't care."

And then he was gone.

Forty

A WEEK HAS PASSED SINCE Jake's kiss landed on my cheek. Since then, I've had little time to dwell on it or the emotion that drenched me like ceaseless waves that night. Apparently neither has Jake, because early the next morning Andy ran over and thanked me for "offering" to help Jake with his birthday party. As Bri would say, sheesh! Well. If Jake can go on as if nothing happened, then I guess so can I.

That's what acceptance is all about, isn't it? Accepting the things that are out of one's control? Speaking of acceptance, I've realized something else. While Mama and I worked fluidly and quickly together prepping flowers for the celebration of Agnes's life earlier this week, our differences became obvious. While she brightened at the prospect of yet another floral bundle to unwrap and clean and trim, I wilted under the yoke of tedium.

Still, knowing that Mama's impending arrival is permanent has made me both thrilled and scared to bits.

Bri, on the other hand, is in her glory knowing there's a quick replacement for her Aunt Dot, who flew back to Miami. Oh, Bri thought her auntie was heading off to the mission field again, but as it turns out, she had a "friend" waiting for her in Grand Gables, one of Miami's swanky retirement communities.

Ahem.

So while Bri gets Mama's room ready, I spend the day puttering in my shop, hoping she'll be pleased enough to stay forever. Once settled, I'll need to address the pending lawsuit, my dwindling capital (although thank you, sweet Agnes for thinking of me!), along with my need for a new apartment. But at least I'm one step closer to my art school dream.

These thoughts swirl around in my head as I take a refreshing stroll to the beach, the evening sun still restless and warm. Oh, baby, that's what I'm talkin' about. Haven't been to the sand since Bri and I ran into each other last week. Since that day when I met the Lord so powerfully—and then Bri and I had our little talk about getting to the root of things—I've changed. Confronting my mother was my first step in finding truth in the rumors around me, and I'm not averse to uncovering more. Which is precisely why I speed up when I spot Meredith zipping around the corner in full jogger-girl attire.

"Hey, Meredith," I call out.

She screws up her face at me, then slows while turning off her iPod. She smiles big. "Wanna join me?"

Uh, no. "I've never jogged a day in my life."

"Really? Well, you look healthy. Must be all that kayaking you're doing."

"Heard about that, huh?" Great.

She's nodding vigorously now. "Everybody knows about it. I'm glad you didn't get yourself killed. It's usually not so rough out there. I think you just hit a bad day."

"There's something else I wanted to talk to you about, Meredith."

"Shoot."

I stop and fold my arms, while she jogs in place and watches me with a questioning lift in her eyes. "Why did you cancel your plans to have me do your wedding flowers?"

Meredith's face falls, although her cadence doesn't slow.

"I mean, did Iris say something about my work?"

She stops and bends over, bracing her hands on her knees as if to catch her breath. "Not at all, Gaby. I called off the wedding, that's all."

I suck in a breath. "Oh? I'm so sorry. I had no idea."

She shrugs one shoulder. "No biggie. Just wasn't meant to be, that's all."

She stands, and I look her straight in the eyes. "That must have been a very hard decision to make, Meredith. I really am sorry for the pain it must have caused you."

She gives me a lopsided, sad smile. "I appreciate that, Gaby. More than you know."

Later, when I'm combing the shore for treasures—something I love to do but have had little time for lately—my sight falls on Kit and Iris, and my heart sinks. Would it be too obvious if I darted down the nearest lane toward home? They're ambling along, their heads down, so maybe they won't even notice.

Then Iris sees me. As they approach, Kit glances up too and her expression shifts between sullenness and suppressed cheerfulness.

"Hello, ladies."

Iris nods. "Gaby."

Kit offers me a noncommittal, "Hey."

Water laps near our feet as Iris speaks in a knowing tone. "Had quite the adventure the other day, I heard."

"Yes, I sure did. I'm even starting to laugh about it now."

"You need to be careful, Gaby. Next time Andy may not be around to rescue you."

"Oh, I know. He's amazing, though."

Iris huffs. "For a drug addict."

My eyebrow arches, and Kit's expression crumbles into a grimace.

Iris continues. "The man lived many years of his life in the gutter until a drug overdose nearly undid him. Such a shame. It's a wonder he's alive today."

I smile. "He's a walking miracle, then, isn't he? Thanks to God for that."

Kit pipes up. "Ya got that right. Let it rest, Mom. It's not like he's still doing drugs."

Iris pats her daughter's back. "Not that we know of, dear."

Despite her often-dour expression, Kit has burrowed her way into my heart. My mind wanders to Kit's revelation about her mother's divorce, and I consider the depths of that kind of trauma. Those who dish out the most painful barbs are often suffering themselves. So maybe Iris's animosity toward me (and others) has more to do with her and the destructive way she deals with rejection.

Thank you, Jesus, for pointing me toward hope and not destruction. The desperate sentiments from Iris's latest blog post streak across my mind, and I purposely catch eyes with her.

"I've been meaning to tell you what a terrific friend your daughter has become," I say. "You are a really great mom to have brought up such a sweetie, Iris."

The lines around her mouth soften. "Thank you, Gaby." She glances at her daughter, those large eyes of hers wide and expressive. "She's my good girl."

"Yes, I agree with you there." I begin to walk away. "You two ladies enjoy your time together, okay?"

Iris beams. "We will, Gaby. We will."

I head down the beach, leaping out of the path of a crashing wave, the spray of water reminding me of Andy's chivalry of a week ago. He doesn't look like a drug addict, but how would I know anyway?

From the first day I met him, aside from his choice in dated clothing, Andy's just been one of those guys that seem happy no matter what. A true optimist. It's obvious that the life he leads now, though, is the outcome of something deeper and ominous from his past. Can't fault him for that, now, can I? I mean, doesn't everybody deserve another chance to get it right?

"Yo, Gab-bay!"

"Hey, Gibson!" I shout to Max's son, whose sun-drenched locks stick to his temples.

"Waves are awesome today."

He says this as if they're not that way every day, in his mind at least. "Sorry I missed you out there. Nathan with you?"

As I ask this, Bri's son jogs up and drops his board behind me, splattering wet sand on my calves. "Hi, Gaby. Mom says to tell you the extra room's all ready. She's makin' brownies. Wanna walk with us?"

"You know it!"

A cryptic glance passes between them as we trudge along through the sand toward Bri and Doug's house. Snicker. Gibson obviously knows that when I show up there'll be fewer brownies for the two of them.

At Bri's house, I slip out of my flip-flops and into her foyer. "Hey, Bri-Bri!"

Livi peeks around the corner, a Coke in her hand, a tray of brownies in the other. "Bri's upstairs. I was just coming out to the patio, so why don't we sit out there? I'm bringing your favorite."

On the front patio, we listen to the saga of unrequited love play out between a couple of squawking seagulls, passing the time until Bri joins us. Livi's dressed like she's been showing houses all day, all except for the hair, which is in its usual ponytail state.

Livi feasts on her second brownie, giving me pause. "Wow. You must be celebrating a big sale today or something, huh, Livi? I'm not used to seeing you tear into calorie-rich foods like that. What's the occasion?"

She frowns. "Just the opposite, Gaby. You know that mentor I told you about, that great boss who was going to teach me all her tricks of the trade?"

"Yes, I remember."

"Well . . ." She sighs and stares off into space. "It just didn't work out. That's all."

I open my mouth to respond when a car pulls into the drive. Beachgoers hunting for parking pull down these narrow lanes all the time and use Bri's and her neighbors' driveways to turn around, so I don't give the approaching car much thought. Until it stops and its engine's familiar hum throws me back.

Hesitantly, Max steps onto the patio. "Gaby?"

I don't move. "Hi, Max."

He glances at Livi, then back at me. "Didn't know I'd be seein' you here."

Right back atcha.

Livi holds up the tray of brownies. "Better hurry. Only a few left, and you wouldn't want to miss out."

Max clears his throat. "It's all right. Not very hungry." He twists around. "Doug here yet?"

Livi takes over as hostess, and it's a good thing, as I have no intention of doing so. "Haven't seen him, and Bri's upstairs. Why don't you pull up a chair and we can just meet out here?"

I jerk a look at Livi, hoping Max won't see the disappointment in my eyes, and swallow my last brownie bite. "Am I interrupting something?"

Bri suddenly trots out the front door and makes a beeline for the tray of brownies that sits on the table. She pulls up like a wild pony when she notices me there, hands folded in my lap, questioning smirk on my face.

"Gaby!"

"Hi, Bri."

Her head turns this way and that, first at Livi, then at Max. I can tell she's dying for a brownie, but she has some explaining to do, does she not? "Heard we're having a little . . . party."

Livi twitters. "Not exactly. I should have told you, Gaby."

My chest hurts from my sinking heart. It's not that my feelings for Max have resurfaced; it's just that this matchup has Bri written all over it. She so much as told me that she didn't think Max was right for me, but couldn't she have waited longer to put on that matchmaking hat of hers? I turn my attention to Livi, my generous helper at the shop, the friend who sacrificed so much time and energy to help me keep things afloat, and wonder when she had been planning to tell me that she'd begun pursuing a relationship with Max.

Bri chimes in. "Livi's boss turned out to be a real shark, and she's thinking about turning from real estate to property management." She rests her hand on Max's shoulder. "I invited Max to come by because of all his experience with that type of business. Thought maybe he could help Livi with the transition."

Plausible? Sure. Likely? No. I roll my eyes at Bri, and she steps in front of Max to block his view, widening her own eyes in my direction, as if silently begging my forgiveness.

"I almost forgot," Livi suddenly says. "Jake told me that you and he were throwing a big bash, Gaby. I'm so excited. *Grazie, grazie*, I get to come!"

All eyes fall on me, and the smirk has slipped off my face and onto Bri's. My best friend's face can hardly hide its excitement. "So you stopped by to invite us all, isn't that right, Gaby-girl?"

Forty-One

KIND OF HARD TO PLAN a party together when you're not on speaking terms with your co-host. But even Livi heard about it, so something tells me Jake's inviting a ton of people. Friends of *his*. So I look at it this way, while I may have lost a little ground in my efforts to heal from a cracked heart, at least I gained four partygoers.

I'm thinking about this while sitting out on the deck, wrapping seashell truffles in clear cellophane. While Jake may still be moping, clearly his money-spending skills have not suffered. I found this large box of specially ordered truffles on my stoop this morning along with a polite note asking that I prep them for party favors. Since I've no money to contribute, not to mention the fact that Andy pretty much saved me from my own clumsiness, it's the least I can do.

Speaking of seashells, a double batch of the real thing showed up on the dock this morning, and again, I could see no sign of a similar delivery at any other home within view. The plot thickens.

Mama started full time today, and though I've longed for this day for years, trepidation managed to draw me out of bed earlier than usual. I'm still surprised that she agreed to leave her roadside stand behind to manage my tiny store. In reflection, getting her to agree seemed too easy.

"There," I say into the air. I tie the last bundle of shells with raffia and set it into the original box. A splash draws my attention to the water, and I pop up and nearly skip over to the handrail, stopping just short of the ramp. Ever since my kayaking accident, I haven't been able to make myself get any closer. "Sweet Thing?" I call out. "Where've you been, my friend?"

A circle of water expands at the spot where Sweet Thing dives beneath the surface.

"You and that lion! It's too much." Shonda's on her deck, wagging her head at me, but even from here I can see the grin on her face. "Maybe you were one of them in another life."

If I believed in reincarnation, then wouldn't I have chosen to come back as someone wealthy? And married? And blond? Well, at least Shonda's smiling at me for once. That's something.

She continues to raise her voice in the morning quiet. "Word on the street is you and the Jake-man are throwing the bash of the year next weekend. I wouldn't miss that for the world. Should be some kind of show."

I nod and shrug. "Not sure what you mean by 'show,' but there'll be lots of good food, I'm sure, and music. And friends, of course."

"And Iris. Don't forget your nemesis." She laughs far too loud in the quiet channel.

"What do you mean, exactly, Shonda? I've got nothing against Iris. Actually, I've enjoyed getting to know her daughter, Kit. Very much so." I glance around, wondering how many of my neighbors have stepped out onto their decks for their morning gossip.

"That's all well and good, Gaby, but I wouldn't be putting her up on the mothering-pedestal too fast. She's not going down without a fight, that's for sure, so my advice to you is be careful how chummy you try to be with that one."

The old me would've let that comment slide, no matter how confusing. But the new me, the one trying to get to the heart of matters, can't let it go. "What fight is that, Shonda? Iris and I aren't fighting over anything."

Her laughter shrills. "Yeah, nothing except Jake!"

Lovely Readers,

It is with a heavy heart that I inform you of my plans to close this blog. Although my intentions for this forum did not completely come to fruition, I consider it to have been an honor to serve your advisory needs. Time will tell how my own life will unfold.

An hour later, after swallowing Shonda's crazy observation and after digesting Iris's final post, I am flitting with Mama around Florally Yours preparing for our first full day of working together without a mountain of orders to fill. We meet Rudy there with a truckload of fresh flowers, and she questions him like a dogged reporter. "You bring the fresh stuff?"

"Yes."

"The gerberas?"

"Yes."

"The purple irises?"

"Yes."

"More flower strippers and water tubes? I need vases! I need wicker!"

Rudy's stamina amazes me. "Yes, Yolanda. It's all there."

She juts her chin out. "Good. You go now and take care of my stand."

I press my lips together as he nods congenially. When Mama turns her back, Rudy sends a wink my way and I press my lips harder so as not to smile too big.

She turns to me. "You can go now."

"What?"

"I work better alone. Go, go. You go do your art." She places her hands on her hips and surveys my shop. "Lots to do, Gabrielle. Lots of work ahead of me."

I gulp. Why do I suddenly feel like a third wheel in my own business? Like I'm an intruder in the one thing I've managed to build, however poorly. Then again, isn't this what I wanted? My heart has not been in floral design in ages, and the shop's just barely surviving, so why not let Mama loose with it?

I cross my arms in front of me. "I can't just leave you here on your first real day."

Her finely painted eyebrows rise slowly and I sense my legs turning to jelly. How can she still have that effect on me after all this time?

I drop my arms. "Well, if you're sure. I have some bookkeeping to do, and I've been thinking of framing a few sketches."

"You do that. These walls are empty, empty, empty! They need art. Lots of your art, with beautiful frames. We will sell them. And I like what you do with all those seashells in your arrangements. We will sell more of those designs too. Now go!"

I glance around. I'm a stranger in my own store, a castaway with nowhere to land. Then again, I've never thought of hanging my own artwork in here, let alone selling it, and the thought of it . . . ? Well, it just sends a little thrill through me, I tell you.

I kiss her on the cheek. "Thank you, Mama. But I'll be back midday, with lunch for us both. You sure you're going to be fine?"

She nods. *"Yo también te quiero,* and I would like a meatball sandwich with extra sauce. No cheese."

With those loving sentiments, I slip out the door.

Lackey that I am, I return three hours later with Mama's sandwich and a Cobb salad for me.

Mama's bent over, dusting my lowest shelf, and when she hears me call out that the lunch wagon has arrived, she stands and glares at me. "How come you didn't say anything about lawyers?" One fist rests on her hip, trembling slightly. "Two stupid people come in here this morning."

Summer and Eric? I cringe, wondering how much more I'm going to have to pay them after a confrontation with my mother. Although wouldn't I love to have been a fly on the wall this morning! "What happened?" I ask cautiously.

"They say they come to talk about the lawsuit, and I say, 'What lawsuit?' and that huge woman says you gave her ugly flowers on the very best day of her life. Aww-ah! I tell her that my daughter would never do such a thing!"

Oh. My.

"And then I tell that husband of hers to go put some pants on."

"He wasn't wearing pants? What?"

Mama shakes her head, and she reminds me of a bobcat that's just spotted a bunny rabbit. "He lets that woman run his life, like she wears the family pants. I shamed him, and then I ran them out of here after that. No more lawsuit. You tell your lawyer that he's fired. Is it Bri's husband? Then I tell him tonight!"

Air releases from my lungs, and my shoulders droop. "I wish it were that simple, Mama."

"What do you mean you wish it were that simple? I tell you, the lawsuit is no more. Done." She holds up a sheet of plain white paper. "I make them sign, right here."

I rush forward and grab the paper from her. "Let me see that!"

In exchange for Gaby Flores's promise not to seek recovery of court costs, we will file a dismissal of our case against Florally Yours.

"H-how did you know what to write?"

Mama waves me away. "Aww-ah! I asked that no-good ex-husband of mine. He used to be a paralegal. He owed me, that one."

I lunge for her. "Mama! You're a genius!"

Despite the annoyed arch of one eyebrow, Mama's tight hug and pinched smile tells me she's mighty pleased with herself.

Forty-Two

ONE ISSUE DOWN, A GAZILLION more to go. In her first day managing my store, Mama saved me (potentially, anyway) thousands of dollars. Money I didn't have in the first place, I might add. Of course, a few things need to happen to make it all official, but Doug tells me he's confident that the matter will be closed very soon with some kind of dismissal filing. *Thank you, Jesus!*

So although admitting my failings at running Florally Yours has done a number on my pride, I am reaping the rewards already. Mama has this way about her that just makes a place shine and customers satisfied, and in the week that's passed, sales are already up, up, up!

Still, I'm worried about the tremble in her arms and hands. After Andy's party this coming weekend, I must get Mama to the doctor.

My mother's voice cuts into my thoughts as we lean against the workbench and strip thorns from yellow roses until my fingers cramp. "I've decided to come to your party on Saturday, Mijita, to meet all your friends. I will help cook."

"That's not necessary. My landlord has all the food taken care of, but you can help me with decorations if you like."

When she doesn't answer, I look up.

"Tell me about this landlord. Does this man have a name? And why are you and he giving a party together?"

"It's for a mutual friend of ours." I don't tell her that I'm indebted to said friend for saving me from the choppy harbor waters. "And yes, my landlord's name is Jake."

"And Jake can cook for many people?"

I continue stripping the foliage in my hands. "I think so. He's been in the restaurant business for years as a chef and entrepreneur. He's actually a pretty good cook."

"He has cooked for you?"

My finger lands on a jagged thorn. I suck the place where it stuck, tasting blood while trying to avoid my mother's lingering gaze. "I've had some of his leftovers, and they haven't been too bad." Actually, they've been great, but am I obligated to say so now?

"I will make enchiladas."

"Jake made enchiladas for me once."

Mama darts me a look.

Do I tell her they were a peace offering after thinking he had poisoned me? I clear my throat. "Anyway, they tasted good. Not like yours, of course, but decent. I'd expect that with his kind of experience, wouldn't you?"

"Did he marinate the chicken with fresh chilies or those canned ones from the grocery? Was it hand shredded or just poured out of some package?"

I bite my lip, suppressing a giggle. Maybe I should unleash Mama in Jake's kitchen. Sweet revenge.

Jake and I have been trading e-mails for two weeks, their content as personal as a stock transaction. So when his voice shows up on the other end of my cell phone, I'm speechless.

"You there, Gaby?"

Breathe. Breathe. What *is* this? "Hey, Jake."

"Listen, we're only a few days away from the big shew, so I thought maybe we ought to meet to discuss the rest of the details." His friendly demeanor sounds forced. Or is it just me?

"Okay. Will you be home tonight?" And just why did that sound so much like a worried wife checking up on her hubby at the office?

"Sure thing. After my hot date."

"Oh."

"With the new dinner staff at La Cofradía."

Bu-dum-bum. "Great!" Okay, that didn't sound too anxious now, did it?

"It's been warm lately, so let's meet outside on the deck around eight o'clock. Okay by you?"

"Sure. I can do that."

"Good. Bring a sweater, and if you're a good girl, I'll bring the dessert."

When I don't answer, Jake breaks back into the conversation. "I didn't mean to . . . that wasn't meant to come across as offensive. I hope . . ."

"I just wondered if you'd be bringing chocolate."

Jake's laughter resonates through the airwaves. "Absolutely. Only the best . . ."

His words trail off, and I wonder if he wanted to add "for you."

"My mother would like to assist you in the kitchen."

"Your mother, huh? Well, if she's anything like you . . ."

"No, actually, she's nothing like me. I'm an okay cook, while she's top notch, and I won't lie—she'll make it rough on you."

He chuckles. "I'm shakin'."

It's already nine o'clock. Jake and I have been out on this deck feasting on tiramisu and making plans for Andy's party, and I'm wondering if he'll slap my hand for pilfering yet another shaving of semi-sweet chocolate. I need the energy if we're going to get everything done in the next two days. I know, I know, Jake's quite the party thrower. Still, if only we'd been talking to each other all week. . . .

Jake's voice cuts in. "So Jane will be here tomorrow. I have to drive down south in the morning. Can I leave her pay with you tonight?"

I picture myself rifling through Jake's underwear drawer in the morning, searching for cash. The recollection of Iris watching me from the street below makes me shudder. "Please do."

He nods. "Check. Now, will you be decorating the dock? We hadn't discussed this before, but I usually like to run some lights along the edge. If I do that, would you hang some tropical flowers, maybe hibiscus or something, along the wires?"

I hesitate and glance down at the dock. Haven't stood on it since my little dance with rough waters, and would he think I'm being a baby if I said as much? I gulp.

"What's wrong?" He follows the path of my vision, then glances back at me, a questioning look in his eyes. "Not afraid you'll fall in, are you?"

I shake my head and make a note on the pad in front of me. "It'll be fine. I'll think of something." And someone to do the decorating for me.

He clears his throat. "Okay, so don't forget there's a mess of supplies in the shed all ready for you. I'll leave extra cash in case you don't find what you're looking for. Oh, and I almost forgot—a crew'll be here on Saturday to deliver and set up tables. In case I'm not around, would you make sure they leave a wide path for limbo?"

I snort, then immediately cover my mouth with three fingers.

Jake stares at me, and the corners of his mouth twitch. "Gaby, you don't fool me for a second. You'll probably win the thing."

"I haven't limboed since I was ten."

Jake's smile brightens the dark. "Then it's about time you got back in the game. Well, it looks like it's all under control, doesn't it?"

I nod and glance out to sea, but truthfully I'm not really sure of anything. We're two strangers throwing a party, something I have little experience at even on my own. Jake's the one with the reputation, and he's not even sure if he'll be around on Saturday morning. Tension rides up my back, but when I let my eyes fall on Jake another emotion vies to take over.

Jake's looking out over the channel. "Thanks for meeting me so late, Gaby. I'm sure you're a busy lady these days with your own business to run. Hope things are looking up for you there."

Our eyes catch. "Yes, they are. And you're right about me being busy, but Andy's a great guy and the neighborhood's abuzz over this party so . . ." I shrug. "I'm glad to be a part of it. And I just want to say that"—Deep breath in. Start fresh—"I didn't mean to hurt your feelings the other night."

The line of his mouth lies flat. "I know, Gaby. I get it. No hard feelings here. None at all. You're a trooper for putting up with all this." He sweeps his hand across the deck. "After Andy's party on Saturday, I hope you feel free to go on your merry way."

I watch him stick his notepad under one beefy arm, stack up our dishes, and head back into the house, leaving me here on my own.

This is what I wanted. Right?

I can't sleep. I search the swirls of plaster on the ceiling above me, but no peace comes. Hastily, I pull on workout clothes (they've been lonely lately), sneakers and a light jacket, and head downstairs.

Minutes later, I stand overlooking Ventura from high atop the hill at Grant Park, where the historic cross stands. An evening event has wound down, and I'm one of the few still in the park.

What brings me here, I do not know. I wrap my jacket tighter about me and stare out over this town that is my home, its borders hugged by the vastness of that great ocean out there. I shiver. Despite the gusts that bounce through the park, the cross at its helm stands steady and towering. I think about its history and the travelers who used it as a road sign in the days before navigational systems and, well, cars.

I follow the length of the vertical post with my eyes, all the way to the top. "I don't deserve you, Lord," I nearly shout. One party straggler scurries off the grass as I continue. "And yet I've got friends who care, a mother I love more than words, a roof over my head, and . . ." I almost say *Jake.* I drop my gaze to the ground. "Lord, whether I've listened to you or not, you've been steering me in the right direction all along. From here on in, I trust you to show me the way."

Forty-Three

WHAT WOULD MEG DO AT a time like this? I am, of course, talking about Meg Ryan, the queen of romantic comedies, in my humble opinion. I've always aspired to her quirky idealism and romantic finesse, and in a situation like this, she'd know what to do. I know it.

Max holds a bouquet of red roses out to me. "These are for you," he tells me. So what if I can get them wholesale? This magnificent bunch still wears thorns, as if plucked straight from the field. They're fresh, and that says a lot.

"They're lovely. Come in, Max."

Even as we cut through Jake's living room to the deck out back, past a couple of servers that Jake's brought in to help with the party, I sense Max's eyes on me. "You look beautiful."

"Thanks. That's sweet." And oh, I feel beautiful too. Shonda loaned me this stretchy black tank dress, and it offers me just the right amount of swing when I walk.

"Hey, Max!" Bri gives him a kiss on the cheek, but not before noting the roses in my hand and giving me an *oh no you didn't* frown.

"Hi, buddy." Doug, appearing more relaxed than ever, shakes Max's hand.

The deck is beginning to fill up with guests, some I know, others not so much. There's Shonda, looking exotic in a creamy white pantsuit cut down to there, and the towering man at her side who can't seem to pull his eyes away from her. . . . Oh, Lord, please let that man be her elusive husband.

Willy's hanging over the rail, pointing to the various docks where he delivers the *Reef Report,* his mother, Terry, by his side. Her curls bounce in the sunlight as she nods, and let me just say, the way she hangs on to her son's words reminds me so much of the enviable relationship between Bri and Nathan. Sigh. I want some of that.

Over at the corner of the deck, the guest of honor, Andy, looks tan and spiffy in white shorts and an equally blinding collared shirt, its neck open enough to display two shiny gold chains. Some people get stuck in another era and just can't get out, you know? His fashion decisions haven't hurt his love life, though, because a Kate Bosworth look-alike leans casually on his shoulder and whispers something apparently quite amusing into his ear.

Bri grabs me by the elbow and steers me away. "What's up with you and Max?" she hisses.

"Nothing. He just gave me a hostess gift."

"Roses? Sheesh. Mighty creative of him. And I thought you two were done."

"We are. I guess he's just being nice."

"Right." She drags me into the house.

"And what about you? Fixing up Max and Livi? What's up with that?"

"Ugh—I knew you'd draw that conclusion. It just looked like that! I was just asking Max to help out Livi. I swear."

"And I'm supposed to believe that, Bri-Bri?"

She sighs. "Max has a hard edge to him these days, but deep down he's a good guy. Try not to hate him, 'kay? Just know he's low on my matchmaking priority list right now because of all his issues."

Okay. Whatever.

"Oh, and Jake needs you. He just asked me where you were, but hey, before you go, why've you been keeping him such a secret?"

My eyebrow darts up. "He's not a secret."

"He's hot, Gaby-girl, like you haven't noticed. Pffst! When he introduced himself I nearly fainted from the heat."

I cut in. "He's also the neighborhood Don Juan, Bri-Bri, and you'd know this if you ever ventured away from the beach to where the rest of the world lives." Who am I kidding? Don Juan or not, my resolve to keep my distance from Jake has nearly ebbed away.

We're in the living room now, a long shell toss from the kitchen, and Bri slides a look at Jake as he stirs something over a medium flame. "You sure about him?"

"Go. You're bothering me."

She sticks out her tongue. "Am not. Speaking of bothering, I think your mama's giving him a good talking-to. Hee-hee."

I dart a glance at my mother, who's wearing a plain apron over a pair of capris with a tag hanging from the side and a vibrant floral blouse, and I wonder just when she had time to shop. She stands inches from Jake, her chin jutting upward at him while giving him the what-for about the benefits of raw onions.

"Only gringos sauté their onions before filling the enchiladas!"

"I know that Yolie . . ."

Yolie?

Jake continues, " . . . but not everyone here can take their sharpness. I'm sure that you and I could, but the rest? I'm afraid most of our guests are gringos."

"Aww-ah!"

I butt in. "Anything I can help with in here?"

Four eyes land on me. My mother is the first to speak after lowering herself from her tiptoes. "This Jake of yours has too many ideas."

Jake of mine?

"And your mother's quite the chef. We could use someone like her at La Cofradía."

I shake my head. "Don't even think about it! I need her at Florally Yours."

"Gracias, Gabrielle. I won't be going anywhere, so never you mind." She wipes her forehead with the back of one hand, and I notice the brief, almost imperceptible shake before she takes up the knife to begin chopping again.

"Mama, why don't you take a break from here? Let me get you some lemonade, okay?"

She shushes me away.

Jake offers me a wink, but the decidedly cheery look on his face fades when he sees the concern on mine. He follows the line of my gaze to my mother's shaky hands and then glances back at me, his expression sober.

"Tell you what, Yolie, I think we've got enough onion, so would you mind taking over here at the stove? I need to get some coals started out back."

"Aww-ah." Mama takes the wooden spoon from Jake's hand and stirs the onion sauté a little more, but not without giving some guff. She mutters quietly as we step away from the kitchen and out onto the deck, Jake's hand securely tucked beneath my elbow.

"Surfin' USA" blares all around us, and as we pretend to watch the boats go by, Jake leans toward my ear. "Has she been shaking like that long?"

I nod, trying to hold back the swell of tears.

He reaches around my back, continuing to lean close so I can hear him above the music and guests. "My guess is you haven't had a chance to discuss this with her."

This time I shake my head, no.

He rubs my arm. "Don't worry, Gaby. My grandmother had thyroid trouble for years, and your mother's shaking reminds me of hers."

Thyroid! Agnes used to take medicine for that, and come to think of it, she used to shake sometimes too. Somehow, I'm not comforted by this, until I remind myself that it was her heart that ultimately gave out.

He continues. "I have a great doctor you can take her to, if you don't know anyone." He pauses. "You okay?"

I look into his eyes . . . and maybe I've gone mad, maybe I'm still suffering from another case of ignorance, of being unable to decipher the difference between Mr. So Right and Mr. So-So Wrong, but if I didn't know better, I'd say that Jake's eyes are filled with one heaping dose of compassion right now. And it's the most attractive thing in the world.

I open my mouth to thank him, when Iris appears at Jake's side. "I'm here now, Jake, and ready to help, just like I promised. Here's the wine I said I'd bring." She holds out a bottle of "Two Buck Chuck" and he takes it from her. "So, Gaby," she says, whisking a glance at me. "You did a decent job with the flowers. Decent, indeed."

At least her smile appears genuine. "Thank you, Iris."

"And that dress looks darling on your figure."

I nod, inwardly pleased at the turn of her attitude toward me.

Then she leans forward and in a not so quiet voice says, "Still having legal troubles?"

Okay, some changes don't happen overnight. At Iris's comment, surprise registers on Jake's face, but I just give a nonchalant shrug. "Not at all—hey, isn't the DJ fabulous?"

"My, my, he is!" Iris exclaims. "Come on, Jake, let's get this old drudge of a party started! Remember how much we liked to dance to 'Barbara Ann' back in the day?"

Jake smirks as Iris grabs his hand. She pulls him toward the designated dance area, a.k.a. the limbo stage, and he quickly hands over the wine while tossing me a withering look. All attention turns to them, especially as Iris's Hawaiian dress in shades of Pepto-Bismol clings to her as she shakes her booty to the Beach Boys like she's lost in some *Laugh-In* time machine. Has she been watching Elaine dance on reruns of *Seinfeld*—or what?

The two become encircled by spectators, some holding their sides from laughter and gasping for air. But I focus solely on Jake. Watching him is another experience entirely. He's gorgeous and brawny with wild hair and a dimple a woman could get lost in. One I could get lost in. And from what I've been so liberally told, he's also the consummate entertainer. So it's not surprising that he can gyrate with the best of them—or in this case, the worst.

Iris's awkwardness blended with Jake's finesse does nothing to still the crowd as voices rise to the crescendo of "Barbara A-a-ann!" I'm thanking God it's not me that everyone's staring at when I notice Kit slip in from the side gate. Willy's sudden interest in our newest guest isn't lost on me as we both step around the dancers—if you can call them that—and over to Kit.

I reach her first, setting her mother's bottle on an empty table. "Hello, my friend."

"Hey—" She spots her mother on the dance floor. "Oh gross."

Willy cackles. "Wanna dance?"

Kit glares at him, and he jerks his head upwards and back, presumably to knock the hair out of his eyes. Despite some teenage gawkiness, Willy's eyes dance with a kind of tenderness rare for a kid his age. At least, for the boys I knew—back in "the day."

I'm laughing to myself, recalling Iris's words to Jake, when a steady arm hooks my waist and pulls me toward the dance floor.

"What . . . what're you doing?"

Jake holds me against himself, laughing in the breeze, and even though I pull away, I can't deny how good this man smells. Like the woods after a rain. He laughs as I put up a lame fight and then reluctantly give in to his leading.

The deck's awash with revelers now, most of them strangers, and I'm wondering if someone just threw open the side gates and now we've got party crashers. Jake's entire face smiles, and apparently he doesn't care about all the strangers surrounding us. I wonder if he even notices.

In a flash the music slows and Jake cinches me closer as "Surfer Girl" flows from the four corners of the deck. I resist him, keeping my body and head as rigid as possible. Or maybe I'm just resisting myself here? Bri catches my eye, but she's not smiling. She's not frowning either. The angelic expression on her face reminds me of a woman watching her daughter walk down the aisle—a little sentimental, a little sappy, a bit of happiness all rolled into one expression.

"Dance with me, Gaby," Jake says, his voice husky.

My shoulders relax, as does my neck, and so I gently lean against him as we sway to those harmonizing Beach Boys. I shut my eyes, the music soothing, and suddenly all the chatter and the worry and the wondering . . . it all drifts away. I came here to start fresh, and I have. So I've had a few bumps along the way? Thanks to Mama, my business may not die after all. And despite Iris's penchant for gossip from day one, I've cut through and made friends anyway—one even saved my life. Soon I'll be applying for art school, and who knows what doors will open on that path?

Love, perhaps?

Inwardly, I shake away the notion. *Don't tempt yourself, Gaby-girl.* If it happens, it happens and as I've learned, all my searching and prying and hoping won't bring me any closer to marital bliss.

We sway to the song's final falsettos, one of Jake's hands at my waist and the other now buried in my hair and resting at the nape of my neck. Need I mention just how right his touch feels? This is the part where I long to tip my chin up and gaze at him. If he were The One, this is the moment he'd lean down and kiss me lightly—or maybe not so lightly—offering me a thank you for the dance. And a promise of more to come.

Instead the music fades and I pull away without looking up.

"Not so fast." Jake's hand slides down my arm and catches me at the wrist. He pulls me forward and swiftly kisses me on the highest part of my cheekbone. My eyes flutter open to see him hovering there, inches from me, and I'm reduced to butter.

A question flips through my head, but I suppress it and lift my chin toward his, letting him know that maybe I've been wrong about him. Maybe there's a chance for something more between us. But before he can take advantage of the moment, Iris's voice breaks through. "Jake, there's someone here to see you."

Forty-Four

I'VE SEEN THE GIRL BEFORE. I'm not sure when or where, but I *know* I've seen her.

Bri appears by my side as the music changes and Jake rushes off the dance floor and into the arms of a young woman, her long blond strands tangled between them. He crushes her to him like she's a fresh breath of air after a smoggy day.

"Why didn't you tell me?" Bri's watching me, not Jake and what's-her-name. What is her name, anyway?

"Tell you what?"

"Gabrielle Flores!"

Both of my eyebrows shoot north. "What, mother?"

Like that mythical fairy godmother she so loathed, Mama appears from nowhere. She steps between us. "Oh, so now she's your madre? *¿Desde cuando?*" Since when?

I try to laugh. Just who is that young woman with Jake?

Bri ignores me and talks to Mama. "Mrs. Flores, don't you think it's pretty obvious that Gaby and Jake are, well, more than landlord and tenant?"

I gasp. "Bri!"

Surprisingly, Mama's nodding. "Those two are perfect. They just don't know it yet."

"I know! I know!" Bri's saying. "Ooh-la-la, when I saw the way he caressed you with his eyes, and the way he held you when you danced . . . . Woo-hoo, all I kept thinking was what color for the bridesmaids, missy? Oh, and you'll just love being married to an older man." She glances at her husband, Doug, and licks her lips. Gross.

Iris waltzes over and we all take a step back to allow her in. "Looks like you'll be having to share deck space over here."

Okay, I'll bite. "And why's that?"

"You don't know who she is?"

I try to bury my disappointment, and shake my head tightly.

"That's Jessie, Jake's prodigal daughter." She stage whispers now. "Got herself in all kinds of trouble, especially with her derelict boyfriend, Sammy. Not exactly sure what, but she hasn't been around in a while."

Sammy. . . . Sammy? . . . Sammy!

She shrugs. "But like you said about Andy the other day, she's a miracle, isn't she? Word to the wise, you may want to find yourself another place to rent. You do prefer to rent now, don't you, Gaby?"

"Would you excuse me?" I pat my mama's arm, briefly catch eyes with Bri, and dash inside, but it isn't long before my best friend finds me in a crumpled mass on the couch bed she loaned me.

"Gaby, I don't know what to say. Should we call the police? Maybe I should go talk with Doug . . . ?"

Deep breath in. Start fresh. "Don't. I've no idea whether she actually helped Sammy rip me off or not—the police couldn't prove that another person was involved—but at least now I know why she looked so familiar. She worked in a bar, so I only saw her a few times when she was awake during the day."

"Maybe Jake doesn't know about her ties to Sammy?"

I give Bri a "nice try" look. "I should have followed Iris's advice fully on this one. Jake knew something—I could feel it in my gut—but I . . . I was starting to think that maybe . . ."

"Yeah, I know. Maybe he's the one."

I won't cry. I. Will. Not. Cry. "Bri, would you give my regrets to everyone? I'm just not in the mood for partying right now."

"No, I won't."

Excuse me? "Why not?"

"This is your home too, Gaby. And you worked hard on this party, so I'm not going to let you cower up here as if you're the one who's got something to hide."

Cower? Who's cowering?

"Now put a smile on that pretty face of yours and get your bum down there. We've got some serious partying to do."

I blow my nose and buy myself a few more minutes. She's right, really. I'm tired of crawling into a shell every time my life takes a dip. Tried that for a while and it was lonely. Truly lonely.

Bri hugs my arm as I stand at the window watching the boisterous, growing crowd two floors down. "Go touch up your makeup. I'll wait." When I don't move, Bri looks out the window. "Another new guest?" she asks about a woman who just stepped in.

"That's Sarah. She lives next door but has been mostly a hermit since I moved in. Well, until some guy pulled a prank on her and nearly crushed her spirit. I ended up helping her figure out what to do." I smile, and turn to Bri. "Did I ever tell you that she plays characters at children's parties? You should see all the fun outfits and props she has in her house."

"Well, hurry up and finish your makeup so you can introduce us."

I reenter the party with fresh makeup and a forced smile. No one would know that beneath my summer dress, my heart breaks. I spot Sarah and give her a big hug. "Thanks for coming. Have you seen Andy yet?"

"Oh, no-no-no. And where is the birthday boy, now, hmm?"

I point him out and she leaves me there to fake slap Bri.

Bri's snorting with laughter. "What was that?"

"I told you, chica. She runs children's parties."

Bri's laugh is catchy, and despite the heaviness of my heart, I'm starting to laugh too. Maybe it's just relief flowing through me that once again, I've dodged a relationship bullet. Jake's nowhere in sight, Iris is ordering the DJ to get the limbo started as she's already begun forming a line, and the sizzling sounds and aromas of delicious food being carried out onto the deck have alerted my senses to what lies ahead.

Tomorrow I can face my debt outlook.

Tomorrow I can start searching for a new place to live.

Tomorrow I can forgive myself for considering that just maybe I'd been wrong about Jake. My heart clinches at the thought.

Max breaks into my musings. "Gaby, could I talk to you?"

"Okay. Are you having fun?"

He captures me with those chocolaty-eyes. "I am. It could be better, though. I'm not much of a dancer, but would you . . . ?" He reaches for my hand and I allow him to take it.

We move awkwardly to "Two Less Lonely People" by Air Supply. He seems distracted and stiff, like he's counting each dance step. "You're beautiful tonight," he finally says.

He told me that already, but who am I to reject a second compliment? "Thanks, Max. How's Gib? Oh, and tell me how Rover's doing?"

"Fine. Fine. They're fine. Gaby, I'm not really sure why I'm here. I don't even know the guy who's having the birthday. . . ."

"I can introduce you." I stop and try to pull Max off the dance floor, but he halts us both.

"Let me finish. I'm here because I think we've got some unfinished business between us. I guess that was pretty forward of me to invite you all the way to Mexico."

I nod.

"Sorry. I'd like to start again with you, Gaby. Maybe take it slower, if you're up for it."

Up for it? I sigh. "Max, you are definitely a great catch . . . for somebody. Just not me."

Max drops my hand. "Can't say that I'm not disappointed, Gaby." He looks away. "Life's been difficult over the past few years. Really bad at times, but I thought . . ." He swings his gaze back to meet mine. "I thought that you and I could overcome things together. I'm sorry I was so impatient with you at our last dinner. You must think I'm a heel."

"You know what I think, Max? I think that when you find the right gal for you, and if she has the same convictions as mine, you'll wait. You won't hesitate—am I right?" He stares at me with those chocolaty eyes, and this time . . . ? Nothing.

Max nods, and I almost see the relief pour out of him. "You might be right there, Gaby," he says. "Just might be." He gives me a brief hug, and I watch him walk off. Just as he does, Livi arrives after having cared for Florally Yours all day. I watch her face light up when she catches sight of Max moving toward the back gate, and forgive my Bri-moment here, but instinct suggests those two lost souls may have just found each other.

"There you are."

The familiar deep voice causes my body to freeze, yet my heart to race.

"Talk to me."

When I turn and make eye contact with Jake, everything in his stance—the slumped shoulders, the cloudy eyes, the shifting feet—tells me that guilt has ensnared him. The DJ plays the old version of "Tiny Bubbles," but I'm in no mood for the hula, so I stare back at him.

He tugs on my arm and I follow him inside, past the servers he hired for the day and into the foyer. "I wanted to tell you of the connection, but I couldn't."

I exhale. "Why not?"

"It's complicated."

"You know, I don't understand any of this, Jake. You never told me anything about your daughter, or that you knew she was connected to Sammy."

"I didn't know where she was all this time, Gaby. If I had known, I would've tracked down that boyfriend of hers and turned him over to the authorities right away."

"Come on, Jake. What kind of father would turn in his own child?"

He drops his gaze to the ground, pain etching his forehead. "Jessie made some very bad decisions, but I know she wouldn't have burglarized your store. We just spoke, and she told me that Sammy did that all on his own. She didn't even learn about it until after they'd run off together, and she desperately wants to apologize to you."

A curious thought drops into my mind. "When did you learn about Sammy burglarizing my store, Jake?"

He raises his chin, and his eyes find mine. "Before you even moved in. A detective called to see if I might know where Sammy had headed. I didn't, but he mentioned you as the victim. Then I saw you quoted in the paper after your apartment building burned down, and my heart broke for you. I just wanted to help, so I sought you out through Livi, who was working at my Realtor's office."

"Livi knew about this?"

"Not all of it, but I did ask her not to mention that I was specifically seeking to offer you my loft to rent. She seemed to think it a nice gesture."

My world just tipped on its axis. Just who can I believe anymore?

"Gaby, listen to me. Like Jessie, I've made some terrible decisions in my life, and I've had to pay my dues. My life's different now. I'm a redeemed man."

"Redeemed's a strong word. From what Iris has told me, it would take quite a bit for you to change."

"You've systematically dismissed Iris's chatter about all those folks out there," he says with a wave toward the outside, "but not me. Why can't you see me for who I am, Gaby? Why do you let someone else's opinion guide yours about me?"

"For starters, with the exception of Doug and a few others, all the men I've known have had trouble with the truth. My mother's husbands, my various boyfriends, my previous landlord—that one's lie nearly killed me. I move in here, and the first thing I learn is that you're the neighborhood lothario. Then I learn that you and Iris are—or were—having an affair."

"Iris and me?" He shakes his head quickly, as if erasing the memory.

I continue. "I was actually thankful for the advance warning."

Jake's eyes fly open. "No more half-truths, then. I want to come completely clean with you. Right here. Right now."

"Is there more about Sammy and your daughter?"

"No. It's about Iris . . . and me."

TMI, baby! I hold up both palms. "Not necessary, Jake. Iris was separated from her husband, and you two have a history . . ."

He wraps his hands around mine and stills them in the air. "There's absolutely nothing between us, but there once was, many years ago." He inhales and lets it out. "You know I grew up here . . . Well, I was a dumb kid with too much money and time. Iris was my first fling, only to her it was more and she thought I'd marry her, that all of this would be hers." His smile is sad. "I ended up marrying someone else before I even hit twenty, but that never seemed to stop Iris from keeping track of me, even after her own marriage, and my divorce. Man, I traveled the world, but she'd still manage to find out where I was and drop me a postcard!"

He stares at the floor. "There's no excuse for how I led her on back then. None. But a few years ago, when I'd had my eyes opened to just how empty my life was despite my money—no wife, a daughter heading down a dangerous path—I swallowed my pride and went to church. And wouldn't you know it? I discovered someone bigger out there than my ego."

My eyebrow darts toward the heavens.

"God."

I release the breath I'd been holding.

Jake continues. "Anyway, life's just not been the same. Eventually I realized how much I'd hurt Iris, and how she'd carried that with her all these years. So I apologized. It's all I could do. I couldn't give her back the years, and I couldn't love her the way she wanted me to, but I could tell her how deeply sorry I was for hurting her."

No man has ever confessed his failings to me. Flaunted them, yes, but admit his hidden screw-ups? Never. Instead of an overconfident man about town, in Jake I'm seeing a gentle giant, a man with humility, and have I mentioned his intriguing dimple?

"Please, don't say anymore," I tell him.

"Wait, one more thing. This is important. I may have bungled this, I should have been more upfront with you, but I only wanted to help you, Gaby. I never meant to, I never knew I'd . . ."

"You'd what, Jake?"

He inhales as if gathering strength. "I'd fall in love."

Forty-Five

You know that part at the end of *Sleepless in Seattle*, when Meg Ryan and Tom Hanks—finally—meet face-to-face on the top of the Empire State Building? He says to her, "It's you," and she replies, "It's me."

This is that moment.

Only Jake gets it right. Instead of taking my hand and walking me toward the nearest elevator like in the movie, he finds my mouth and kisses me with passion I've never known. He doesn't stop, and the more he kisses my lips, my eyes, my cheeks, the more hungry I become. My skin tingles, my breathing accelerates, and my fingers hang on tight. At this moment, it would take more than winning the lottery to pry me from his embrace.

Unfortunately, we've got a deck full of people to entertain. Bri sticks her head into the doorway, and let me just say, she's beyond ecstatic. Trust me, I know. "You two wanna join your own party? The guests are demanding dessert."

Reluctantly, Jake releases his grip on me, but not totally. With one arm around my waist, he ushers me out to the deck. "Well then," he says, "let **them** eat cake!"

The next morning I'm lying on a chaise lounge out on the deck, gazing at the few paper lanterns that managed to survive the night. Jake's inside cooking breakfast with Mama at his side, probably teaching him the finer points of frying bacon to the correct crispness. Our friends stayed late into the night, but Jake never left my side. He didn't really have to with Mama around.

The walk to my loft last night was long and lonely. Mama stayed in a second-floor guestroom, Jessie in her room with all its pinkness, and I in my tower seemingly far away from Jake. Unless something changes soon, I'll have to move out of here for different reasons entirely.

Jake steps onto the deck with two plates brimming with eggs, bacon, and sliced mango. He slides into the chaise lounge next to mine and hands me my breakfast. "You look like you could get used to this," he says with a wink.

"You know it."

Jake chuckles. "You're honest."

"It's the new me," I say with a laugh. "Where's Mama?"

Jake just shakes his head. "She insists on eating in the kitchen. Can you believe it? Says she's going to clean the kitchen the right way and then give that Jane a 'talking-to'."

Oh. My.

"I hope you don't mind my butting in, but I talked with her about her symptoms."

I sit up. "You did?"

"She's got Graves' disease, Gaby."

An invisible vice grips my lungs. I can't breathe.

"It's completely treatable. Yolie's doctor gave her medication, but she was afraid of the side effects and hasn't started taking it. I nudged her into agreeing to, though. She looked like she wanted to smack me, but when I told her how worried you were, she relented."

I let go of the breath I'd been holding, all my tension alleviated by Jake's pronouncement. "So the tremors are . . . ?"

"Just one of the symptoms. She tried to wave me away, but when she did her hand shook."

Relief continues to flow over me. "I . . . I don't know what to say, Jake, other than thank you. Thank you so much." I sigh. "You keep on surprising me, don't you?"

He chuckles. "All part of the plan."

When a splash just beyond the railing draws my attention, I hop up and set my plate aside. "Sweet Thing?"

My sea lion friend swims in a continuous oval in the channel below.

"You named her?"

"What can I say? I like to call my friends by name. Besides, I think she's been bringing me seashells."

"Physically impossible."

"Well, what-ev! All I know is that every time she's around, it seems, a mound of pretty shells shows up on this dock. I've been bringing them to the shop to use in some arrangements." I turn to him. "Unless you think they're for you?"

"I hate to burst the idealism in that pretty head of yours, but they're from Kit. Don't tell her I told you."

"Kit? No way."

"Way. She's a hard kid sometimes, but she likes you. You've been nice to her, so she wanted to surprise you with them. I caught her early one morning."

Well, who knew?

He grabs my hand. "Come on. Let's say hi to ol' what's her name."

"It's Sweet Thing, and that's okay. I think I'll just stay up here."

Jake pulls me close. "Don't be scared. I'm comin' with you."

"I'm not scared!"

"Oh no? I haven't seen you anywhere near that water since the kayaking incident. If you're going to be living here I want you to face that fear."

"Yes, about living here . . ."

"I've got a surprise. Wait here." I watch him dash off to the side yard, the one spot I've never ventured over to because, frankly, it looks like a debris graveyard. Minutes later, he hauls out a long purple kayak and two paddles.

"Gee, Jake, you really do know how to surprise a lady."

"You think? Let's go, just you and me."

"Go where?"

"Out on the kayak together. This is the tandem I used to take Jessie out on, and now I'm taking you."

"I . . . I don't think so. Not this morning, anyway. It's cold. Brrrr."

He stares at me, the sun beating down on his browning shoulders. I sigh, loudly. "Please, Jake. Let's not ruin such a nice morning."

"I want you to trust me, Gaby."

"I do."

He holds out a paddle. "Then show me."

I'm in the front as we move steadily down the channel, Jake steering from the rear. Sweet Thing pokes her head up twice before disappearing altogether, and the waters lie calm all around us. If I didn't have the memory of my kayaking fiasco so close to the surface of my mind, I might actually be able to relax. A pelican glides close to the water as we enter the main channel, and I wish I could be so calm.

"Isn't it a beautiful morning? Makes me think of that worship song, 'Indescribable.' Know it?" Jake calls from behind me.

I can't turn around for fear of tipping us, so I just nod, because he's right. The words of that song always get me, especially the part about creation revealing God's majesty. The air, the water, the sky above, it's all laid out before us in swaths of muted morning blue. *You rock, God.*

"Still trusting me?"

We're heading closer and closer to the jetties, the breakwater in view, and little ripples of fear bubble through me.

"Gaby?"

I nod again. I do trust Jake, it's myself I'm not quite sure about as we bob along toward the harbor's mouth. Left, right, left. I've survived for years without a father, with little money, with my own poor decisions. Can I really believe that this time the good stuff will stick? *Jesus, help me believe.*

No powerful wind kicks up after that prayer, no treacherous storm or other challenge. We just continue to watch the sea's playground come alive as we paddle toward Mom's Beach. I hold my breath as we pass the south jetty, ride over a cresting hill of water, and glide effortlessly around the rocks and within site of the protected beach, where local moms can safely bring their toddlers to romp around.

Jake steers us onto the sand and we come to a stop with a soft thud. He's already out of the boat and offering me his hand.

He kisses me softly. "You did it, Gaby. I'm so proud of you."

I glance around at the deserted beach, then down at our fingers intertwined. His large hands holding mine make me feel secure and safe. And have I mentioned petite? I raise my eyes to smile at him, but he's lowering himself, on one knee, to the soft earth below.

"What are . . . ?" I drop my eyes to meet his.

"I've been waiting for you all my life, Gabrielle. There's no doubt in my mind. None at all. I've wanted to tell you this almost from the start but was waiting to know that you trust me. You do trust me, right?"

I nod, despite a tinge of shock.

He exhales, a smile spreading across his cheeks. "I love you, Gaby Flores."

I blink. "I-I don't deserve you, Jake."

He shakes his head. "It's the other way around, but I'm on my knees here hoping you'll love me anyway. Will you?"

I've never told a man that I love him. Until now, when I whisper, "I love you too, Jake!"

He releases his breath, draws in another, then asks, "Marry me?"

My tears fall onto his stubbly cheeks, and I begin to shake and to laugh, and I just can't stop. The shell that I've built around myself, the one meant to protect me from life's setbacks, suddenly cracks and falls away. Life's not always safe, and sometimes things don't make sense, but what I know is this: I love this man! This was worth waiting for.

When I've finally caught my breath, I cup Jake's bristly face with my hands and look into those fervent eyes of his. "Yes!"

He pulls me down into his bear-like arms and crushes me close. Then together we climb into our kayak and paddle home.

Acknowledgments

Special thanks to my father, Dan Navarro, and my uncle Hap Navarro for help with *mi español*. My late grandmother, Mary, tried to teach me to speak Spanish when I was young. Unfortunately, I was too busy making up stories to pay much attention. Ah well. Grandma Mary did manage to make one phrase stick, though, and that is *"Te quiero,"* meaning "I love you." So to Dad and Uncle Hap, *"Los quiero mucho a los dos."*

To my husband, Dan, thanks for help with legal matters, for being my best friend, and for all those promotional photos you took without receiving official credit—until now. And kisses to our kids, Matt, Angela, and Emma, for being my support crew at events and at home.

Loads of gratitude also go out to:

Joseph Torres, my cousin and chef extraordinaire, for insights into your fascinating foodie world.

Sherrill Waters, my friend who stayed up way too late pouring over Gaby's story in its final stages, yet I'm so glad you did!

Tracy Burchett, faithful friend who read and critiqued this story in various stages. (Thanks for the cool eye cream, too.)

The fabulous team at Bethany House: Charlene Patterson, editor, you're so easy to work with, and I'm grateful for your support; Sarah Long, fellow Mexican food lover, I appreciate all your work on making Gaby's story ready to be read; and Karen Schurrer, for your copy editing expertise.

Steve Laube, my gifted and hard-working agent; Karen Robbins, fellow ACFW member, for sharing your floral expertise; Rachel A. Marks, fellow ACFW member, for your insights into an artist's mind; Kathryn (Katie) Cushman for meeting me for a seaside lunch when it was all over—so yum; and Trufflehounds Fine Chocolates in Ventura, for sweet temptation.

My readers—here's to the beach chick in all of us!

And my God, who made the sea and everything in it. Your inspiration is endless.

JULIE CAROBINI is an award-winning writer whose stories often spotlight her family, the sea, and God's timely work in the lives of those around her. *Chocolate Beach,* which features Bri's story, was her first novel. She lives in Southern California with her husband, Dan, and their three children.

Questions for Conversation

1. Despite all the turmoil in Gaby's life, she's outwardly resolute that God is in control. Yet there's evidence she doesn't completely believe this. Have you ever felt unsure about God's involvement in your life? What happened to change your mind—or not? Do you feel closer to God when you are happy or when you are troubled?

2. Gaby has been on her own for a long time, and she finds it tough to ask for help. Are you comfortable turning to friends or family when you're facing difficulties? Does talking about your problems help?

3. Gaby's a dreamer. She finds comfort in romantic movies with a happy ending, yet she's tempted to "settle" in her own love life. Have you ever settled in an area of your life only to find out that something better was waiting for you?

4. Agnes Tilley is a church lady with a heart for God's people. To Gaby, she represents someone who lives her faith every day. Who do you know who has put feet to his or her faith? Has knowing them changed how you live? In what ways do you act out your faith?

5. First impressions can be deceiving. Gaby's not impressed with her landlord, but her opinion about him eventually changes. Have you ever met a person, judged them (not on purpose, of course!), only to discover they are not who or what you thought? On the flip side, have you ever felt judged? Can you think of a time when you've been surprised by someone's generosity toward you?

6. Gaby longs for her mama's approval. Have you ever sought the approval of someone else? Or felt that someone is seeking yours? In what ways did Gaby's mama show her approval and love for her daughter? How are Gaby and her mother different? The same?

7. Do you have a favorite spot that you go to pray or think or just get away? What do you like about this place? Do other people know about it?

8. What is your favorite romantic movie? Favorite type of chocolate? Favorite beach?